Praise for Christine McGuire's Novels of Suspense

UNTIL THE BOUGH BREAKS

"Her plot is full of the sort of twists and insider looks at a criminal investigation that fans of legal thrillers adore." —*Booklist*

UNTIL DEATH DO US PART

"Starts with a bang—literally–and never lets up. . . . McGuire, an experienced criminal prosecutor, provides fascinating forensic details and juggles her plotlines skillfully, never sacrificing clarity, as the book speeds to its conclusion." —*Publishers Weekly*

"A gripping drama. . . . Readers are treated to three-dimensional human beings filled with fears, doubts, and flaws." —Amazon.com

UNTIL JUSTICE IS DONE

"What sets McGuire's novels apart from the pack is the level of realism she brings to the legal aspects of the story." —*The Sentinel* (Santa Cruz, CA)

UNTIL PROVEN GUILTY

"A tense, nerve-jangling thriller that should satisfy fans of *The Silence of the Lambs*." —Peter Blauner, bestselling author of *The Intruder* and *Slow Motion Riot*

Books by Christine McGuire

Until Proven Guilty
Until Justice Is Done
Until Death Do Us Part
Until the Bough Breaks
Until We Meet Again

Published by POCKET BOOKS

UNTIL WE MEET AGAIN

CHRISTINE McGUIRE

POCKET BOOKS
New York London Toronto Sydney Singapore

This book is a work of fiction. Names, characters, places and
incidents are products of the author's imagination or are used
fictitiously. Any resemblance to actual events or locales or
persons, living or dead, is entirely coincidental.

An *Original* Publication of POCKET BOOKS

POCKET BOOKS, a division of Simon & Schuster Inc.
1230 Avenue of the Americas, New York, NY 10020

ISBN: 1-4165-0174-6

This Pocket Books paperback printing May 2004

10 9 8 7 6 5 4 3 2 1

POCKET and colophon are registered trademarks of
Simon & Schuster Inc.

Front cover illustration by Gerber Studio
Front cover photo by ICL/Zephyr Images

Printed in the U.S.A.

This novel is dedicated to
the
Survivors of sexual abuse

Acknowledgments

With deep gratitude to
my literary agents
Arthur and Richard Pine
and my editor
Jason Kaufman

UNTIL WE MEET AGAIN

Prologue

―――

"*Have a nice day and don't worry about me, Nita.*" *Carlotta hugged her sister tight and kissed her on the cheek. "I'll be fine. I'll go to school as soon as I feel better. It's just an upset stomach."*

"Don't go to school, Carly. You're never sick. Stay home and relax," her older sister advised. As an after-thought, she added, "And cook us something special for dinner. I'll call you on my break."

Carlotta watched her sister walk down the path from their apartment and drive away in her old Toyota. She waved good-bye, but Anita never looked back.

She leaned her forehead briefly against the jamb, then closed the door and engaged the dead bolt. She lowered and latched the windows in the living room, bathroom, bedrooms, and kitchen, then opened the door of the old Frigidaire and removed a container of orange juice. Carefully, she washed and dried a cut-crystal glass, filled it with juice, and walked to her bedroom.

Her bedroom was immaculately clean and unmis-takably feminine. The bed was covered with a bright floral spread, fluffy pillows, and stuffed animals. She moved the pillows to the far side of the bed next to the wall, picked up a plastic pill bottle from the nightstand, and leaned against the headboard, swinging her legs onto the bed. She shook two pills into her left palm, reconsidered, shook out four more, popped all six into her mouth, and swallowed them with a large gulp of orange juice.

"That wasn't so hard, was it?" she asked the teddy bear nestled on her tummy. She washed down another four pills, followed by four more, then four more, pausing briefly to be sure she would not throw up. Then she swallowed the remaining pills and set the empty container on the stand.

She tuned the cheap digital radio alarm clock to station KESP, which played rap music, slid between the fresh clean sheets and fluffed the pillow under her head. She relaxed and closed her eyes. Shortly, sleep overtook her, and darkness unlike any she had ever known obliterated her consciousness.

The final thought Carlotta Escobedo ever had was that she hoped she wouldn't get in trouble for cutting school.

1

"Hold still, you grouchy old nag," Todd laughed at his bay gelding as he cinched the saddle up tight. The horse snorted angrily, blowing snot on his owner's shirt, and tried to bite his arm.

"Too quick for you," Todd told him, jerking his arm away. He slipped the bit into the horse's mouth and swung up onto his back. Sonny plodded reluctantly to the green Powder River corral gate, which Todd unlatched and swung open.

Bill Todd, airline pilot and part-time rancher, surveyed the panoramic view of the bay from his corral at the top of Mount Cabrillo. He could see from the farms on the outskirts of Española to the open space beyond Santa Rita that swept up the hill toward the university campus. The circular bay stretched south from narrow sandy beaches toward Monterey and Pacific Grove, across twenty miles of sparkling azure water.

It was a stroke of flight scheduling luck that Todd could spend the morning mending fences around his forty-acre gentleman's ranch. The downside to his lifestyle was the drive to work. The skinny old road snaked across and down the hill from Mount Cabrillo Park at the top to south Santa Rita. No guardrails separated the roadway from the sheer cliffs, which in some places dropped vertically several hundred feet.

Todd spotted dangling wire and four metal fence posts pushed over, the result of seven tons of hungry cattle poking their necks through the fence. "Damn cows are just like people, they always think the grass is greener on the other side," he said to no one.

He swung out of the saddle and tied the horse to a tree. Sonny nuzzled his left arm and grunted. "Oh, so now you like me? I know what you want." He reached into a saddlebag and pulled out two green apples, which he cut into quarters with a pocket knife and held one piece at a time in the palm of his hand. Sonny grabbed them with his agile lips and chewed with surprising delicacy.

After the repair, they made their way to the corner of the ranch, a small, level meadow studded with century-old white oaks hidden from the roadway by a row of apple trees. The meadow abutted a precipitous drop into a narrow canyon, which was bisected by a creek about twelve feet wide and six inches deep. From the sharp curve in the roadway above, the drop to the bottom was fifty feet or more.

Sound carried well in the open air, and Todd heard a car on the road. It idled for several minutes, then the engine roared, tires screeched, and Todd looked up just as a shiny white car sailed past the edge of the roadway over the tops of the trees and manzanita brush. It seemed to hang in the air momentarily, then it rolled slowly to its left, pitched forward, and hurtled end over end toward the ground. He saw it land on its wheels, bounce, and settle on its passenger side in the muddy water.

"Jesus Christ," Todd muttered to himself. He yanked a cellular phone from a leather case on his belt and punched in 9-1-1.

"County Communications," a female voice answered.

"There's been an accident near the top of Mount Cabrillo," he reported. "A car went over the cliff."

"What's your name and address, sir?" the dispatcher asked.

"William Todd. Fourteen-seventy-seven Mount Cabrillo Grade Road."

"Are you at the location of the accident now?"

"I'm on a cell phone in the pasture behind the house. I can see it from here."

"Okay, don't hang up." After a minute, she was back on the line. "I dispatched the Highway Patrol. Can you wait and show them the accident?"

California Highway Patrol Officer Sterling looked over the edge of the cliff at the car below, whistled, and exclaimed, "Holy shit!" Then he asked Todd, "Is there any way down there?"

"Yeah, there's a trail over there. Follow me."

The two men slid down the steep slope and Sterling surveyed the car, which rocked precariously on its side. "I've got to call this in." He lifted the portable radio. "County Comm, four-lincoln-twenty-two. I'm at that accident on Mount Cabrillo. The car's on its side at the bottom of a gully in Cloudy Creek. It's pretty shaky. If I climb up on it, it's gonna roll over. Alert County Fire Search and Rescue, they'll need to get to the crash site up the creek bed in all-terrain vehicles. I think they're gonna have to airlift the victims outta there, so notify the S.O. to spin the chopper up. I'll wait here."

"Ten-four, I'll contact the Sheriff's office. County Comm out."

After about ten minutes, Sterling picked up the faint whine of a small four-stroke engine. He poked Todd and pointed downstream. "There they are."

Todd saw one, then three more chartreuse Honda four-wheel ATVs scream upstream, right wheels on the dry creek bed, left wheels kicking out rooster tails of brown water, engines howling in protest. The first unit careened to a halt alongside and slightly upgrade from the rear end of the car. The second, piloted by a fire fighter with "PARAMEDIC" stenciled on his jacket, slid to a stop alongside, followed by the others.

The firefighters acknowledged Sterling and Todd, but went quickly to work. One pulled a yellow polyvinyl rope from the back of an ATV, tossed it over the top of the car, tied one end to the car's frame and the other end around a large tree to stabilize it temporarily. The second cranked up a portable generator, while the other two secured the car to solid oak trees with two quarter-inch wire cables on the uphill side and another two downhill.

Once the car was stable, Paramedic Johnny Wong climbed onto the car and peered into the interior through the driver's window. He saw two bodies inside the car, arms and legs akimbo, and blood everywhere. He could tell one was a man and the other a woman, but little else. He braced one foot against the rear window frame and yanked hard on the driver's door handle. It wouldn't budge. "Fuck," he said aloud. "Hey, Legs, hand me a crowbar."

Fire Captain Shirley MacLain, dubbed "Legs" for the movie star after whom she was named, grabbed a tool from her ATV and handed it up. Wong pried around the perimeter of the door, but it refused to open.

"Break the driver's window." MacLain suggested.

"Can't, Cap. Glass'd fall on 'em. Need the Jaws," he said, referring to the hydraulically operated scissors they called the Jaws of Life. "And we can't get these people outta here without the chopper. Where's it stand? Those people are hurt bad, if they're alive. Once we get 'em out of the car and stabilized, they've gotta get to the hospital in a hurry."

"I called it in," Sterling told him. "It should be overhead by the time you extricate them."

MacLain handed Wong the Jaws of Life, which looked like a giant steel woodpecker with a hydraulic hose stuck up its rear end. It could effectively crush, or pry and separate, exerting enormous force in either direction.

Wong stuck the tips of the Jaws into a gap between the driver's door and the frame, and mashed the hydraulic actuator lever. The portable power unit bogged down under the heavy load, and the Jaws inched opened. As they spread, the gap grew until the door finally sprang loose with a metallic crunch.

Wong dropped the Jaws on the ground, flopped the door open, and dropped into the car's interior. MacLain climbed up to help, while the other firefighters prepared stretchers with Todd and Sterling's help.

"He's got a pulse," Wong shouted. He wrapped a collar around each victim's neck, inflated them, then lifted the man out the door. MacLain helped lower him to the men below, who placed him on a stretcher. They repeated the process with the woman, then carried the stretchers away from the wreck and lay them on a level dry spot.

Wong listened to the woman's chest through a stethoscope and lifted her eyelids. "No heartbeat, pupils fixed and dilated. Shit, man, she's dead. Get blankets on 'em. Notify County General Emergency that one of the victims is alive. Rig the slings, I hear the chopper. This guy's got to get to the hospital, stat! Rig her, too, just in case."

A green and white Bell helicopter swooped over the ridge, dropped down, and hovered about forty feet above the car. The downdraft kicked water and gravel in every direction. A sheriff's deputy dropped cable from a davit on the chopper's starboard side to the firefighters, who hooked it to the man's stretcher sling. Then he winched it up and dragged the stretcher through the cargo door. He winched the woman up next. As soon as the second stretcher disappeared inside, the machine banked and roared toward Santa Rita.

As the search and rescue team assembled its gear, Sterling asked Wong, "He gonna make it?"

"Maybe," the paramedic answered. "but he's hurt pretty bad.

2

Assistant District Attorney Kathryn Mackay sipped a cup of coffee and gazed at the early Monday morning fog from her office desk in the concrete bunker they called the County Government Center. The tiny, grimy, non-opening window was one of the few perks conferred on the senior lawyer in charge of prosecuting the county's worst murderers and sexual predators.

District Attorney Harold Benton poked his head past the partially closed door. "Good morning, Kathryn. Can you spare a minute?"

Mackay recognized her boss's soft southern drawl, and surreptitiously stuffed her half-eaten bagel and a copy of *California Lawyer* magazine, which was opened to the "Professional Opportunities and Positions" section, into the pencil drawer, then turned to the door.

"Sure, Hal, come in."

Benton settled into a leather chair in front of her desk. He was dressed impeccably, as usual, in an expensive dark gray double-breasted suit, a white shirt, and a maroon tie.

"I trust you and Emma had a pleasant week-end?" he asked, referring to Mackay's ten-year-old daughter.

Mackay smiled, as she often did, at Benton's easy-going nature and gentlemanly manners, which were glaringly incongruous in an office where the clients were scared, confused crime victims, and thieves and drug dealers often called the attorneys by their first names.

"Yes, we did," she answered. "One of the first in a long time I didn't get called out."

Benton crossed his right leg over his left and smoothed the crease in his trousers. "I had a break-fast meeting this morning with Sheriff Purvis to discuss my opposition to the Board of Supervisors' proposed no-questions-asked needle exchange pro-gram. Purvis asked me to make you available to assist the S.O. in an investigation."

"Do you know what it's about?"

"No, I'm afraid not. I was more interested in getting his support and didn't ask. Give Lieutenant Earheart a call, will you?"

"Sure. Anything else?"

Benton stood and strode toward the door, turning with his hand on the knob. "Nope, thanks. I consider this a favor, so I owe you one, Kathryn. Now, I'd better get back to my office."

Watching his receding back, Mackay reflected on her good fortune in working for Harold Benton, a man whom she thought of as a friend and mentor, but only rarely as her boss. Then she picked up her desk phone and punched in a four-digit extension.

"Earheart," he answered gruffly without preamble.

"Good morning, Walt. That's some telephone demeanor you've got there."

"It's early, Kathryn, I haven't warmed up yet. Damn wet fog goes right through you."

"I know. You wanted to talk to me?" she asked as she checked her desk drawer to be sure the magazine was out of sight, as if Earheart could see it through the phone line, and pulled out the bagel remains.

"Can you meet me at the morgue ASAP? Doc Nelson just called me. He's about to start an autopsy, and I'd like you to be there." Morgan Nelson was the forensic pathologist who functioned as the County Coroner.

"Sure, Walt, I was hoping I could start my week out with a visit to the Hellhole. What've you got? I didn't hear about any murders over the weekend, and I was on call."

"My deputy coroners just picked up a body from County General Hospital. Car wreck. A sixteen-year-old student at Española High School. Her name's . . . Esther Fuentes."

"Sounds like there's no one to prosecute if she's already at the morgue."

"There was someone else in the car. Male Hispanic name of Raymondo Miranda. He's at County General in the Intensive Care Unit. Serious but stable. Looks like he'll live."

"Was he drunk or high?"

"Neither. Looks like a mutual suicide."

Kathryn took another sip of coffee and a delicate bite of bagel before saying anything, buying a little time to think.

"Under certain circumstances, the survivor of a

mutual suicide attempt is charged with murder. I'll be there in half an hour."

Mackay hung up the phone and wolfed down the rest of the bagel and lukewarm coffee. She dropped a chunk of bagel on the floor and slopped coffee on her shirt.

"Dammit," she muttered out loud, "I've been hanging around cops so long I'm starting to eat like they do." She grabbed her jacket from the back of a chair it was draped over and slipped it on, noting with satisfaction that it covered the coffee stain.

Halfway down the hall, she spotted Dr. Robert Simmons, head of the Santa Rita County Department of Public Health, walking up the hall in the opposite direction. Simmons was a personal friend of District Attorney Harold Benton's. He was tall and slender, with striking blue eyes and dark brown hair, and wore a conservative dark suit.

"Good morning, Doctor," Kathryn said. "If you're looking to catch Hal, I believe he's in his office."

"I expect so—we have an appointment." He held up two cups of coffee he carried on a paper tray. "But at least we can enjoy a cup of coffee."

Mackay nodded politely, checked out with her secretary, and hustled to the parking lot.

3

———

When Kathryn pushed open the door to the lobby of County General Hospital, which housed the morgue, she saw Earheart in the elevator aiming his finger at the down button.

"Hey, Walt, wait a sec and I'll ride down to the dungeon with you," she shouted. People who conducted business at the morgue on a regular basis had a lot of nicknames for it, many of which couldn't be repeated in polite company.

Earheart grinned and stuck his shoe into the sliding doors to keep them from closing. Walt was a mid-sized teddy bear, a short, pudgy man with a shiny, bald dome and plastic-rimmed glasses on his nose. He'd been a cop for more than twenty years, and in Mackay's opinion was as good as they get.

When the elevator doors slid open in the basement, the familiar stench of the morgue wafted into their nostrils. Earheart caught it and scrunched up his face.

"Damn, I hate that smell. I never get used to it.

Can't figure out if it smells more like a bottle of toilet cleaner or the toilet itself."

"Count your blessings," she responded as they stepped from the elevator. "At least we don't have to visit the VIP suite. I can't get that odor out of my nose for a week." She was referring to the special isolation unit, where bodies that were in the advanced stages of decomposition or were known to be harboring infectious diseases were evaluated.

They headed down the sterile tile-floored hallway toward Morgan Nelson, who leaned against the door-jamb of an open autopsy suite. A Highway Patrol officer stood beside him. Mackay smiled, despite the purpose for her visit, as she almost always did when she first saw her friend Morgan.

"Good morning, Kate. Walt." Nelson wore green surgical scrubs and matching green rubber-soled shoes. His eyes looked like giant bloodshot saucers behind his wire-rimmed bifocals, and a fringe of short-cropped gingery hair stuck out around the bottom of his green skull cap. "This is Marlon Sterling. He's the CHP officer who responded to the accident scene."

Sterling was a handsome black man with short-cropped hair. He was massive, but not fat, and looked like a dark Arnold Schwarzenegger, threatening to burst the seams of his tight tan uniform shirt. His Glock pistol and handcuff case rode high on his waist in basket-weave leather. He shook hands briefly with Earheart, then stuck his hand out and grabbed Mackay's in a firm grip.

"Nice to meet you, Ms. Mackay. I've heard a lot about you." He smiled, flashing perfect white teeth, and added, "Judging from your reputation, I figured you'd be at least seven feet tall and have fangs like a saber-toothed tiger. You look pretty normal to me."

At five three and a hundred ten pounds soaking wet, Kathryn Mackay wasn't an imposing figure, but her reputation as a hard-nosed prosecutor over-whelmed many of the younger cops. Officer Sterling clearly wasn't intimidated.

"Don't let my looks fool you. And call me Kathryn, please. Makes me feel old when officers call me Ms. Mackay," she told him as she retrieved her hand and checked it for broken bones. "You were the first person at the scene?"

"No, a rancher saw it and called it in. The car went off the old road on the back side of Mount Cabrillo, fell fifty or sixty feet and landed at the bottom of a gully. I wasn't far away when I caught the call, so I was there within a few minutes. Had dispatch call MAIT and Search and Rescue. Victims were airlifted out."

"MAIT?" Mackay asked.

"Multidisciplinary Accident Investigation Team. There are four of us on the team. We're called out on accidents like this."

"How did you ID the victims?"

"The paramedic grabbed a purse and sent it along. Miranda's wallet was still in his pants pocket when he arrived at the hospital. When I got to the emergency room, Miranda was in surgery. Fuentes was already on her way to the morgue."

She nodded. "What about his clothing?"

"I thought you might need them, so I got them from ER and put 'em in evidence bags."

"Good. CSI might be able to locate some fabric

transfers inside the car," she replied, referring to the Sheriff's Crime Scene Investigation unit. "That would help us determine who was behind the wheel. Then what?"

"Well, my lieutenant directed me to assist in contacting Miranda's parents. Turned out by the time I got to their house, County Comm had reached them by phone. They were already on their way to the hospital. I went back to County Gen and found them in the OR waiting room."

"Walt said you found a note?" she asked.

He nodded. "It was in his backpack. It had Sea-Hawks logos all over it—he's a student at Portola Community College. I found some personal stuff inside along with two textbooks. An accounting principles book, one for English lit, and a notebook."

He opened his briefcase and handed Kathryn a spiral-bound notebook. It had doodles, names, and phone numbers scribbled all over the cover.

"Looks just like mine did when I was in college," she observed. Inside the front cover, he had written in neat block letters, "PROPERTY OF RAYMONDO MIRANDA, FALL SEMESTER, ACCOUNTING 1B."

Sterling continued, "I was just passing the time, sitting with his parents while their son was in surgery. They were pretty upset and I figured they could use a little moral support. Anyway, I flipped through it and found the note on the last page. There weren't many class notes—must be a boring class."

Mackay thumbed through the book. The note was written in neat script:

Aug 31 - Dear Mom and Dad: Please forgive me but I didn't know what else to do. I know God

can never forgive me but I hope you can. I take
full responsibility.

Love, Ray

Kathryn arched her eyebrows and handed the notebook to Earheart. "I don't remember much about suicide pacts or assisted suicide from law school, but I know a criminal admission when I see one."

She thought for a moment, then turned to Nelson. "Before I can determine what crimes Miranda might have committed, I need to know if he was driving the car. Fuentes's injury pattern should confirm whether or not she was the passenger, right?"

Nelson nodded and motioned with his forefinger for the three of them to follow him into the autopsy suite, explaining as he went. "Sometimes drivers have distinctive chest and abdominal damage caused by steering wheels, foot pedals, gearshifts, and other stuff. They also have unique lower-extremity injuries."

He stopped beside the only gurney in the room. It held a female body covered with a white sheath. Long dark hair matted with blood spilled out from under the sheath over the edge of the gurney and hung almost to the floor.

"Passenger's injuries are more likely to be to the head and extremities. The differences in injury patterns between the driver and passenger can be significant. Hospital records will tell us what Miranda's injuries are. I'll determine Fuentes's through autopsy."

Nelson slid the sheath off the nude body and said, "I've already taken a full set of x-rays."

"She must have been beautiful," Mackay said

softly when she saw the dead girl. What once had
been flawless olive skin was now covered with
bruises and lacerations.

"Cranial trauma and subdural hematoma was most
likely the cause of death," Nelson speculated, picking
up a scalpel with a gloved hand. "But we'll open up
the thoracic cavity first, before removing the skull."

Kathryn turned to the highway patrolman. "Officer
Sterling, there's no need for you to stay. I need you to
return to the accident scene and hook up with your
team. If I'm going to file charges, I'll need your
investigation results. Keep me posted."

Sterling nodded. "I'd be happy to miss this. I doubt
they've got the car out of that gully yet. They needed
two or three big tow rigs, and that'd take a while. I'll
go back to the scene and oversee the recovery and
have the car towed to our garage for inspection."

Sterling said good-bye to everyone and left the
room just as Nelson sliced a straight, deep incision
straight across Esther Fuentes's lower abdomen from
hipbone to hipbone. Then he incised an intersecting
deep cut on a right angle from the top of the pubis to
just below the center of her breastbone. Next he cut
two Y-shaped incisions from the sternum to the tops
of each shoulder, laid the scalpel on a stainless steel
tray, and folded the flaps of skin back like a peeled
orange. The subcutaneous fat was yellow and ugly.

Before Nelson could examine any internal organs,
the wall phone chirped.

"Aw, shit," he swore under his breath, snapped off
his latex gloves, and flipped them into a stainless-
steel trash container with a foot-operated hinged top.
"Gotta answer that. I instructed the receptionist to
only put emergencies through."

He answered, listened briefly, looked at Mackay, and said, "Yeah, she's here." He nodded and listened another minute or so, then his jaw dropped open and he turned white. He looked at Kathryn again and said into the phone, "I'll tell her," then hung up.

Kathryn knew something was seriously wrong just by the look on Nelson's face. She knew him to be an open book when it came to emotions. She raised her eyebrows. "Doc?"

He put his hand on her shoulder and looked directly into her eyes. "Kathryn, that was Nancy, Hal Benton's secretary. They need you back at the office right away. I'm not sure how to tell you this, so I'm just going to come right out with it." He paused, drew a deep breath, swallowed hard, and continued. "Hal had a heart attack."

Kathryn gasped and clutched the front of her shirt so hard her knuckles turned white. Benton was at the prime age for a heart attack, but he was in excellent health and took meticulous care of himself.

"How bad?" Mackay preferred to get the worst news right away so she could deal with it up front. Besides, it was her theory that things are usually not as bad as they seem. This time she was wrong.

"He's dead, Kathryn," Nelson answered.

Kathryn grabbed her purse and headed for the door, leaving Morgan Nelson and Walter Earheart standing in stunned silence beside the mutilated remains of Esther Fuentes.

4

Kathryn Mackay exploded from the front door of County General Hospital at a dead run, charged down the steps and across the parking lot to where her red Audi was parked in the law enforcement area. She jabbed her key at the door lock, but her trembling hand dropped the key ring and it bounced under the car.

"Damn," she swore, and knelt on the pavement to retrieve them, ripping a gaping hole in the right knee of her pantyhose.

She started the car and raced into the four-lane street that fronted the burgeoning medical complex around the hospital. Just as she entered traffic, she was startled by the deafening blast of an air horn and screeching tires, and instinctively slammed on the brakes, the Audi coming to rest blocking both westbound lanes. She looked up at the gigantic radiator of a Peterbilt ten-wheeler loaded with gravel two feet from her door. The truck was askew in the lane, brakes smoking.

The truck driver was a white-haired guy with a

long ponytail, a white beard, and a red headband. He looked like Willie Nelson. He leaned out the driver's window and hollered, "You dumb broad! I damn near hit you. Get the fuck outta the street." He cranked the stalled engine and it belched a huge black cloud out the chrome stack when the diesel fired.

Heart pounding, Kathryn lowered her window and mumbled, "Sorry," but the word was lost in the rattle of the truck's engine. She restarted her car and roared off without looking, lucky there was no on-coming traffic on the normally busy street. The truck driver blasted the air horn again, and she looked in her rearview mirror just in time to see him flip her the finger.

As she pulled into the county parking lot, she spotted a chartreuse County Fire Department para-medic unit parked at the main entrance to the admin-istration building, rear doors ajar and lights flashing, alongside a white Santa Rita Sheriff-Coroner van.

Kathryn ran past the two empty vehicles and through the double doors into the building. Halfway down the wide polished concrete hallway she spotted two uniformed paramedics pushing an empty gur-ney.

As they passed, she whispered, "Oh, no," and sprinted to the end of the corridor, charged up the gray stairs two at a time, and exited on the second floor. When she approached the DA's security door, an ashen-faced receptionist buzzed her through with-out a word.

The door opened into a hallway where several people stood talking quietly. A tall, attractive woman with long black hair, wearing a sedate blue business suit, broke away from the group and put her arms around Kathryn.

"God, Kate, Hal's dead." Mary Elizabeth Skinner was the DA's legal advisor and Kathryn's closest friend in the office. A woman whose introspective, unassuming demeanor belied her technical competence, she had joined the DA's office just months before Kathryn and was close only to Mackay and Benton.

Kathryn clung to Mary Elizabeth for a moment, then said softly, "I have to go down the hall. I'll get back to you as soon as I can. We have to be strong."

"I know, I'm okay. Go ahead."

Kathryn gave her friend a squeeze, then headed toward Benton's office. The District Attorney's office occupied two-thirds of the second floor of the huge, square building. Two perpendicular hallways divided it into approximately equal quadrants. Giant concrete pillars about twenty-five feet apart supported the overhead, which in reality was the floor of the Sheriff-Coroner's Office, which consumed the building's entire third floor. Exposed air circulation ducts and electrical conduit hung from the ceiling, which was coated with an ineffective gray soundproofing that county officials denied contained harmful levels of asbestos.

Institutional gray and green semiportable metal panels bolted to the floor and ceiling chopped the interior into a helter-skelter labyrinth of offices, conference rooms, a law library, an employee lounge, and various other work areas.

The wider and longer north-south hallway, which terminated at the door to Harold Benton's office, was flanked by the Assistant DA offices, arranged so the senior lawyers enjoyed the largest spaces, nearest the District Attorney himself.

Kathryn rushed past her own office, which was adjacent to Benton's, and encountered half a dozen senior attorneys clustered around the door, silent and solemn. Her eyes locked onto those of Don Whitaker, a tall, gangly blond man whom she especially liked. In his early to mid thirties, he had already earned a reputation as a tough and spectacularly effective trial attorney.

She gently pushed her way through the crowd. "Glenn?" she said tentatively.

Glenn Horner, sergeant in charge of the Sheriff's Coroner Section, was talking softly to Robert Simmons. Simmons sat in a leather chair beside Benton's desk, shaking his head to something Horner was saying. Deputy Coroner Rockwell Staley stood beside a gurney in the far corner of the office.

Horner turned and nodded at Kathryn, then stood and walked to where she waited in the doorway. "Kathryn, I'm glad you're here. We can't locate Mac," he said, referring to Benton's Chief Deputy in Charge of Operations, Neal McCaskill.

"Neal's at a Commander's meeting this morning," Kathryn replied. She stared at the shiny black vinyl body bag on the gurney. It was zipped up the middle from top to bottom and obviously held Harold Benton's dead body. The early morning sunlight reflected off the bag's metal zipper into her eyes.

"What happened?"

Horner grasped her by an elbow and led her around behind the office door where they couldn't be overheard. He glanced furtively at Simmons. "As near as I can figure it, Hal collapsed about thirty minutes ago. Someone from down here called our section right afterward. Don't know who. I grabbed Rocky and came down."

Kathryn glared at him. "Jesus Christ, Sarge, why didn't you make them put him in an ambulance? Maybe they could've saved him!"

"Take it easy, Kathryn," Horner said, touching her on the forearm. "You know as long as there's a chance a person is still alive, the medical people are in charge. The Coroner doesn't assume jurisdiction until someone is pronounced dead. There wasn't anything I could do at the time."

"Yes, but—"

"When I got here, Hal was obviously dead. No question in my mind; taking him to the hospital wouldn't have made any difference. Paramedics said when they arrived, Hal was gone but Simmons was still trying to resuscitate him. They had to make him quit. Once he stopped, he pronounced—"

Horner's voice caught, and he cleared his throat before continuing. "—he pronounced Hal dead. Then I assumed jurisdiction. I sent Rocky over to the motor pool to get the van and gurney. There really wasn't anything more any of us could have done."

"I'm sorry, Glenn. I'm pretty upset, I guess. No offense meant."

He smiled. "None taken. We're all pretty upset. Especially Dr. Simmons. Christ, he tried to resuscitate Benton for fifteen or twenty minutes. It was hopeless from the start."

"What does Simmons say?" Kathryn asked.

"I haven't really had a chance to talk to him except to calm him down. He thinks it's his fault somehow.

You know he and Hal were pretty good friends. Maybe you and I could interview him together." He paused and looked at Kathryn intensely. "Are you up to it?"

She drew in a deep breath and forced her eyes from the body on the gurney. "I'm fine. Really. I'm okay."

Horner stared at her for another moment, then nodded and turned. He gestured at Deputy Staley with a slight toss of his head. Staley nodded and rolled the gurney from the room, closing the door behind him.

Kathryn pulled two chairs over and placed them in front of Simmons, who stared absently out the office window. He was pale, his eyes wet and bloodshot. His suit coat was tossed on the floor, and the tail of his shirt was pulled out of the waist of his trousers.

"Doctor?" Horner began gently. "Doctor, could we talk with you? Are you all right?"

Simmons looked at them and his eyes cleared. "Sure. Hello, Ms. Mackay." He sighed and shook his head sadly. "You'd think I'd be used to death by now, after all my years in medicine, but I guess I'm not. I can't believe Hal's dead."

"Doctor," Kathryn interjected softly, "can you tell us what happened?"

"Well, I came up to talk with Hal this morning about an important matter. I got here right after nine o'clock, but first I grabbed coffee at the Starbucks cart in the atrium because I figured we'd be tied up for a couple of hours. I recall passing you in the hall on the way. Anyway, . . ."

"Can you tell us what you were meeting about, Doctor?" Kathryn asked.

"Next Tuesday the Board of Supervisors is going to vote on a very controversial needle exchange ordinance. One that legalizes the free distribution of sterilized needles to intravenous drug users, no questions asked."

Horner looked confused. "So what did that have to do with you and Hal?"

"Hal and I disagreed about the proposed ordinance. I'm afraid . . ." Simmons's voice caught and he swallowed hard, then continued. "I really didn't realize how far apart we were until this morning."

"What do you mean?" Mackay asked softly.

"Hal was lining up law enforcement support to appear with him at the Board meeting in opposition. I came up here this morning to try to talk him out of his position. It's that simple."

"Were you able to do that?" Kathryn asked him.

"No. In fact, quite the contrary. The more we discussed it, the more resolute he became. I had no idea he felt so strongly. We . . ." He cleared his throat again. "We argued."

Kathryn's eyebrows rose slightly. She knew Benton to be a powerful trial attorney but not personally argumentative, nor did she perceive Simmons as confrontational.

"You argued?"

"I'm afraid so," he replied in a shaky voice. "Vigorously. At one point he threatened to throw me out of his office. Said he didn't want to associate with 'a flaming-ass out-of-control liberal with no public conscience.' That angered me, and I said a few things I shouldn't have. It got out of control."

"And?" Horner prompted.

"As I said, it got pretty heated. Hal was extremely agitated. I was sitting here across from him in front of his desk. Suddenly, his face turned pale and his eyes got large. He grabbed at his chest and stood up suddenly, and tried to say something, but couldn't speak. Then just as suddenly, he sat back down and collapsed face down on his desk. I recognized the symptoms of a myocardial infarction immediately."

"Oh, God," Kathryn said softly.

Simmons continued, "I ran around behind his desk and laid him on the floor and ripped off his shirt and tie. He wasn't breathing, and he was unconscious. I started CPR, but he didn't respond. At one point I stopped and ran to the door. It was closed; Hal closed it when we started to argue. Someone was walking by, I don't know who it was, but I told them to call an ambulance, that Benton had had a heart attack. I resumed CPR and I guess maybe it was ten minutes or so before the paramedics showed up. Glenn arrived shortly after. I . . ."

Kathryn slid her chair closer to Simmons and touched him on the arm. "Dr. Simmons, I know this is hard. Take your time."

"No," he said, "I'm all right. Anyway, they literally pulled me off Hal; it was obvious he was dead. I just didn't want to give up. I guess I felt . . . I feel responsible. If we hadn't been arguing, maybe . . . Well, he was dead, so I pronounced. Then Sergeant Horner took over. That's about all I can recall right now."

"That's fine, thanks," Kathryn assured him. "You'll contact us if anything else—"

The office door slammed open and Neal McCaskill rushed into the room, breathless and shaken. He looked at Simmons, then at Horner, momentarily ignoring Mackay. "Glenn. Doctor. Is it true? Hal's dead?"

Horner nodded. "It's true, Mac. He was with Dr. Simmons when it happened."

McCaskill thought for a minute, then unbuttoned the jacket of his expensive charcoal suit, loosened his tie, and unbuttoned the top button of his shirt. He ran his fingers through his hair and sighed, collecting his thoughts. Then he acknowledged Kathryn Mackay for the first time. "Kathryn, I'd like to talk to you right away, please."

"Sure, Mac, I'll be there as soon as we're finished here. It won't be long."

McCaskill turned, his hand on the doorknob, looked at her, said, "Five minutes. In my office," and closed the door.

The young Hispanic woman clutched herself tightly around the chest and shivered uncontrollably, although she was not cold. Her breasts were large and tender and she felt them weigh heavily against her forearms. She wore loose-fitting sweatpants and a matching sweatshirt over a T-shirt that said "What, me worry?" on the front.

Her baby fussed. "Quiet, baby, it won't be long now." The baby ignored her and kicked again, harder. She smiled tolerantly, as mothers do. "Silencio, niño, calmese. No se asustado, tu madre es aqui."

A heavy wave crashed into the concrete riprap below, spewing a fine spray on her face. It felt cool and familiar. She sucked in a deep breath and licked her wet lips. They tasted salty.

Remnants of gigantic Pacific storms, born fifteen hundred miles to the west, speed eastward, gaining momentum and anger, eventually venting their accumulated fury on the central California coast. The water, at a constant temperature of sixty-six degrees, takes your breath away when you enter it.

A well-conditioned, strong, powerful swimmer without a wet suit might survive four or five minutes in the cold water before succumbing to hypothermia. Weak swimmers are sucked into the severe undertow created as the roiling green waves retreat and regroup for another assault. They lose consciousness within two minutes, and drown within five. Sometimes their bodies are swept out to sea, never to be found, and sometimes they wash up on the beach at Santa Rita. Either way, anyone who falls or jumps into the ocean at Lighthouse Point is doomed, and the woman knew it.

Although she had been a high school athlete, she was not in her best physical condition, and could not swim. She leaned forward and peered down the fifteen-foot vertical drop into the swirling, foaming luminescent surf.

She had made her decision. She felt light-headed but calm, peaceful, and completely in control for the first time in months. "Are you ready, baby?" she asked. The baby responded by kicking her. She chuckled.

The woman interwove her fingers, cupped her hands under her baby's tiny head, at the same time supporting her own distended stomach, closed her eyes, turned her face skyward, and said, "Forgive me, God." Then she stepped over the cliff into the Pacific Ocean.

She held her breath as long as possible. When she could hold it no longer, she exhaled and took a deep breath, dragging sand and seawater deep into her lungs. She struggled briefly but violently, gasped several times, then was still.

Amelia Salazar never felt her unborn son's final desperate kick.

5

Neal McCaskill was forty-five years old, short, and slightly overweight. He worked harder at dressing to conceal his weight than to control it, and he was always handsomely dressed and neatly coiffured. By the time Kathryn Mackay strode into his office, his hair was brushed, his necktie was tightened, his suit coat was buttoned, and he was sitting behind his desk. He looked up when Mackay entered, and motioned her to sit by pointing at the chair in front of him.

Mackay respected McCaskill's professional skills and liked him well enough, although she didn't know him outside the office. A married man, he socialized very little with coworkers, including Harold Benton, but he was considered politically astute.

She slid a chair up to his desk. "What did you want to see me about?"

He interlaced his fingers on his desk and gazed at her for a few seconds. "As the senior chief deputy, I'm Acting District Attorney until the Board appoints me Hal's successor. Do you agree?"

"Christ, Neal, Hal's body isn't even at the morgue yet. Frankly, I hadn't given it any thought."

"Well I have, and I need to get up to speed on the high-profile cases so I can assure the Board there will be no loss of momentum or continuity in the operation of this office when I take over."

"I don't think I'd have new business cards printed yet," Mackay told him.

"What are you talking about? Who else would they appoint?"

"The last time a DA died in office they appointed the Public Defender. Granted, that was a long time ago, but one of the Supes is still on the Board and Hal's alienated some of the others over the years."

"You're being ridiculous," McCaskill replied coldly, picking up a glossy black Waterman fountain pen. He removed the cap and held it poised over a yellow legal pad. "I need you to give me an overview of your unit's most important cases. If I need to delve deeper into one, we can come back to it later."

By eleven-thirty, Kathryn had briefed McCaskill on the murders, rapes, and other serious cases she and her team had in the pipeline.

When the briefing was concluded, Kathryn walked to the Starbucks coffee cart in the atrium, which connected the county's administration and courts buildings, and picked up a double espresso. She carried it back to her office and closed and locked the door so she wouldn't be disturbed. She removed her jacket, tossed it over the back of a chair, and for the first time reacted to the death of her friend. She nuzzled her face into her folded arms on her desk and cried. She never drank her coffee.

The phone buzzed. She considered letting voice

mail take the call, but habit compelled her to pick up before the fourth ring. "This is Kathryn Mackay."

"Ms. Mackay, this is Patty O'Conner from Supervisor Lawrence's office. The Supervisor would like to meet with you in the Board chambers, if that is possible."

Kathryn opened her appointment book. "Sure, when?"

"Right now, Supervisor Lawrence said. Can you be there in five minutes?"

"Of course. Can you tell me what this is about?" Kathryn asked.

"No, I'm sorry, I don't know. Supervisor Lawrence just said for me to tell you it's extremely urgent."

"I'll be right there," Kathryn answered. She held the receiver over the desk set momentarily, then dropped it softly into the cradle.

She quickly reapplied makeup, straightened her shirt, and put on her jacket. Five minutes later, she stood outside the double oak doors emblazoned with the seal of the Santa Rita County Board of Supervisors.

6

═══

When Kathryn entered, the Board chambers were empty except for County Administrative Officer Sharon Brice, County Counsel Dan Burford, and the five supervisors, all seated around a polished oak conference table. Board Chairperson Wilma Lawrence stood from her chair in the center of the table and shook Mackay's hand, then asked her to be seated.

"Thank you for coming, Ms. Mackay. Allow me to say on behalf of all of us how saddened we are. Harold Benton was a fine man and an exemplary District Attorney and his death is a great loss. We also know that you and he were close friends and we want to express our condolences to you personally. If there is anything we can do, please just let us know."

The other four supervisors nodded, and Kathryn answered, "Thank you. I appreciate your thoughtfulness. It really wasn't necessary to call me here, as busy as you are, but I'll be happy to convey your condolences to everyone in our office."

Lawrence glanced at each of her colleagues, then

cleared her throat and looked Mackay directly in the eye. "As you know, Ms. Mackay, it is the Board's duty when a vacancy occurs in an elective office to appoint an interim successor until the next general election in June. As you might imagine, we are not unanimous in our perception of who the best person to assume that responsibility might be."

She glanced at each of her colleagues again. "To cut to the chase, the Board has voted three-to-two to appoint you interim District Attorney. Are you interested?"

Kathryn paused momentarily, hoping her excitement wasn't apparent. In a voice as calm as she could muster, she answered, "Absolutely."

"Ms. Mackay, let me be quite frank," Philip Boynton interjected. "I was one of the two dissenting votes. While your success as a trial attorney speaks for itself, in my opinion Neal McCaskill possesses the administrative skills necessary to run the DA's office and, just as important, he has the political acumen to get himself elected next year. The Board would be deeply embarrassed if we appointed a successor who couldn't or wouldn't run a successful reelection campaign next June. Unfortunate, maybe, but a fact of political life."

Gerald Staley, a distinguished-looking man in his seventies and father of Sheriff's Deputy Rockwell Staley, held his hand up to request the floor. Lawrence granted it with a nod. Staley removed his bifocals and held them in his hand, then smiled.

"Ms. Mackay, Supervisor Boynton and I disagreed about who should succeed Harold Benton, but the Board is unanimous on the matter of reelection. Our offer is contingent on your promise to seek reelection next June and your commitment to make every legitimate effort to succeed in that effort. You will have—you do have—this Board's complete confidence and support both publicly and privately. Any disagreements we had will not be aired in a public forum."

"One more thing, Ms. Mackay," Chairperson Lawrence added. "Neither you nor the Board can afford to appear indecisive on such an important matter. We need your answer before you leave our chambers."

Kathryn contemplated, then leaned forward and placed her elbows on the oak table. "I can only make a tentative commitment at this time, Madam Chairperson. I'm a single parent, and I promised my ten-year-old daughter that she and I would talk about all the important decisions that affect our lives. I'm certain she will agree that this is a wonderful opportunity for both of us, but I need to discuss it with her before formally accepting your offer. I can't give you an answer now."

Lawrence smiled. "What's your daughter's name?"

"Emma."

"Emma. My daughter's name is Sheila. Of course, she's a bit older than Emma. Thirty-one, with two children of her own. I consider it admirable that you have your priorities straight. I believe that is exactly the kind of person Santa Rita needs as a District Attorney." She paused, then stated officiously, "The Chair will hear a motion to allow Kathryn Mackay until 8 A.M. tomorrow morning to accept the Board's offer of appointment as interim District Attorney. Do I hear such a motion?"

"So moved, Madam Chair," proposed Staley, with a

smile at Kathryn. "And I concur with the Chair's comments with respect to appropriate priorities."

The motion was seconded by Supervisor Janet Gutierrez, who represented the largely Hispanic fifth supervisorial district, which included Española. The motion was approved unanimously, and Kathryn was excused with a directive to meet with the Board at exactly eight o'clock the next morning.

Kathryn excused herself, walked down the three flights of stairs to the second floor, went into her office, and closed the door. Then she picked up the phone and called Emma's after-school care to tell them she planned to pick up Emma early that afternoon.

Kathryn walked into the school yard at four-thirty and spotted Emma talking with her best friend and two other girls Kathryn didn't recognize. Kathryn's face brightened and she waved her hand. "Hi, honey," she shouted.

Emma said something to one of the girls to which they both rolled their eyes, grabbed her backpack, and shuffled slowly toward her mother. Kathryn bent over to kiss her on the cheek, but Emma pulled away.

"What's wrong, honey? Is everything okay?"

"You just ruined my life, that's all. Did you absolutely *have* to try and kiss me in front of all my friends like I'm a child or something? I'm so mortified." Emma tossed her backpack into the back seat and climbed into the front seat beside her mother.

Inwardly Kathryn laughed, recalling all too well how much she hated shows of affection at that age. "Buckle up, Em," Kathryn told her.

Emma pulled the shoulder harness over her chest

and snapped the buckle in place. "I got an A on my math exam. Want to see it? I really studied hard."

Kathryn smiled. "I know you did, Em. I'll look at it when we get home, if that's all right. Maybe we should stop at Sophie's and get a couple of quesadillas so we don't have to cook. I'd like to talk with you about something tonight."

"That sounds good. Can we get dessert at Baskin-Robbins?" She paused. "Steven Billups asked me if I could dance with him at the fifth grade graduation party. Do you think I should?"

Kathryn eased onto the freeway on-ramp headed south and glanced at her daughter's beautiful freckled face. "That isn't for another eight or nine months. Can you put the decision off for a few days?"

Emma rolled her eyes in exasperation. "You don't understand anything. If I don't answer him, he'll ask someone else."

"Well, in that case, I think it would be all right to promise him at least one dance. But why do you want to? I thought you hated boys."

"Not Steven. He's different. And he's cute."

7

―――

"Mom, let's sit here," Emma suggested, plopping her tray on the table closest to the window, which faced the Baskin-Robbins across the courtyard. Without waiting for her mother, she stuffed three chips into her mouth.

"Emma, that wasn't polite," Kathryn admonished. "Couldn't you at least wait for me to sit down? Try some guacamole. And don't eat so many chips, or you won't want your quesadilla."

"Yuk! I hate guacamole. It's all green. I'm starving." Emma took a long pull on her Diet Coke and a bite from a quesadilla wedge.

Kathryn hadn't eaten all day, but she could hardly stand the thought of food. As she absentmindedly sipped her Coke, she glanced around the taqueria and was overwhelmed by a wave of nostalgia and anger. Sophie's had been her and Emma and Dave's favorite place to grab a bite to eat together.

DA Inspector Dave Granz had been Kathryn's lover, friend, and confidante who, except for Morgan Nelson, was the only person with whom she had discussed important personal matters. Several months before, Dave had been shot and almost killed by a woman named Julia Soto, a stalker with whom he had a brief affair and then rejected. He had assured Kathryn that the affair was over, but she knew she could never trust him again, and broke off their relationship. Now, she could no longer turn to him. "Damn you, Granz, damn you. Why did you do that?" she thought.

"Honey, can I talk to you about something?" Kathryn said, returning her attention to Emma, who had a mouth full of food. "I have sort of a hard decision to make, and I hoped you could help me out."

Emma took another swallow of her drink, then put the glass on the table. "Sure, Mom. Is it something about my school? You know I'm trying really hard to get good grades."

Kathryn patted Emma's hand. "It's nothing like that, sweetie. You're doing fine in school, and I'm proud of you. This is about my job."

Emma looked at Kathryn intently but said nothing, so Kathryn continued. "Something happened at work today that I need to tell you about. You know how in my job I'm called a District Attorney?"

Emma nodded.

"Well I'm actually an Assistant District Attorney. The District Attorney is . . ."

"I know, Mom, the District Attorney is Mr. Benton. He's your boss, huh?"

Kathryn sipped from her Coke. "Well, honey, this is a little hard, but this morning Mr. Benton had . . . he had a heart attack and . . ."

Emma's eyes grew huge, and her mouth dropped open. Although she did not know Harold Benton well, on the occasions they had been together, they seemed to make a real connection. "Mommy, is Mr. Benton dead? I read in a book that when people have heart attacks they die. Did he, Mommy?"

Kathryn grasped both her daughter's hands in her own and squeezed. "Yes, Emma, I'm afraid he did." Tears welled up in Kathryn's eyes and ran down her cheeks.

Emma wiped her lips delicately on a salsa-stained paper napkin and walked around the table to sit beside Kathryn. She pulled her mother's head onto her shoulder and put her arms around Kathryn's shoulders. "It's okay to cry, Mommy. I'm here and I understand."

Kathryn's chest seemed to swell to the point of bursting with love and pride for her daughter. She allowed herself to sob briefly, then raised her head and wiped her eyes. She looked directly into her daughter's beautiful brown eyes and saw a maturity and compassion that startled her in a ten-year-old. "Thank you, Em. It's so important for me to know that I can count on you. I'm all right now. Go on back and eat while we talk."

Emma resumed eating, and past a mouthful of chips she said, "Okay, Mom, what do you want to talk about?"

"Well, honey, someone now has to be *the* District Attorney, to take Mr. Benton's place. And they have asked me to do it. But I told them I'd have to talk with you, first, that you and I make all our important decisions together. What do you think?"

Emma consumed the final piece of her quesadilla, and nibbled on a chip thoughtfully. "Would you be the boss?"

"Yes, I would."

"Would you still put criminals in jail?"

"Of course. That's what District Attorneys do."

Emma looked at her mother. "Do you want to be District Attorney?"

"Yes, honey, I do. It would be an honor for me, and I think you would be proud, but I need to know how you feel about it."

"I think you should take it, Mom," Emma advised, then asked, "Would you still get your name in the paper and be on TV a lot?"

Kathryn was surprised by the question. "That's an interesting question, Em. I hadn't really thought about it. I'd probably be in the paper and on TV even more, because even though the other lawyers would do most of the trials, I'd be their boss, so the reporters would want to interview me. I know it embarrasses you for me to be so well known, that your friends tease you about it. Would this make it harder for you at school?"

"Oh, Mom, I just say that. I think it's neat to have kids at school say, 'Hey, Em, I saw your mom on TV.' It's sorta like we're famous." Emma paused. "Can we go to Baskin-Robbins now? I saved just enough room for ice cream."

"How about a frozen yogurt instead?"

"Same thing," Emma opined. "When we get home can I show you my math test? I got an A, you know."

As soon as they got to their condo, Kathryn opened the sliding door to the deck, which afforded a glimpse of the ocean, and the cool evening sea breeze washed over her body, eliciting a deep, soulful sigh.

Once Emma was settled in her room studying, Kathryn walked straight through her bedroom to the adjoining bathroom, ignoring the unmade bed and small pile of dirty clothes, and stripping naked as she went. She bent over the sink and splashed cold water on her face. With a cool, wet cloth, she removed her makeup and washed her face, then removed her contact lenses and put on plastic-framed glasses. Finally, she wiped her entire body with a damp washcloth and put on a pair of dark blue sweatpants and matching sweatshirt with nothing underneath.

Feeling clean and unencumbered, Kathryn spent the rest of the evening reviewing Emma's math exam, helping with her spelling homework, doing two loads of wash, and cleaning up after Sam, their sixty-pound yellow lab. The dog had been Dave's gift to Emma following the courtroom shooting death of Emma's father, Kathryn's ex-husband, several years before. Once again, Kathryn said, "Damn you, Dave, damn you to hell," only this time she said it aloud to herself.

"Emma, what are you doing in your bedroom? Do I hear the television after you told me you were going in there to study?"

The TV sound went silent and Emma stuck her head around the kitchen door. She answered sheepishly, "I wasn't really watching it, Mom. It was turned down really low." Seeing the stern look on her mother's face, she added, "Besides, I'm all done with my homework."

"Okay, honey, then go take your shower, and we'll watch TV together."

"Aw, Mom, do I hafta? Can't I take my shower tomorrow morning? Please? You might need me around just in case you need to cry some more."

Kathryn smiled. At the ripe old age of ten, her daughter had mastered the fine art of manipulation.

But she knew Emma's offer was also motivated by unselfishness, one of the traits Kathryn loved most. "All right, sweetie, go put on your PJs. What should we watch?"

"Yay!" Emma exclaimed. "*Sister, Sister.* There's two of them tonight. Can we watch them both?"

By the time Emma had changed, Kathryn sat on the beige leather sofa with her legs curled up under her. Sam sat on the floor with his huge head on her lap, his tongue hanging out the side drooling on Kathryn's sweatpants. Emma crawled up and tucked herself into the curve of her mother's body. Sam assumed it was a family get-together, and before the first commercial he was curled up on the sofa alongside Emma, snoozing noisily.

When the second episode of *Sister, Sister* ended at nine o'clock, Kathryn said, "Okay, Em, jump up and brush your teeth, then call me when you're in bed so I can tuck you in."

"Aw, Mom, can't I stay up till nine-thirty? Nine o'clock is too early for bedtime. I'm not a kid anymore, you know."

"Not tonight," Kathryn answered. "I'm awfully tired. As soon as I tuck you in, I think I'll go to bed myself. Now run along."

"I love you, Mommy," Emma said after she crawled into bed.

Kathryn leaned over her daughter and allowed her head to be drawn down by the strong little arms around her neck. "I love you, too, sweetie. More than anything in the world. Now, go to sleep so you aren't cranky in the morning."

As her mother was about to close the bedroom door, Emma said, "Mom?"

Kathryn turned. "Yes, Em?"

"I'll bet Mr. Benton would want you to be District Attorney."

"Thank you, honey. Now go to sleep."

By nine-fifteen, Kathryn had crawled between the cool sheets of her bed. It seemed like hours before she drifted into a fitful sleep, her turbulent emotions swinging wildly between anguish over the loss of her friend and the pride and anticipation of becoming Santa Rita County's first woman District Attorney.

8

"Good Morning, Santa Rita. It's 5:42 A.M., September eighth, the world is spinning, the sun is up, and radio station KSRC is set to begin another broadcast day. Today on the Central California Coast we'll see dense early morning fog, with clearing by mid-morning, followed by—" Kathryn snapped off the clock radio and listened. Emma apparently wasn't disturbed.

She wiped her brow with the towel draped around her neck and walked back to the spare bedroom, which served as office, playroom, and exercise room. She had awakened before five o'clock and, abandoning hope of more sleep, had drunk a cup of black coffee, then, clad in a black leotard, she had turned on the treadmill for ten minutes. Now she switched to the Stairmaster, set the counter, and started climbing. She preferred at least thirty minutes of aerobic exercise each morning, but usually settled for fifteen to twenty minutes, two or three times a week.

At six-thirty, Kathryn awakened Emma, who had burrowed under the covers and had her head at the foot of the bed. Sam reluctantly climbed off the bed and slunk to his own bed when Kathryn opened the door. "Emma, time to get up."

"I'm sick, Mom. I can't go to school. I feel awful."

Kathryn feigned concern. One or two mornings each week Emma had a new ailment that threatened to keep her in bed the remainder of the day. "I hope it isn't something too serious. What do you think it is?"

Emma giggled. "I think I have scruples."

Her mother laughed, too. "What sort of symptoms accompany this disease?"

"My eye hurts and it's blurry when I close my right eye. See?" She squinted and squeezed her left eye shut. "It's red, too, huh? It's for sure I have scruples."

"Wait here," her mother answered with mock concern, "I'll get the medical book and see what to do."

Momentarily, Kathryn returned with a gigantic blue home health care book and flipped to the index. "Let's see," she read, "eyes, eye emergencies, here we go, let's see . . . page 761 . . . ah, here we are. Scleritis, also known as scruples. Symptoms: pain in one or both eyes, redness, blurred vision. Sounds like that's what you've got, all right. But it says here, 'under no circumstances should children with scruples stay home from school, which only worsens the condition.'"

"Mom, you're making that up!"

"How do you know?"

"I looked it up. That's where I learned about it, but I couldn't 'member how to pronounce it."

"Out with you, faker," Kathryn ordered, jerking the covers back, "and into the shower while I make us breakfast." When Emma had run into the bathroom, Kathryn shook her head and smiled. "At least I can count on certain things remaining constant," she said to herself.

Already dressed in a Ralph Lauren charcoal gray pinstriped suit, white silk shirt, and medium-height black heels, Kathryn returned to the kitchen and took out orange juice, a whole-wheat bagel and orange marmalade for herself, plus Cheerios, milk, and a banana for Emma. Although her stomach churned and she was still not hungry, it was her and Emma's daily ritual to eat breakfast together while discussing other's plans for the day.

Just as the shower started to run, Kathryn was startled by the chirp of the portable phone. She reached for it, pulled back, then reached for it again, knowing that calls at home usually meant work.

"Kate, this is Morgan. Did I wake you?"

"No, I was making breakfast for Emma."

"And something for yourself, I hope."

"I'm not very hungry."

"That's why I called, Katie," he answered, addressing her with the familiar nickname that was his special privilege, "to see how you're doing. I haven't talked to you since . . . well, since you left the morgue. Are you all right?"

"I'm doing okay, but I still have a hard time believing Hal's gone. How about you? The autopsy on Hal's body must have been pretty hard for you."

"I didn't autopsy him, Kate. It's not required when someone dies in the presence of a physician. Simmons signed the death certificate. Hal's family was anxious to hold services, so I withdrew fluid samples and released the body this morning."

"That makes sense. Simmons was there the whole

time." She paused. "I have something to tell you, if you have time."

"I always have time for you, Katie."

"After Hal . . . after . . . oh hell, right after Hal died, I met with Neal McCaskill. He wanted to get up to speed on the murder and rape cases my unit's working. Well, anyway, he said he expected to be appointed DA by the Board of Supervisors."

"That's probably a given."

"That's what I thought, but just before noon, the Board called me to their chambers and offered me the appointment. Lawrence said it was three to two, but they were firm in their offer. They gave me until eight o'clock this morning to give them my answer."

"What did you tell them?"

"That I needed to talk to Emma."

"What was her reaction?"

"She told me to accept, and I'm going to."

"Congratulations, they couldn't have made a better choice, in my opinion. How do you think Mac'll react?"

"Well, he thinks he's entitled to succeed Hal, and he's convinced that's what Hal would have wanted. He expects the appointment."

"Bull! Mac has no more right to be DA than you. It's not a kingdom that's passed down from monarch to monarch."

"I know. He'll be pissed, but I suppose I can handle it."

"Of course you can. Now you're sounding like you have second thoughts. What's the problem?"

"No problem, really, but I'm a trial lawyer, not a politician. Hal spent every waking minute politicking. I don't want to destroy my personal life, and I don't know the first thing about politics."

"You can learn. Hal had one great failing, Katie; he didn't know how to delegate. Surround yourself with good, carefully chosen people, tell them exactly what you expect of them, give them the authority they need, then step aside and let them do their jobs. You'll do fine."

"Thanks, Doc, I know I will, but I wanted to hear you tell me so."

Kathryn strode into the Board chambers at exactly eight o'clock and sat in front of the assembled body. As before, the County Administrative Officer and County Counsel were present, but in addition, Judge Jemima Tucker sat beside the CAO. She smiled at Kathryn but said nothing.

Chairperson Lawrence turned on the reel-to-reel tape that recorded all Board meetings, rapped her gavel on the oak table, and announced, "The Santa Rita County Board of Supervisors is convened pursuant to the Brown Act in closed session to discuss a special personnel matter, namely, the appointment of a District Attorney of Santa Rita County to fill the vacancy created by the untimely death of District Attorney Harold Benton. The record shall reflect that present are Supervisors Gutierrez, Staley, Jones, Vice Chair Boynton, Chairperson Lawrence, County Administrative Officer Sharon Brice, County Counsel Daniel Burford, Judge of the Superior Court Jemima Tucker, and Assistant District Attorney Kathryn Mackay."

Lawrence sipped from her ice water and contin-ued. "The Board has tendered an offer to Kathryn

Mackay to serve as the District Attorney until the general election on June sixth of next year. Ms. Mackay has agreed to apprise this Board of her decision to accept or decline this appointment at 8 A.M. this morning. Ms. Mackay, what is your decision?"

The tension in the room was palpable, but Kathryn sat straight in her chair and her voice was confident, strong, and clear as she spoke into the microphone in front of her. "Madam Chairwoman and members of the Santa Rita County Board of Supervisors, I am honored to accept your appointment as District Attorney. I will serve to the best of my capability."

All five supervisors broke with protocol and stood to extend their hands in congratulation. Kathryn shook each one warmly, as well as Brice's and Burford's. Judge Tucker did not offer her hand.

Chairperson Lawrence once again rapped her gavel and announced, "The County Administrative Officer is directed to announce the action taken in closed session here today and to publicly post notice of that action in accordance with the law. The Board is adjourned." She turned to Kathryn and said, "Step this way, please, Ms. Mackay."

By the time Lawrence and Mackay rounded the table and stepped to the center of the raised dais, Judge Tucker had donned her black robe.

Lawrence smiled and said, "We were a bit premature, I guess, but we hoped and assumed you would accept. Judge Tucker has graciously agreed to administer the oath of office."

"Raise your right hand, and repeat after me, please," Tucker ordered.

Kathryn repeated, "I, Kathryn Mackay, do solemnly swear to uphold the Constitution of the United States and the laws of the State of California, and to carry out the duties of District Attorney of the County of Santa Rita, California, to the best of my ability, so help me God."

Jemima Tucker smiled and hugged Kathryn Mackay in an unusual show of affection and whispered, "Good luck Kathryn. You can call on me anytime, but you're going to do just fine." Aloud, so everyone could hear, she said, "Congratulations, Ms. District Attorney. I'll see you in court."

9

When Kathryn returned to the DA's office, she sat behind her old government-issue desk, forgoing for the time being the privilege of moving into Harold Benton's office.

She considered it crucial to meet one-on-one with key members of her office so they learned about her appointment directly from her rather than through the grapevine.

But the first telephone number she dialed was extension 5735.

"Granz."

"Dave, this is Kathryn."

"Good morning, Kathryn," Dave answered tentatively. Interaction between the two had been sparse and tense since their relationship ended.

"Dave, there's a rather important matter that I need to discuss with you. Could you come to my office right away?" The inspectors' offices were at the far corner of the complex, although Chief of Inspectors Norm Podnoretz occupied an office adjacent to Mackay's.

Kathryn heard voices and paper shuffling in the background. "Jeez, Kate, I'm up to my ass in alligators right now. Could this wait till tomorrow or later this afternoon?"

"No, it really can't, Dave. I need to see you right now."

"Okay, sure, I'll be right there," he answered, then asked, "Should I pick us up some coffee, babe?"

"No, thanks. I'll see you in a minute," she answered, ignoring his attempt at intimacy.

In the three minutes since speaking on the phone, Granz's attitude had changed from sweet to sullen. Uninvited, he flopped into one of her beige leather chairs and slouched down. Despite the early hour, his tie and shirt collar were loosened, and he wore no jacket. His blond hair was uncombed, as usual. He looked frazzled. "What's up, Kathryn? I'm busy," he stated unceremoniously.

She ignored the attitude, assuming correctly that it stemmed from her rebuke of his advance. "Dave, I've just come from the Board of Supervisors chambers. I want you to hear the news directly from me. I have just been appointed District Attorney to replace Hal. Judge Tucker swore me in about ten minutes ago."

Granz looked at her briefly with a blank look on his face, then uncrossed his legs and sat upright in the chair, arms on the elbows. "You what!? You are the District Attorney?"

"As we speak."

"What about McCaskill? Everyone assumed he had a lock on it. Hell, I'd have bet my 49ers season tickets on it. Does he know?"

Mackay shook her head. "No, you're the first person I've told here. The Board gave me an hour to advise management before it's announced."

Granz thought for a minute, then despite himself he smiled the lopsided grin that Kathryn had always found so appealing. "So, you're my boss. Damn, that's an interesting twist. That'll really complicate our relationship, won't it?"

"Dave, let's get something clear between us right now. When I said we could never be together again after that . . . that Soto mess, I meant it. There is no relationship between us, and there never will be again."

"Okay, then what the hell did you call me here for? Podnoretz is the Chief of Inspectors, not me." His voice grew soft, as it did when he was angry. He stood up abruptly and the chair toppled over. "Call Norm, Kathryn. I need to get back to work."

"Dave, please. Sit down, so we can talk. I called you because I wanted you to be the first to hear. And because it's important we both know what to expect from each other."

"Okay," he answered, then despite his best effort another smile broke through. "I'm sorry, Kathryn. You deserve congratulations, not hassles. You'll do a great job. You can count on my help."

"I appreciate that, thank you. Dave, you're one of the most gifted police officers I've ever known. Under normal circumstances I'd offer you Chief of Inspectors in a minute, but I know that couldn't work, and so do you."

"Kathryn, you know I can handle it."

"I know, but too much has happened between us

for any reasonable professional relationship to have a chance, and I need to feel one hundred percent comfortable with all the division chiefs."

"What about Podnoretz? You gonna keep him?"

"He was Hal's appointee," she answered. "Besides, Norm's close to retiring. My guess is he'll pull the plug now that Hal's gone."

Granz ran his fingers through his blond hair and reflected. "Yeah, you're right about that. Pod told me lotsa times that if Hal ever retired, he would, too. Who you got in mind?"

"I was hoping you'd give me some advice on that."

"It's a no-brainer, Kathryn. Jim Fields is your guy. He's the best there is—not counting me, that is. You offer it to him, he'll grab it and you'll never be sorry."

"I agree," she said. "Are you going to be able to handle this? It could get a little uncomfortable for you."

"There's something I need to tell you, too. Walt Earheart has submitted his resignation to Sheriff Purvis. Says he wants to spend more time on his spread up in Montana hunting and fishing. He's going to retire as soon as Purvis finds someone to take over as Sheriff's Chief of Detectives. Purvis offered it to me, but I turned it down. I think I'll reconsider."

"Dave, I'm not trying to run you off. I just wanted to be up front about our situation here. I'm sure we can work together."

"I know that, but it's hard, you know? I still have feelings for you, Kate. I think I still love you in my own way. And . . ."

"Dave, please," Kathryn said softly, "Don't. It's been

just as hard for me. But I've let it go, and you should, too."

"I know, and I have, except in moments of weakness, like this morning on the phone. I'm sorry, sometimes you bring out the worst in me, and sometimes the best. I never know which part of me will appear. I'll call Purvis as soon as I get back to my office."

"Dave, maybe you should think it over."

"Don't need to. It's the smart thing to do. I started my career in the S.O. I wouldn't mind finishing it there. And it'll make it easier for both of us."

Kathryn nodded and folded her hands on her lap so he wouldn't see them tremble.

"You can consider this my two-week notice, Kathryn. I'll put it in writing if you prefer."

"That's not necessary."

Dave walked around the desk and kissed Kathryn on the cheek. "Congratulations, Ms. District Attorney. You deserve it. Call me any time I can help. I'll be there."

"What the hell do you mean you're the District Attorney?" McCaskill's face turned beet red, and he jumped from Mackay's leather chair as though shot from a cannon. "Who the hell says so!"

His strong reaction was exactly what she had expected, and she was prepared. "Sit down, Neal, and lower your voice, please, so we can discuss this."

He sat, but on the edge of the chair as if he intended to leap at her and tear her throat out. "What's to talk about? This is ridiculous, a fucking mistake."

"Please stop swearing. It's no mistake. As I said, the Board offered me the appointment yesterday but gave me until this morning to decide. I was sworn in at about eight-twenty by Judge Tucker."

Mackay and McCaskill sat in silence for a few moments, which he broke. "You had no right, Mackay. That was my appointment. I worked for years for this. How dare you sneak around and stab me in the back!"

"Neal," Kathryn said, "I never approached anyone about this. They called me, and I was more surprised than anyone. I assumed they would appoint you, and I would have supported you if they had. You owe me the same respect."

McCaskill stood and glared calmly at Mackay, "I owe you nothing! Nothing. You screwed me, and we both know it, so quit the bullshit. So what now, Ms. District Attorney, am I demoted to trying drunk drivers in municipal court?"

"Absolutely not. I want you to remain as my chief deputy. We'll work this out, believe me."

"Believe you? Why should I?"

Kathryn grew stern. "Because it's your only option unless you *do* want to try drunk drivers. As of now, I am the District Attorney of Santa Rita County. You have until noon today to decide whether or not you want to continue as chief deputy. If so, you'll get my full support, and I shall accept no less from you. I'll expect you to drop by my office before you go to lunch and give me your decision."

James Fields was stocky, with thinning hair and a dark-complexioned face that bore the aftermath of teenage acne. The right sleeve of his suit coat was neatly gathered and tucked into itself where his right hand should be. He looked handicapped but wasn't. Loss of his right hand in a courtroom bombing, followed by intense rehabilitation, had taught the naturally right-handed cop to do everything left-handed. Following rehab, he was restored to full duty as a DA inspector.

"Kathryn," he began, then reconsidered. "I mean Madam District Attorney. If the Board had asked me, I'd have told them up front that you were the best choice. You have my complete support. Is there anything I can do to make the transition easier for you?"

"My name is still Kathryn, Jim. Judge Tucker didn't change it when she swore me in. And, yes, now that you offered, there is something you can do for me."

"Name it," he responded, expertly flipping his leather-bound notebook open with his left hand and retrieving a roller-ball pen from his shirt pocket.

"You can accept my appointment to Chief of Inspectors, effective immediately."

Fields looked at her, retracted the pen and clipped it back into his shirt pocket, then closed his notebook. He crossed his legs, sat back in his chair, and placed his left hand over the empty sleeve of his right arm. "Kathryn, I'm flattered and honored that you would think of me. But I've worked with Norm Podnoretz for eighteen years and I owe him a great deal. My loyalty to him would preclude me discussing this with you without his knowledge and approval. Even then, I would not consider such an appointment if I thought by doing so I was costing Norm his job. I'm sorry, but that's how I see it."

Kathryn smiled. "I know that, Jim, and believe me,

I hope I can expect the same loyalty from you. Norm asked to speak with me a few minutes ago. He's decided to file his retirement papers as soon as I get someone in place to take over for him. You're my choice, Jim. What do you say?"

"I say 'yes.' Thanks for clearing that up with Norm. He's a great guy."

"I agree. Is it all right with you if I announce your appointment, or would you prefer me to wait?"

"Go ahead, Kathryn. No point in waiting." Standing to leave, he added, "I need to get back to my office and begin reassigning cases. I'll let you know as soon as that's done, and you can brief me on where you want to go."

At twelve-twenty-five, just as Kathryn was preparing to go to the cafeteria for a sandwich, Neal McCaskill stuck his head around the corner of her door and peered in. "Is now a good time? I can come back if you're tied up."

"No, now's fine, Mac. I'm going to have to get used to missing a lot more lunches than I did before. Come on in and sit down."

McCaskill was clearly more composed than the last time they talked. He cleared his throat. "Kathryn, I want to apologize for my outburst earlier, I . . ." he cleared his throat again.

Kathryn spread her fingers, palms out, and shook her head as if to say, "No problem, I understand."

"Anyway," he continued, "hearing about being passed over was a shock, as you can imagine. It hurt my pride, I admit, but I know you had as much right to be considered as anyone, including me. And ultimately, it doesn't really matter who did what or who lobbied the Board and who didn't; it was their call and they made it. If the offer is still open to be your chief deputy, I'd like to accept."

"I'm glad. Of course it's still open, and you are my chief deputy. Thanks for being so forthright. How would you like to handle notifying the managers and staff? I'll leave it to your discretion."

"Well, I've thought about that. The easy way would be to let you do it, and for me to just kind of slink around with my tail between my legs. But that's not my style, and it isn't conducive to effective leadership. You've got plenty to do, and it's my job. I'll take care of it. Anything special you want me to say on your behalf?"

"No, only that as policy decisions and assignments are made they will be communicated through the chief deputy."

"Done. And, Kathryn? Move into the office next door. That's always where I look for my boss when I need him, uh, her."

After McCaskill departed, Kathryn contemplated his latest reaction. The anger she had expected, but the conciliation she hadn't. Did he mean it? Cautious optimism is the best approach, she decided; hope for the best but prepare for the worst.

10

After talking with McCaskill, Kathryn quickly stuffed her framed newspaper clippings and other personal belongings into cardboard boxes and buzzed Nancy Torres, Harold Benton's secretary.

Nancy stuck her head in the door. "Can I come in?"

Kathryn looked up. "Yes, please. I assume you've heard."

Nancy sat across from Kathryn and began nervously. "Yes, I have. Kathryn, I'm so happy for you. You'll make a wonderful DA. I know you might want to choose your own secretary like Mr. Benton did. If you do, I'll understand. But I want you to know that I'd be proud to work for you if you want to keep me."

"I was hoping you'd feel that way, Nancy. I'd really appreciate it if you'd stay."

Nancy beamed. "Thanks. The first thing I did each morning was go over Mr. Benton's schedule for the day with him so he didn't miss a court appearance or an important appointment. He had a couple of things scheduled for today you need to know about. I'll go get my calendar."

"Yes, here we are," she said when she returned. "Two things. Oral arguments on the Banyon case in Judge Tucker's court at 1 P.M. You may recall Mr. Benton wanted to handle it himself because it's our first sexually violent predator petition. I can ask Mac to handle it, if you want."

"No, I'll do it, Nancy," Mackay replied, glancing at her watch. "What else?"

"A grievance hearing before the civil service commission at two this afternoon. Remember, Warren Silva was demoted from Attorney II to Attorney I and put on probation? Well, he filed a grievance."

"Give it to Loomis. Ted's the Administrative Chief Deputy. That's his job. Don't make any other appointments for me today. I want to settle in. Call Fields and ask him to round up a couple of trustees from the jail to move the boxes and stuff from my old office. See if they can do it while I'm in court."

Kathryn spent a few minutes sifting through Harold Benton's desk. The desk drawers contained only a few personal items: a red Swiss army knife, maps, a fountain pen, a bottle of aspirin, a scuffed baseball autographed by St. Louis Cardinals slugger Mark McGwire. They filled less than a shoe box; a sad collection, Kathryn thought, for a man who sat at this desk for almost twenty years. She carefully sealed the box with tape, which she would ask Fields to personally deliver to Benton's widow that afternoon, then secreted his appointment book in a locking drawer to review later.

Superior Court Judge Jemima Tucker was a beautiful black woman with flawless skin, perfect features, a quick wit, and an even quicker temper. A graduate of Bolt Law School, she was a woman on the rise in the judicial profession, and she tolerated no nonsense in her courtroom.

At one o'clock she convened her courtroom and announced, "The District Attorney has filed a petition to commit William Banyon pursuant to Welfare and Institutions Code Section 6600, also known as the Sexually Violent Predators Act."

The door flew open and Kathryn Mackay hurried down the aisle.

Judge Tucker paused, glanced at Mackay, then continued, "This is the time I set to render my decision on the petition. Does anyone wish to be heard before I proceed?"

Kathryn stood beside the prosecution table. "District Attorney Kathryn Mackay, Your Honor. I wish to make a few comments."

"Proceed, Ms. Mackay, but please be brief."

"The defendant has been evaluated by two psychiatrists, who concur that he has a mental disorder, pedophilia, such that without appropriate treatment and custody, he will likely engage in sexually violent behavior upon his release. The defendant claims the Sexually Violent Predator Act illegally imposes a new punishment for an inmate who has already been convicted and served his sentence."

Kathryn paused briefly, then continued. "The People disagree. The SVP law is a reasonable approach to dealing with those who prey on the innocent. Rather than await a re-offense and offer condolences to the new victim's family, the People merely seek to remove a violent sexual predator from society, while at the same time ensuring that he receives whatever treatment is available for his disorder."

Judge Tucker put on her reading glasses and flipped quickly through the case file. "The defendant will please rise," she ordered.

The defendant and his attorney, Public Defender Michael Books, rose simultaneously. In a bright orange jail jumpsuit, with a long ponytail and scraggly handlebar mustache, Banyon stood in dramatic contrast to his clean-shaven lawyer in his expensive suit. Banyon stared impassively at Tucker.

"I agree with the People," the judge stated. "We cannot call ourselves a civilized society unless our citizens can walk the streets without being victimized by violent criminals. My decision today will prevent the defendant from preying on a new victim. The defendant will be committed to Atascadero State Hospital, with his treatment program to be reviewed in two years."

The judge then turned to Mackay. "Does the District Attorney have other matters before this court this morning?"

"No, Your Honor," Mackay answered.

"Then I'll call the next case on calendar. And by the way, District Attorney Mackay, your office prevailed today, but don't expect the same result every time you walk into my courtroom."

Jesus, that was the shortest honeymoon period in history, Kathryn reflected to herself as she grabbed a coffee at the Starbucks cart on the way back to her office.

Pink "while-you-were-out" slips were stacked neatly in the center of Kathryn's desk when she returned. A Post-it stuck to the top said, "The first two are the important ones. The rest can wait. Nancy."

She flipped through them: "Call me at the S.O.:

Dave"; "URGENT: CALL STEVE WALLACE OR
ARLISS KRAFT @ CHANNEL 7! 342-7777".

Kathryn groaned. The media already. She decided
to put that one off, and dialed the Sheriff's Office
instead. When Granz answered, he sounded tense.

"Kathryn, one of the reasons I called was to tell you
that I'm Acting Chief of Detectives as of right now. An
hour ago, to be exact. Earheart's leaving in thirteen
days, and Purvis wanted him to teach me the ropes
before he left. I told Fields, and he said it wasn't a
problem."

"Jesus, Dave, this is a bit quick." She paused, then
said, "That's one reason you called. What else?"

"A dead body washed up on the main beach and
some guy stumbled over it this morning while he was
jogging."

"A homicide?" she asked.

"Can't be sure until Doctor Death does the autopsy."

Morgan Nelson's unofficial nickname always angered Kathryn, but she didn't react. "Man or woman?" she asked.

"Woman," he answered. "Young and pregnant,
looked almost ready to deliver. She was pretty beat
up, but the surf in there is really bad and the
shoreline is rocky. Could be an accident or suicide,
although suicide by drowning is pretty rare. I'm
treating it as a homicide until foul play can be ruled
out."

"Okay, thanks, Dave. Keep me informed. Let me
know when Dr. Nelson autopsies her. I want to be
there." Kathryn made a point to refer to Nelson by his
proper name and title in response to Granz's charac-
terization. She hung up and sat for several minutes. It

wouldn't be the same without Dave—maybe better, maybe worse, but definitely not the same.

Eventually, Kathryn could no longer delay her call to Channel 7. She picked up the receiver and punched in a new number.

"Channel 7 News."

"Hello, this is District Attorney Kathryn Mackay returning Mr. Wallace and Ms. Kraft's phone call. Is either of them available?"

"One moment, I'll check," the receptionist answered. The line clicked and strains of Montovani's "Moon River" filled the earpiece. Momentarily, the phone was picked up on the other end.

"Ms. Mackay, thank you so much for returning my call, although I was hoping to hear from you earlier. Our six o'clock segment is already pretty much set, but I'm sure we can squeeze in your response."

Warily, Kathryn asked, "Response to what, Ms. Kraft?"

"We received a call this morning from your chief deputy, Neal McCaskill." Kraft waited for a response, but Mackay didn't take the bait. "He told us he intends to oppose you in the District Attorney race next June. We taped an interview with him during the noon hour which will run as the lead story on tonight's six o'clock local news segment. We'd like to air your response, although time is a little tight right now. We could probably work something out if you could drive to our studio so we can do a quick film shoot."

Son-of-a-bitch, Kathryn thought. That's why that snake was so conciliatory. He knew announcing as chief deputy would make him a more credible candidate.

"I see," Kathryn answered noncommittally. "I'm sorry, but I can't make it down. I'm sure you understand that there is a lot to do here."

"We could send a film crew to your office," Kraft suggested.

"I'm afraid that won't work, either. I'm sorry."

"Well, can we record a statement over the phone?"

"Ms. Kraft, it's premature for me to comment on an interview that has not been broadcast, and which I haven't had time to properly consider."

"Why are you being so difficult?" Kraft asked testily. "Channel 7 is the only TV station that provides in-depth local news coverage. District Attorney Benton and Chief Deputy McCaskill were always quite forthcoming."

Mackay drew in a deep breath. "This is a new administration, Ms. Kraft. From now on it will be the District Attorney's policy to not grant exclusive interviews. If anything on tonight's news justifies a response from this office, I will call a news conference and make my announcement to all the media simultaneously."

"You mean you intend to let a challenge like that go unanswered?"

"As I said, any public statement by this office will be made after Mr. McCaskill's interview is broadcast, if a statement is necessary. Was there anything further I could help you with?"

"No, there wasn't," she answered, and hung up.

Kathryn sighed and checked her watch. She needed to be home in time to catch the local six o'clock news.

11

Kathryn and Emma sat on the living room sofa with the television turned to channel 7, watching a Toyota commercial.

"I really like your new job, Mom," Emma told her.

"I'm glad. Why do you say that?"

"'Cause we get to watch TV while we eat."

The Channel 7 News logo, a stylized sailboat superimposed over a setting sun, flashed on the screen, followed by the picture-perfect face of Steve Wallace, picture-perfect Arliss Kraft at his left shoulder with a standard news-anchor smile pasted on her face. Kathryn thought of them as Ken and Barbie.

"Good evening, ladies and gentlemen," Wallace opened. "Tonight we look at a controversy already swirling around today's appointment of senior trial attorney Kathryn Mackay to replace Harold Benton as District Attorney."

"Benton was one of the most visible District Attorneys in the state," Kraft interjected smoothly, "and was reportedly in his last term when he was struck down by a fatal heart attack. He was fifty-four years old. Steve?"

"Harold Benton was a law-and-order, lock-'em-up kind of DA. As you will learn in our first segment, some of his colleagues believe his intolerance for criminal liberalism led to retaliatory fallout and the appointment of a marginally qualified successor."

The picture cut to a video cam close-up of Neal McCaskill. Off camera, Wallace asked, "Mr. McCaskill, you are the Chief Deputy District Attorney, is that correct?"

McCaskill looked at the camera. "Yes, I served as Harold Benton's chief deputy for more than ten years. Naturally, Kathryn Mackay asked me to continue in that capacity, and it's my duty to assist her. Although she's a good trial attorney, she has no experience running a DA's office."

"Why would the Board of Supervisors appoint someone who lacks experience?"

"Because District Attorney Benton and I opposed their ill-conceived needle exchange program, which will guarantee an increase in illegal drug use. Maybe certain Supervisors assumed Ms. Mackay could be manipulated."

"What do you intend to do about this situation?" Wallace goaded.

McCaskill cleared his throat and stared into the camera. "I have decided to announce my candidacy for District Attorney. I plan to run against Ms. Mackay in the general election next June. I have considerable support, and I believe once the voters are given a choice, they will select the more experienced and qualified person for District Attorney."

The shot faded to frame McCaskill in front of the

County Courts building, the county seal and American and California flags visible over his left shoulder. Then the image switched to live studio. Wallace and Kraft sat at a semicircular table. Inserted in the upper right quarter of the screen was a head-and-shoulders still shot of Kathryn Mackay.

"Hey, Mom," Emma commented. "That's you, but it's not a very good picture. You look awful. Guess you were wrong."

"About what, honey?"

"You only got your new job yesterday and you're already on TV."

Kathryn nodded and patted her daughter on the head. "Eat your dinner, honey, and let's listen." *God, I look like a crazy woman.* The shot had been taken two years earlier, during a contentious murder trial. She was answering a reporter's question about certain controversial testimony, and the camera operator caught her with her hair flying and her mouth wide open. It was more than unflattering; it was the worst piece of film footage ever taken of her.

". . . and newly appointed District Attorney Mackay refused to comment when contacted at her office by Channel 7 News this afternoon," Wallace was saying.

"Thanks, Steve," Kraft told him gratuitously, turning to face the camera to end the segment. "That was fine reporting."

Kathryn aimed the remote at the TV and flipped it off, then turned it back on. "Sorry, Em. Put it on whatever channel you want. I'm going to make a cup of coffee." While she was filling the kettle with water, the phone rang.

"Kate, this is Morgan."

"Hi, Doc," she said sullenly.

"You see the six o'clock news?" he asked.

"I saw it. That SOB."

"You can't afford to let something like this tear your office apart. What are you going to do?"

Kathryn poured hot water through the Melitta filter, and dark, black, decaffeinated coffee dripped into the clear glass mug. "I'm going to call him into my office first thing tomorrow morning and demote him. Appoint a new chief deputy."

"I don't know, Kate. He thought this through before making that announcement. He's committed. He'll swear the demotion is punitive. He'll file a lawsuit faster than you can complete the paper work."

"Probably, but that's better than letting him run amok, undermining my authority." Kathryn splashed a dollop of Mocha Mix into her coffee and swirled it until it was a light milk-chocolate color. "I don't see that I have a choice."

"I suppose you're right. Good luck."

Kathryn picked up her coffee and started to sip it, but she was interrupted by the phone ringing again. She picked up the portable, carried it into the living room, and sat beside Emma, who was engrossed in a rerun of *Full House*.

"Hello."

"Ms. Mackay?"

"Yes."

"This is Robert Simmons."

Kathryn sat up straight. "Hello, Doctor. How can I help you?"

"Please call me Robert. And I'll call you Kathryn, if

that's all right. This is strictly a personal call, so if you're busy I can call another time."

A personal call? "No, now's fine. My daughter and I are watching TV. It's one of her favorite programs. She doesn't even know I'm in the room."

"I just called to congratulate you. Harold always spoke highly of you. I'm sure you'll do a great job."

"Well, thanks. That's very kind of you."

"And . . . um . . . well, actually this is a little awkward. It's been so long since I've asked someone . . . well, just to be perfectly blunt about it, I was wondering if you and I might get together for a glass of wine some evening and chat. Maybe get to know each other."

Kathryn sat her coffee cup on the coffee table and was surprised to see her hand shake slightly. *He's asking me for a date. How long has it been since that happened? I can't. I haven't even spoken with a man that way since I met Dave, what, six years ago? Simmons is attractive, but I couldn't—I don't have the time.*

"Yes, I think I'd like that. Could you call me tomorrow so we can arrange a time?" *That wasn't my voice saying that.*

"How about tomorrow after work?" he blurted. "We could meet at Clouds. They have a wonderful wine cellar."

Kathryn paused. "Can you hold for a second?" She kissed Emma on the cheek, but Em was oblivious to her. She placed her hand over the mouthpiece, walked to the kitchen, and leaned against the counter. "There, I can hear better. As I said, the TV is on and my daughter likes it a bit loud." *I don't want my daughter to hear me making a date with a man I barely know.*

"I know it's a bit presumptuous of me, but could we meet tomorrow evening?" he persisted.

She thought, *I can't. I've got to pick Emma up after school, then fix dinner, work on the Miranda investigation, and . . .* She said, "I'll tell you what might work better for me. Maybe we could meet at the Starbucks next to the mall. It's on the way to Emma's school, and I have to confess that a fondness for coffee is one of my great character flaws."

Simmons laughed. "Great! Me, too. So, I'll see you tomorrow at about five-fifteen at Starbucks. Oh, and before I forget, I want you to know I saw Neal McCaskill's interview on channel 7. It's none of my business, but Harold wouldn't have been happy about it. He would have been pleased to have you appointed his successor."

"See you tomorrow. Good night."

12

When Nancy Torres arrived at the office Wednesday morning, Kathryn summoned her with instructions to bring a steno pad. "I want to dictate a press release. Ready?"

"Shoot," she answered, pen poised over her notebook.

Kathryn dictated, "Santa Rita County District Attorney Kathryn Mackay this morning announced the promotion of Mary Elizabeth Skinner to Chief Deputy in Charge of Operations, the first woman to serve in that capacity in Santa Rita County. Skinner is an honors graduate of Southwestern University School of Law in Los Angeles. She has been employed by the District Attorney's office for twelve years. For the past four years, she has served as the DA's legal advisor and is highly respected among her colleagues. Former chief deputy Neal McCaskill has been reassigned to the municipal courts.

"Did you get that?"

Nancy looked at her boss questioningly but answered, "Yes, ma'am. Anything else?"

"Not for now, Nancy. As soon as you have it typed up, give it to Mary Elizabeth to review. Tell her I said you may release it to the media as soon as she has indicated her approval by initialing a copy. Thanks."

Kathryn heaved a heavy sigh and decided to let voice mail answer the ringing phone. Then she remembered that her voice mail had not been switched from her old number, and she picked up. "Kathryn Mackay."

"Good morning, Kathryn," Morgan Nelson answered. "So, did you take care of Mac?"

His direct and no-nonsense approach was one of Nelson's qualities Kathryn liked best. "Yep, bumped Mac back to Attorney IV and promoted Mary Elizabeth."

"Good choice, Katie. But the reason I called is that Granz said you wanted to observe the autopsy on that drowned girl. I'm ready to cut this morning."

"Girl? Granz said 'woman' when he called me," she said.

"She looks sixteen, maybe seventeen years old."

"Granz said she was pregnant."

"He was right about that. Real pregnant."

"I'll be right there," she told him.

"Allow some extra time if you can. I'd like to go over my findings on the Fuentes autopsy, too."

Kathryn hung up, then buzzed Jim Fields's extension. When he answered, Kathryn asked him to assign an inspector to the Miranda/Fuentes investigation to accompany her to the morgue.

"Already done. I put Escalante on it. She's reviewed the police reports and is ready to go."

Kathryn paused. "Donna Escalante? I don't know, Jim. She's never been the Investigating Officer on a major investigation before."

"Trust me, Kathryn. She's a natural. Better instincts than most cops with twenty years on the job. She'll be at the morgue in ten minutes."

Tall and slender, with short straight black hair, Donna Escalante was in her early thirties but looked younger. Her pleated trousers and charcoal double breasted jacket failed to conceal her athletic figure. Except for lipstick, she wore no makeup, and while she wasn't exactly pretty, she was attractive in a scrubbed, wholesome way.

Escalante gazed around the autopsy suite, which looked like a hospital room except for the twelve-inch stainless steel drain in the floor, then walked to the sink and picked up a plastic jar. Dave Granz, who had arrived a few minutes earlier, joined her.

"Human brain. They all are," Nelson told her, indicating the half dozen containers lined up on the counter. He and Granz were already dressed in scrubs and latex gloves, with masks hanging around their necks.

Nelson tossed the two women green gowns, surgical masks, latex gloves, and paper booties. He saw Mackay begin putting hers on, but Escalante hesitated.

"SOP in an autopsy suite. We disinfect the body and take various steps to prevent aerosolization of potentially infectious particulate matter, but some release of airborne material is unavoidable, especially when the cranial vault is opened. Go ahead, put them on."

Escalante struggled into the gown and slid on the gloves.

"Your first autopsy?" Nelson asked.

"Yes," Escalante answered.

Nelson motioned them to a gurney in the middle of the room, which held the nude body of a pregnant young woman, lying on its back.

"As I proceed, I'll explain everything I'm doing. That way you'll be of some use next time you're assigned to observe an autopsy."

Escalante nodded.

"Okay. The first objective of a forensic autopsy is to identify the deceased. Sometimes we do that with a personal identification by the next of kin. But it's surprising how often a relative identifies the wrong body."

"What do you do if you can't locate a next of kin?"

"We take full-body photographs before any autopsy procedures are conducted, even when there is a next-of-kin ID. Also, we fingerprint every body we examine. I've already photographed and printed this girl."

"Of course," Kathryn interjected, "with someone so young fingerprints usually aren't helpful. But if she has a driver's license, DMV might match the autopsy photo in DIPS."

The state motor vehicle department's new Digitized Identification Photograph System computer scanned driver's license photos and converted them to digital files, which it stored in a database. Law enforcement agencies could submit photos of unidentified persons, which the system digitized, then attempted to match in the database. Such IDs achieved a reliability level approaching that of fingerprints.

"She looks old enough to have a learner's permit," Escalante speculated.

"I'll get on it as soon as I get back to the office," Granz said.

Nelson covered his nose and mouth with the mask, and the other three followed suit. He switched on two intense white overhead lights and pulled down a microphone.

"The body is that of an Hispanic female, approximately seventeen years of age. Height, five feet six; weight, approximately one hundred fifty pounds. Black hair, brown eyes. In advanced stage of pregnancy, estimated eight and one-half months. Preliminary external examination indicates trauma to the head, chest, and extremities. Two upper incisor teeth broken off at the gumline. No obvious external disease, no visible scars or tattoos. Genitalia normal."

Nelson switched off the microphone and pulled out a black-handled Buck hunting knife, which he honed briefly on sharpening paper. To test the razor-sharp edge, he drew it down the middle of a piece of white copier paper. It severed cleanly, and he nodded his satisfaction.

"I've tried everything over the years," he said. "Scalpels, butcher knives, you name it. Buck hunting knives work best."

Nelson switched on the mike and described the procedure as he went. He sliced a deep V-shaped incision in the body beginning at each shoulder and ending at the top of the abdomen. He completed the Y with a vertical cut from the bottom of the V to the top of the pubis, then made a horizontal incision from hipbone to hipbone.

Nelson flipped the loose skin flap from the chest over the face and tugged the other flaps away from the rib cage.

"Okay," Nelson advised, "better stand back a little." He switched on a small battery-powered circular saw. The saw blade whined. It bogged down as it bit into cartilage and bone, but within seconds the rib cage was removed, exposing the inner organs and a large fetus, which Nelson rolled from side to side.

"The fetus is near term, well developed, no apparent abnormalities, no obvious infection or inflammation of the umbilical cord, membranes, or placenta." He lifted the fetus and placenta and placed them on the table. "I'll autopsy the fetus later."

The lungs were then removed and sliced open, and their contents dumped into a stainless-steel bowl. Nelson stirred the ugly mixture of blood, mucous, weeds, seawater, and sand. "She was conscious when she entered the water, and she went in close to shore. There's no sand in the lungs with deep-water drownings. She died almost instantly."

He reached up into the throat cavity, clipped out a section of the windpipe, and sliced the knobby tube lengthwise, exposing the inner surface. Holding it up to the light, he said, "Sand and seaweed in the trachea. Preliminary opinion: cause of death, respiratory failure due to ingestion of water and foreign materials into the lungs."

"Doc, you said she was dead instantly. I thought it took several minutes for a person to drown. I've read accounts of people being revived as long as thirty minutes after being pulled from the water," Kathryn said.

"Yeah, that's true, especially in seawater. Sometimes a person goes into a sort of suspended animation and they can be resuscitated. But not in a case like this. When the victim inhales heavy concentrations of sand with the water, the respiratory system shuts down completely. Cardiac failure follows immediately, and death occurs with astounding quickness."

"What about the head injuries? Is it possible she was struck on the head, rendered unconscious, and then entered the water?" Escalante asked.

"Good question, but I'd say no," Nelson answered. "Did you notice that her tongue was severely bitten? That's a classic sign she struggled after entering the water. Now look at the head wound. The skin and underlying bone are damaged, but there's no blood accumulation at the site. Trauma causes bruising as long as the heart hasn't stopped, but the same trauma after loss of blood pressure doesn't. Some of her contusions show a bruise pattern, but the head wounds were post mortem. She was conscious when she entered the water, was tossed against the rocks repeatedly by the surf, but she was dead before suffering the head damage."

"Can you fix the time of death, Doc?" Kathryn asked.

"Not precisely, as you know. A body immersed in water cools about twice as fast as one in air, about five degrees per hour. Her body temp was sixty-six degrees, same as the water. It had been at least six hours. Putrefaction starts very quickly and gas accumulates. Since there was no gas formation, my opinion is she fell or jumped into the water sometime last night. Or was pushed," he added as an afterthought.

Nelson rolled the gloves off his hands and shot them into a stainless-steel trash can like rubber bands. "I'll wrap this up later. Examine the heart. The right side is distended, as are the great veins. She drowned, all right, and so did the baby." He gestured for the three of them to follow him to his office.

"You said you wanted to discuss your findings from the Fuentes autopsy?" Kathryn asked.

Nelson shoved a report across the desk. "Here's my protocol. Cause of death: subdural hematoma as a result of blunt-force head trauma. Couple of surprises. Tox screen indicates Fuentes had ingested a massive dose of chlorpromazine."

"Chlorpromazine?" Escalante asked.

"Generic name for Thorazine," he answered. "She ingested the dosage not long before the accident."

"Enough to kill her?" Granz inquired, suddenly very interested.

"No. Enough to make her sleep like a baby for a long time, but not fatal. But that's not the most interesting thing. She was pregnant."

Mackay and Granz exchanged looks, and Mackay leaned forward with her arms on Nelson's desk. "How pregnant?" she asked.

"Second trimester. I'd say about fifteen to sixteen weeks. A fetus, not an embryo."

"Jesus," Kathryn exclaimed, then, seeing a confused look on Donna Escalante's face, she explained.

"Under California law, murder is the unlawful killing of a human being *or a fetus*. That means if Miranda intentionally drove Fuentes off the cliff without her knowledge or acquiescence, he is guilty of murdering her. And if he murdered Esther Fuentes, he also murdered her unborn child. That makes it a special-circumstance crime and . . ."

"And a possible death-penalty case," Escalante finished.

13

Kathryn pulled into the parking lot in front of Starbucks. She wasn't surprised to find the palms of her hands moist; she had looked forward to meeting Robert Simmons with mounting anticipation since early afternoon. She locked the Audi, and as she approached the coffee house, she spotted him at a secluded corner table. *I wonder how early he got here to find an intimate spot.*

Robert stood as she approached, and held out his hand. He grasped hers firmly and squeezed gently, perhaps slightly longer than necessary. She removed her black jacket and hung it over the back of a chair. She wore an opaque white shirt over a sheer lacy bra, which she hoped didn't show through the shirt.

Robert was dressed impeccably. His gray-streaked brown hair was complimented perfectly by an expensive dark brown suit and tie.

"Kathryn, I'm so glad you could make it. How was traffic?" he asked.

"No worse than usual. I remember when you could

jump on the highway in Santa Rita and drive the speed limit all the way to Española. No more."

"That's for sure. Those days are gone for good," he answered. After a brief, tense pause, he asked, "Shall we grab a coffee and maybe a snack? I missed lunch today, and their lemon tarts are the best I've ever tasted."

Kathryn ordered the house coffee and a low-fat fruit scone. Simmons asked for a doppio—a double espresso, twice pulled—and a lemon tart. When they returned to the table, he grinned boyishly. "You've discovered two of my worst weaknesses," he said, "coffee and sweets."

"You'd never know it to look at you—the sweets, I mean," Kathryn replied. *God, that was dumb. Why did I say that?*

"I try to find time to work out."

He took a bite of his lemon tart and wiped his lips on a napkin. "You have a daughter, I think you said? How do you find enough time to be with her?"

"I don't always. Often, we settle for Emma curling up next to me watching TV or reading while I work. I think she'll be a lot more demanding as she gets older. I'm hoping to have a little more control over my schedule now than I did before."

"How old is Emma?" he asked.

"Ten going on thirty-five," she laughed. "Sometimes she amazes me how mature she is. I guess it comes from being an only child that was never talked down to."

Robert gazed at Kathryn. "Does she look like her mother?"

"A spitting image, I'm afraid," Kathryn answered. "Long, dark brown hair, brown eyes, and freckles."

"Well, then she's lucky. If she looks like her mother, she's a very beautiful young lady."

Don't blush. Am I blushing? My face feels warm. Kathryn wiped her lips. "What about you? Any children?"

"No, I'm sorry to say. I love kids. I was only married for two years, right after we finished medical school at the University of Arkansas. We were both residents at Memorial Hospital in Little Rock. Residency isn't conducive to raising children. Or to marriage. I never remarried."

Kathryn let the subject drop. She didn't want to discuss the history of her failed marriage to Emma's father just yet, and she guessed correctly that Robert was too polite to ask if she didn't volunteer.

"Arkansas? That's a long way from Santa Rita. How did you end up here?"

"It's not a very exciting story," he told her. "I was born and raised in Russellville, about seventy miles from Little Rock. So was my wife. My father worked for the U.S. Forest Service. I was the first of my family to go to college, never mind professional school. My parents helped some, but mostly I paid my own way with scholarships, student loans, and odd jobs. After we divorced, she stayed on at the hospital. So I packed up and left."

He sipped at his espresso. "I wound up in San Francisco working at a free clinic, but it didn't take long to realize I couldn't handle the big city. I'm a country boy. So I answered a recruitment ad for a staff physician at the county health clinic here in Santa Rita. The rest, as they say, is history."

"Hometown boy makes good," Kathryn commented. "Sounds sort of like me. I grew up in Kansas

City." She gave him a thumbnail sketch of her career: a brief stint as a public defender in Kansas City; migration to Los Angeles; deputy district attorney in L.A., where she met, married, and divorced; then a move north to Santa Rita to escape what had become an ugly entanglement.

"Tell me about your job, Kathryn. How is it being district attorney for two whole days? I'll bet you're swamped."

"That's putting it mildly. But I feel more like a bureaucrat than a prosecutor. I haven't begun to pick up the ball on investigations Hal was handling personally."

Robert seemed genuinely surprised. "He handled investigations, too? I'd have bet that all Hal did was politic and administrate."

Kathryn laughed. "For the most part, you'd have won that bet. But, on occasion he handled certain sensitive investigations. He called them his 'R-files.'"

"Sounds pretty mysterious."

"Not really. They were usually officer-involved shootings or politically delicate matters. Interestingly, Hal was working on one the day he died. I haven't had time to look for the file. I don't even know what it was about."

Kathryn sipped at her coffee, then said, "Enough about my work. Tell me about yours."

"Well, as you know, I'm head of the county health department. Actually, it consists of several divisions: environmental health, family planning, and mental health among others, plus a clinic that provides free or reduced-cost care to low-income families, mostly Hispanic. I started at the clinic, as I said, and was gradually promoted.

"When I first became clinic chief, patients rarely saw the same doctor twice. That's awful for the patients; they never get to feel as if they have a doctor. I pioneered a program as soon as I took over as head of the Department where patients see the same physician each time, if at all possible. We try to maintain continuity of care so the doctor-patient relationship resembles that of private health care. I think it's worked wonderfully."

"That sounds like a very sensitive approach, but it also sounds like you rarely get to practice medicine."

"Depends on how broadly you define the practice of medicine, I suppose. Like Hal, and now you, I spend much of my time doing administrative work."

"I see," Kathryn said, not knowing what else to say.

"Kathryn, I'm going to be blunt because I don't know how else to do it and still tell you what's on my mind." He took a deep breath. "I find you enormously attractive. More than anyone I've met in years. That's why I asked you to meet me. I'm hoping we can see more of each other and become . . . friends." He reached out and placed his right hand on top of her left. When she didn't pull away, he wove his fingers between hers.

Too fast, Kathryn. Slow down. Think. You don't have time for this. "I, uh, I feel the same, Robert."

He placed his other hand over hers. She was oblivious to her surroundings, but the room was empty of customers, and the staff was paying them no attention. "Kathryn, please tell me if I'm out of line, but given we're both so visible in the community, would you consider the possibility of going away with me for a weekend sometime? Maybe to the wine country or Mendocino?"

No! Absolutely not! I don't even know you, and I haven't been intimate with a man for over a year. I'm not even sure I remember how to make love, much less how to be passionate. And I don't have enough time with Emma as it is. No way. "Can you let me think about it? This is a shock, to say the least, and I wasn't prepared for something like this."

"Of course, Kathryn. I'm sorry if I seem impetuous." He thought for a minute. "No, that's not true at all. I like feeling impetuous. And I like how I feel around you, too. You make me feel . . . you're incredibly attractive, Kathryn, that's all I can say. But remember, we Arkansas Razorbacks are an impatient bunch. Take all the time you need. Is tomorrow morning long enough?" he joked.

They both laughed. It was the first time Kathryn had laughed in a long time, and it was the first time in months she felt like a woman rather than a lawyer, or a mom, or . . . It felt terrific. "Call me tomorrow afternoon."

Robert walked Kathryn to her car and held the door while she snapped her seat belt. He reached out to straighten a twist in the shoulder harness, and when he did his hand brushed softly across her left breast. Her nipple strained against the smooth silk shirt. After what seemed an eternity, he patted her shoulder and closed the car door. *Was that intentional? No, it couldn't have been. It was an accident.*

As Kathryn dove away, she looked back to where Robert Simmons stood waving. She touched herself where his hand had been and found herself tingling. Her stomach churned, but it wasn't from the coffee.

14

At 8 A.M. Thursday, Marlon Sterling and Roselba Menendez greeted Mackay, Escalante, and Granz at the entrance to the Department of Justice complex at 46A Research Drive, referred to by those in law enforcement simply as "Building Forty-Six-A."

Criminalist Menendez wore faded Levi's and a blue T-shirt with a Warren's Salinas Harley-Davidson logo on the front. She stood about five-three and had long hair, light olive skin, and bright red fingernails. Beside the huge, ferocious-looking Sterling in his starched tan CHP coveralls, she looked tiny and fragile, but in this case looks were deceiving. Kathryn couldn't have been more pleased with this investigative team. They were both the very best at their jobs.

"Good morning, Dave," Kathryn said. "I brought Inspector Escalante along so she's up to speed on the investigation. I know it's still S.O.'s investigation at this point."

"I know the drill, Kathryn. I expect you won't create any territorial disputes with me."

Kathryn started to respond to the veiled threat but thought better of it.

"The entrance to the vehicle inspection area is around back," Menendez said. Her voice held the slightest hint of a Spanish accent, and she motioned with her finger for them to follow. She punched her PIC—personal identity code—into an electronic panel beside a roll-up metal garage door. It opened into the spotless interior of what could easily pass for a high-tech Mercedes Benz service bay.

A wrecked but shiny white Chevy Impala rested on dollies and jack stands in the center of the room. A padded mechanic's creeper leaned against a red Craftsman rolling tool chest, and parts were scattered randomly about.

"I had the car brought here because DOJ has the expertise to evaluate the interior—you know, fabric transfers and so forth. And I can do the mechanical inspection as well here as at the CHP garage," Sterling observed. "The car's in pretty bad shape, but it was obviously Miranda's pride and joy."

Sterling looked at Menendez. "Should I go first with my findings?"

She nodded. "That'd probably be best."

"Okay. My job in a case like this is to evaluate the condition of the vehicle to determine whether or not mechanical failure contributed to the event. It took some digging in this case. I've been here since five this morning taking this car apart." He pointed to a pair of filthy coveralls piled on the floor. "Now if we could get started . . ."

They clustered around a stainless-steel workbench. "The three components most likely to cause a catastrophic accident are the tires, steering, and brakes.

Failure of most any other part of a car usually results in nothing worse than a breakdown that leaves you stranded alongside the road."

Sterling indicated the chrome wheels and tires leaning against the workbench. "His tires had more than five-sixteenths of an inch of tread. They were almost new. No problem.

"The steering mechanism is a lot harder to evaluate. That's why the car is on jacks. I disassembled everything from the steering wheel through the steering column, the steering gearbox, swing arms, tie-rods, and ball joints. You can imagine that if steering fails, it's almost always disastrous. Manufacturers know that, so they build 'em like Sherman tanks. They're practically indestructible and need almost no maintenance. The steering system on Miranda's car was fine. That left the brakes—a common cause of accidents."

Sterling slid several odd-shaped parts into a pile. "These shiny discs are the front brake rotors. Car had front disc brakes and drums on the rear, the usual configuration in the early eighties. Front brakes provide at least 70 percent of the stopping power, so that's where I looked first. The rears were okay, but even without them the car could stop as long as the fronts were in good shape."

Escalante picked up one of the rotors and inspected it.

"Run the tip of your finger over the shiny surface," Sterling told her. When she had done so, she handed the rotor to Kathryn and then Menendez and Granz, who followed suit. "What do you feel?"

"Smooth as glass," Granz said.

"Correct. The way disc brakes work is that the disc

rotates between these brake pads. When the brake pedal is depressed, the pads rub against the rotor, stopping the wheel, and thus the car, by friction. After a few thousand miles, the metal embedded in the brake pad material carves little grooves in the rotor. Perfectly normal."

"But there aren't any grooves in these at all," Escalante observed.

"Right," Sterling responded. "That's because the entire brake system is brand-new. Rotors, pads, master cylinder, hydraulic lines, everything was in perfect shape."

"So," Kathryn mused, "if there was no mechanical failure, maybe the driver got out of control, slammed on the brakes, but it was too late."

"Nope. No skid marks at the scene."

"Then maybe the driver fell asleep and just toppled over the edge."

"Not a chance. If that'd been the case, the car would have slowed down before it went over. There would have been gouges in the pavement and shoulder where the car's undercarriage dragged when the front wheels dropped. And that doesn't jibe with the rancher's report. Todd heard the car's engine idle awhile, then race like crazy just before it went off. And he said the thing sailed into the air like a missile. It went over fast. This was no accident, Kathryn. Miranda drove over that cliff intentionally."

"You would testify to that? As an Accident Investigation Specialist, that in your opinion, this car was intentionally driven off old Mount Cabrillo Grade Road?"

"Absolutely."

"You said 'he' drove over the cliff," Escalante said. "Couldn't she have been driving?"

"The car was registered to Miranda. Look at it. It's so perfect, it's probably in better shape than the day it rolled out of the showroom. Lots of young guys put their heart and soul into their cars. I did when I was that age, and I'll bet Dave did, too."

Granz nodded his concurrence, and Sterling continued. "Guys like that are territorial. They don't let anybody pilot their wheels."

"That's not enough to work with," Kathryn said.

"I know you need something more substantive. Follow me." He approached a pile of car parts laid out alongside the left front fender.

"Jeez, look at that steering wheel," Escalante whistled.

"Yep, it's badly deformed. Steering column, too. See that wire mesh stuff? The column telescopes in a frontal impact and the mesh absorbs some of the force. The driver hit the steering wheel hard—real hard—during that accident."

"I agree," Roselba Menendez interjected. "Take a look."

She opened the passenger door and pointed to a huge dent in the dashboard. "Passenger's head impacted here . . . and here, too," she said pointing to the passenger door window where dried blood was clearly visible. Fuentes have serious head injuries?"

Kathryn nodded. "Pathologist established cause of death as blunt-force trauma to the head, and she sustained severe lacerations to the right cheek."

"Figures. Typical passenger injuries. I tested the blood from the dash and window; it was A-positive.

Fuentes's blood type was A-positive, Miranda's was O-negative. Located several strands of long hair stuck in the blood. And that's not all. I retrieved dark blue fabric transfers from the passenger side of the dashboard. Denim. Matched them to the baggy denim overalls Fuentes was wearing. Real popular nowadays. She was the passenger, all right."

"I'll get a search warrant for Miranda's medical records," Escalante said. "They may confirm whether or not he has driver-pattern injuries."

15

Just before noon, Kathryn was settled at her desk when her private line rang. Robert Simmons was on the other end. "I hope you don't mind, but I figured your private number would be the same as Hal's."

"You were right, and I don't mind."

"Even though you said to call this afternoon?"

"The afternoon does seem a long time off, doesn't it? I'm glad you called."

"Good. Now you'll see how presumptuous I can be. First thing this morning, I called my travel agent."

"Your travel agent?"

"You didn't say 'no' when I asked if we might get away some weekend, so I decided to look into some reservations."

"I didn't exactly say 'yes,' either."

"That's true," he said, then asked, "Have you ever been to Victoria, British Columbia?"

"No, but I've heard it's beautiful."

"An understatement, especially this time of year. The restaurants are terrific, and the Empress Hotel is one of the most luxurious in the world. There aren't many flights from the U.S. directly into Victoria, so the best way to get there is to fly into Seattle, spend the night, and leave for B.C. early the next morning."

"How do you get from Seattle to Victoria?"

"On the passenger ferry. It only takes a couple of hours, and the trip up the San Juan Straights is spectacular."

"Sounds nice. I've never been to Seattle, either."

"Kate, I know I'm pushing, but I had my agent book the last two seats on a Reno Air flight from San Jose to Seattle."

"For when?"

He hesitated. "This weekend."

"This weekend? That's only two days away. Robert, you shouldn't have done that. We hardly know each other."

"We've been acquainted for years."

"Professionally, yes, but that's different," she answered. "Besides, I haven't had time to think about this."

"Should I describe to you what I had in mind, or would you prefer to talk about it some other time?"

"I suppose it couldn't hurt to listen."

"I reserved rooms at the Pacific Plaza in downtown Seattle. It's a beautiful historic hotel, European style, a short walk from the ferry terminal."

"Don't tell me, let me guess."

"Right. I booked round-trip ferry passage too. It'll be the highlight of the trip."

"Somehow, I doubt that," she answered, then despite herself, she laughed. "What are we having for breakfast?"

"Whatever you want," he said, also laughing. Then

he added seriously, "I don't want to offend you, Kathryn. I can cancel the reservations if you want."

"I'm not offended, just surprised. And apprehensive."

"Me, too," he told her.

Kathryn looked at her watch. "I've got to return some phone messages. Can I call you this afternoon?"

"Sure, and Kate? If you want me to cancel, just say so."

"I'll talk to you later."

When Morgan Nelson picked up the phone at the morgue, Kathryn said, "Hi, Morgan, am I interrupting your lunch?"

"Of course not. What's going on, Katie?" he asked.

"What do you mean, what's going on?"

"You called me Morgan instead of Doc."

"Escalante's on her way over with Miranda's medical records. Would you look at them and give me your opinion on whether his injuries are consistent with him striking the car's steering wheel?"

"Sure."

"Since Fuentes was pregnant, I may be looking at charging Miranda with statutory rape, assuming he was the father. What's the status of the DNA test?"

"I sent samples from the fetus to DOJ. They should have the results back to us in ten days or so."

"Thanks. Let me know as soon as you get anything."

"Okay. Anything else?"

When she didn't answer, he said, "Escalante could have given me that message, Katie. What did you really call about?"

"It's nothing."

"Can I help?"

After a few moments, she asked, "How well do you know Robert Simmons?"

"Well enough to know he's one of the better county health officers."

"How about personally?"

"Can't help you much there. You know me, I don't socialize much. I know he's unmarried and lives alone. But, from what I do know about him personally, he seems like a nice enough guy. Why?"

Kathryn told him about the rendezvous at Starbucks, and Simmons's proposal for the coming weekend.

"What did you tell him?"

"That I'd call back."

"Then you must be thinking about it."

"Common sense tells me to turn and run, but . . ."

"That's your head talking. Your head and your heart don't always speak the same language. What does your heart say?"

She drew in a deep breath and expelled it slowly. "I think it says, 'yes.'"

"I see."

"Crazy, huh?"

"Out of character for you, definitely, but not crazy. You work so much and your life is so damned structured, maybe a little spontaneous fun is exactly what you need."

"I suppose, but . . ."

"It's been awhile since you and Dave split up, Katie. Eventually, you need to see other men. You can always turn around and come home if it doesn't work out, can't you?"

"Yes."

"Then, what do you have to lose?"

"Nothing except my self-respect, I guess. Thanks, Doc," Kathryn answered, and hung up the phone gently.

By three o'clock, Kathryn had returned all the urgent messages. She picked up the phone handset, replaced it, then picked it up again and dialed Robert Simmons's office number. As his secretary was explaining that he had left the Health Services building for an appointment outside the office, he stuck his head around the door to Kathryn's office. She said a hasty good-bye and replaced the phone handset into the cradle.

"I can come back if you're busy," he said.

Kathryn shook her head in feigned disapproval. "You get an A for persistence," she told him. "I was just talking to your secretary. Come in, please."

"I thought maybe we could both use one of these," he said, handing her a steaming coffee with the green and black Starbucks logo on the paper cup. "Picked it up from the cart."

"Thanks. I don't usually drink coffee after lunch, but I can use the caffeine about now." Kathryn removed the lid, sipped, and made a face.

"Too hot?" he asked.

"No, just a little bitter."

Robert sat in a leather chair, crossed his legs, and gazed at Kathryn expectantly. She rose and walked to the door to tell Nancy Torres she would be tied up for a few minutes and to hold her calls. When she sat, she took a chair alongside Robert rather than behind her desk. As if it were connected to an alien being, she watched her left hand reach out and grasp his, intertwining their fingers.

His eyebrows arched and he smiled, squeezing affectionately. "Have you thought about what we discussed this morning?" he asked softly. "I haven't thought about anything else."

She considered her words carefully. "When you mentioned the Pacific Plaza Hotel in Seattle, you said you had reserved 'rooms.' Was that a slip, or did you mean it to be plural?"

"It was plural, Kate. I reserved two rooms there and at the Empress in Victoria, too. I don't want either of us to feel obligated to, well, to become more involved faster than seems right."

"I agree about separate rooms. We should just relax and see how things develop. No matter what else happens . . . or doesn't happen . . . we just enjoy ourselves."

He looked at her. "Are you saying you'll go? That sounded more like a yes than a no."

"You're not the only one who can be spontaneous and impetuous, Doctor," she joked.

"Terrific! So, let's see, I can pick you up Friday after work and—"

Kathryn laughed and extracted her hand, then walked around behind her desk. "Now, scat so I can concentrate on my work or we won't be going anyplace this Friday."

16

On Friday, Kathryn Mackay and Robert Simmons ate lunch in her office with the door closed. They were discussing the logistics of making it to the San Jose airport by 6 P.M. and getting from SeaTac to downtown Seattle. Kathryn felt more excited than she had in months.

Robert had picked up sandwiches, dill pickles, and old-fashioned carbonated Cokes at a deli. Although she didn't eat the pickle, Kathryn enjoyed the Coke and the bubbles tickled her nose when she drank from the paper cup.

When the phone buzzed she ignored it, but it persisted and eventually she sighed and picked up. "I asked not to be disturbed, Nancy."

"I know, Ms. Mackay," her secretary said on the other end. "But it's important. I think you'd better turn on your TV to channel 7."

Kathryn apologized to Robert for cutting their lunch short. As soon as he left, she aimed the remote at the TV and scrolled through the channels until she saw the familiar face of Steve Wallace. The scene cut to a head-and-shoulders close-up of Neal McCaskill on the steps of the County Courts building, with a microphone shoved in his face. She sat her empty cup down and turned up the volume.

"Mr. McCaskill, Channel 7 News has learned from a reliable source that Kathryn Mackay intends to personally handle the Raymondo Miranda/Esther Fuentes investigation, and if criminal charges result from that investigation, to prosecute the case herself. Can you confirm that rumor?"

"The Chief of Inspectors confirmed to me that District Attorney Mackay has assumed responsibility for the investigation into the death of Esther Fuentes."

"Isn't that a bit unusual, considering Mackay assumed office only a few days ago and is busy, shall we say, 'realigning office duties'?"

"Absolutely. An investigation of that importance should be assigned to a highly experienced, very senior attorney who can devote his full attention to it. It's far too important to the community to allow anything to fall through the cracks."

"By 'highly experienced, very senior attorney,' you mean someone like yourself?"

"Yes, I am the logical choice if the District Attorney wants the investigation conducted properly."

"Was her refusal to assign you to this investigation punitive, like your demotion from chief deputy to staff attorney?"

"No question. It was punitive."

"One more thing," Wallace said. "Will the proper or, perhaps, the improper utilization of office staff resources likely become a campaign issue next spring?"

McCaskill looked into the eye of the camera and smiled. "It already has."

"What do you mean I can't talk to the press without clearing it with you first, Kathryn? Have you ever heard of the First Amendment to the United States Constitution?" McCaskill flopped in Mackay's leather chair, unbuttoned his suit coat, leaned back and clasped his hands behind his head as though he were interviewing a law school graduate about a job.

"Statements to the press pertaining to the District Attorney's office are to be cleared by me personally."

"I didn't make a statement to the press. A channel 7 reporter caught me outside and asked me a couple of questions. I didn't tell him anything he didn't already know."

"I suspect he already knew because someone in this office called him. Don't politic on county time, Neal."

"That interview occurred on my lunch hour. I'm a legitimate political candidate and have as much right to address the press on the steps of the courthouse as anybody. Don't mess with my right to run for public office, or my lawyer will slap you with a lawsuit so fast you won't know what happened. And don't imply that I leaked information. My attorney understands slander laws, too."

"Are you finished?" Mackay asked calmly.

"For now," McCaskill answered.

"Good. I have no intention of violating your right to run for DA or to conduct a legitimate campaign, but I won't tolerate any breach of office policy."

Kathryn stood up behind her desk. "Be clear on this. You do your job, follow the rules, don't politic on my time, and everything will be fine. Don't do your job, and I'll land on you with both feet. And don't ever threaten me again."

McCaskill stood and walked to the door, but turned before opening it. "I intend to do my job. You worry about doing yours. We'll have this discussion again next year, but I'll be on that side of the desk and you'll be walking out this door. Your days as DA are numbered, Mackay. Enjoy them while you can."

After McCaskill left, Kathryn sat at her desk for several minutes, then went to the women's rest room. She knelt over a toilet and vomited, then ran cold water on a paper towel and wiped her face. Then she took three ibuprofen tablets for her throbbing headache, returned to her office, and put her head down on her desk.

17

Approaching Seattle-Tacoma Airport's inner terminal, Kathryn spotted a uniformed man holding a sign that read "Mackay/Simmons."

"You didn't!"

"Oh yes, I did," Robert answered with a smile.

By the time the chauffeur eased the black stretch onto northbound I-5, Kathryn was snoozing, but she awakened when the limo exited on Seneca Street and pulled up to the Pacific Plaza Hotel.

"I slept all the way from the airport?" she asked.

"Almost thirty minutes," Robert answered.

Kathryn yawned and pointed toward a peach-colored overstuffed easy chair in the far corner of the elegant, ornate lobby. "I think I'll sit down while you check us in. Can the concierge arrange to have our bags put away while we grab a bite to eat? I'm exhausted."

When Robert handed her a room key, he said, "Your room is seven-eighteen, mine is seven-sixteen. Ready to eat?"

"Yes, but nothing fancy."

They located a small restaurant a block from the hotel and sat at an outdoor table.

"I'd like to call Emma to say good night." Kathryn said. "She's staying with my neighbor, Ruth, and she'll be going to bed in a few minutes."

"Take your time, I'll order wine."

"Everything okay?" he asked when she returned, handing her a glass of white wine. "Riesling, I hope that's all right."

"Everything's fine." She sipped delicately. "U-m-m-m, very nice. Why don't we order dinner?"

Saturday dawned sunny and clear, and they grabbed coffee at Seattle's Best Coffee before boarding the *Victoria Clipper*. Kathryn felt nauseous, attributing it to seasickness, and Robert gave her medication that made her feel almost normal by the time the taxi pulled onto the cobblestone entry to the Empress Hotel and parked in front of the ivy-covered, arched foyer.

After the bellman escorted them into the huge, elegant lobby, they went to their adjoining rooms to put away their things. Kathryn changed into a white cotton T-shirt and black linen slacks. She and Robert met at two o'clock on the semicircular flagstone stairs leading to the hotel's front entrance. He wore crisp, sharply creased tan Dockers with a dark brown shirt and Timberland shoes.

At five o'clock, following a tour of the city aboard a white surrey hitched to a beautiful gray Percheron, the driver dropped them at the entrance to the hotel.

"Let's have a glass of wine," Kathryn suggested.

They found the Bengal Lounge almost empty and selected a table facing the flower garden. Intense late-afternoon sun streamed through the window, and Kathryn put on her sunglasses. The bartender and waiters in safari khakis chatted at the bar, which perched on an island in the middle of the wood-paneled room. Rolled bamboo shades tied with hemp cord hung from all four sides of the bar. Along one wall, a safari steam table held finger food and an Indian curry dinner buffet. Above the stone fireplace, a stuffed Bengal tiger, teeth and claws bared, stood motionless in a glass case.

"I feel like we walked into a time and space warp," Kathryn commented. "An authentic early-twentieth-century English lodge in India."

They sat silently for several minutes, sipping their wine, enjoying the view of the lush lawn and flower garden. They ordered a second glass of wine and made small talk while they drank and snacked on peanuts and bar mix.

Kathryn finished her wine and Robert asked, "Would you like another, or should we order something to eat?"

Kathryn placed her hand over his. "I have a better idea. Let's have a bottle of champagne delivered to my room. I'd like to drink a glass of champagne while I take a bubble bath."

Robert looked confused. "Sure. But maybe we should get something to eat as soon as you've finished with your bath."

"Actually," she said, "I was hoping you'd join me."

The tub was an antique double claw-foot with Jacuzzi jets. Kathryn poured scented bubble bath into the tub and turned on the jets and hot water while Robert opened a bottle of Tattinger's. He submerged it in an ice bucket along with two stemmed crystal glasses, then rolled it into the large white-marble bathroom on a wheeled cart. Except for shoes, they were both fully clothed.

"Kathryn," he said, "I . . . I'm afraid I don't know exactly how to go about this. Should I—"

She touched her fingertips to his lips. "Shush," she whispered. She unbuttoned his shirt and pushed it from his shoulders, then allowed her fingers to wander down past his chest and stomach to unfasten his belt and pants. He stepped out of his trousers and stood nude before her. "You're beautiful," she told him.

He groaned, and his trembling fingers fumbled with the buttons on her shirt.

"Wait," she said. She led him to the tub, and when he had settled into the bubbly water, she poured two glasses of champagne, then set her glass on the cart beside the tub.

Slowly, she unbuttoned and removed her shirt, jeans, and lacy white bikini panties while Robert studied her every movement. When she was naked, she slid into the hot water facing him, one foot touching each of his hips. Then she picked up her champagne. "To us."

They sipped champagne, devouring each other's bodies with their eyes, then Robert leaned forward and placed his lips on hers. They kissed tentatively at first, then their mouths opened and their tongues touched.

Kathryn searched for him in the hot water and grasped him, stroking slowly at first, then as her own excitement grew, more insistently.

"Robert, here, let me . . ." she whispered. She knelt over him, and guided him into her. "Now, slowly,

slowly," she whispered, and lowered herself onto him, accepting his full length into her body. He rose to meet her and they moved together as if they had been lovers for years.

He leaned back against the tub, looked into her eyes, and began thrusting rapidly. Sensing his urgency, she slowed her hips and moved his hand to where their bodies had joined together. "Touch me there," she urged.

Afterwards, they lay in the hot water and finished the champagne. When it was gone, they called room service and ordered a pizza, which they consumed voraciously while dressed only in white terry-cloth robes monogrammed "Canadian Pacific Hotels" on the chest.

They made love twice more that night, but neither slept more than an hour before morning. Robert's bed was unused when they checked out early on Sunday to catch a cab to the ferry terminal.

When Robert dropped Kathryn off at her condo Sunday evening, he asked, "How are you feeling, Kate? Is your stomach still upset?"

"A little bit. And I still have a headache, too. Maybe I drank too much champagne, and I didn't sleep much last night," she answered. "Nothing to worry about. Robert, I can't tell you what a wonderful weekend I had. Thank you so much."

"It was the best weekend I've ever had," he said. "I hope it isn't the last."

"It's not. Call me tomorrow."

18

Kathryn spent Monday morning and the early afternoon sifting through phone messages and managing the seemingly endless stream of administrative paperwork. At three thirty that afternoon she called Donna Escalante to her office.

"I set a meeting on the Miranda investigation for four o'clock with Granz, Nelson, you, and me," Mackay told her inspector, "but I need you to do something for me first."

"Name it."

"One of the Evidence and Property Reports lists a pill bottle. Have the S.O. property clerk sign it out to you."

"Okay, see you shortly."

Escalante was the last to get to the conference room, Morgan Nelson and Dave Granz having arrived minutes before. She handed her boss a sealed evidence envelope, which Mackay shook, nodding when she heard rattling in the medicine container. She set it next to a stack of reports.

"Thanks for coming, Doc, Dave. I hoped to get up

to speed on the entire investigation, but I didn't get all the reports. Dave, you promised to have your reports to Inspector Escalante by the end of the day Friday."

Granz stared at Mackay. "I said I'd *try*. But this isn't the only case my detectives are working on."

"Can you tell me when I'll have them?"

"When we've completed our investigation. Until then it's the S.O.'s jurisdiction."

Kathryn shot him a look, but refused to start a turf war. An uncomfortable silence followed before she continued. "Let me summarize the investigation so far. A week ago, two kids drive off the cliff up on Mount Cabrillo. One is seriously injured, the other is killed. Looks like a tragic accident, except the CHP finds a note indicating maybe it wasn't an accident, maybe it was a double suicide attempt."

"But suicide isn't against the law," Escalante interrupted.

"True. If they'd both lived—or died—we wouldn't be here. But one of them survived. Trying to kill yourself isn't illegal, but assisting someone else is a felony."

"Suicide, my ass! This was a murder," Granz said.

"I'm not so sure, Dave," Nelson said. "Fuentes was pregnant."

"I know, but girls get pregnant every day. They get an abortion, they don't kill themselves."

"Lots do abort," Nelson answered, "but Latino cultural mores are strong. For some anything is better than an abortion."

"Even dying?"

"Yep, unfortunately. About seventy thousand teenagers have killed themselves since 1992. Lots were pregnancy related."

"Let's move this along," Mackay interjected. "Sterling excluded mechanical failure. Coupled with what I hear CSI will report regarding their evaluation of the site, I believe the car was driven off the cliff intentionally." Mackay referred to the sheriff's Crime Scene Investigation unit's report.

Mackay turned to Nelson. "Doc, can you confirm that Miranda was driving?"

Nelson sat forward in his chair, pushed his bifocals up on his nose, and ran his hand through his short hair. "I can confirm that Miranda sustained injuries to his chest and rib cage consistent with striking the steering wheel. On its own, that's not conclusive, but in my opinion, he was driving."

"It's good enough for me when you add it to the CHP and DOJ findings," Granz said. "I'll have one of my detectives arrest Miranda for murder and book him at the hospital."

"Not so fast, Dave," Kathryn said.

"What do you mean, 'not so fast'? Miranda drives his drugged, pregnant girlfriend over a cliff and kills her and the baby she's carrying. He's good for murder. I'm gonna have my guys arrest his ass."

Ignoring his challenge, Mackay said, "I can't make a filing decision until I know what we've got. We've got to rule out a mutual suicide pact. If they each independently decided to commit suicide and just acted together, she made her own choice and he's not culpable. If you arrest him now, I won't charge him and he'll walk out the door in forty-eight hours."

Granz stood up and headed for the door. "Miranda was the one calling the shots. He was driving the car.

Doc says Fuentes was practically comatose from Thorazine. And you've told me yourself that surviving a suicide pact triggers a presumption that the survivor entered into the pact in less than good faith. This isn't a mutual suicide pact, it's a murder-suicide pact. Let me know when you've worked up the guts to file on Miranda. Meanwhile, I've got other investigations to work on."

"Jesus, that came out of nowhere. What's his problem?" Escalante asked, glancing first at Mackay, then at Nelson, who shrugged.

"Inspector, please give Doctor Nelson and me a few minutes. Thanks."

After Escalante left, Kathryn said to Nelson, "What was that all about?"

"Delayed reaction," Nelson said.

"To what?"

"The breakup of your relationship, for one thing. That you've leapfrogged past him in the law enforcement pecking order for another. He's setting up the boundaries between your new position and his. You can't worry about it now, you've got too much to do."

She nodded. Then she opened the evidence envelope Escalante had given her at the start of the meeting and retrieved a pill container. "It has a Spanish label, from a *farmacia* in Monterrey, Mexico. Looks like a couple of tablets left. Can you analyze them in your lab right away?"

"Sure. What are you thinking they are, Katie?"

"Thorazine. They were in Miranda's backpack when Sterling seized it. If he gave her the Thorazine, his role in her death may be active, not passive. It may be assisting a suicide, or it may be murder, as Dave said."

"What about the fetus?" Nelson asked.

"If he knew she was pregnant and murdered her, he's good for two counts of murder. And if he was the baby's father, he's committed statutory rape."

"You know relationships between older guys and young girls are common in Mexico, Kate. It's the norm in their culture. Besides, he's only four years older than her."

"I know, but can I ignore the statutory rape laws? People have to obey the laws of the country they reside in, even recent immigrants. Wouldn't any other decision open a Pandora's box we'd never get the lid on again."

"So, what now?"

"I convene the grand jury."

"Katie, if you don't mind my saying so, you may be shooting yourself in the foot. McCaskill's demanding that charges be filed against Miranda immediately. You convene a grand jury investigation and he'll holler 'cover-up'—accuse you of being indecisive. It's political suicide."

"Maybe, but it's premature to file. We don't know all the facts, and this is just the kind of investigation that should be handled by a confidential proceeding. It's the right thing to do, Morgan. If it costs me the election, then so be it."

19

––––––

"I've convened the grand jury for next Monday," Mackay told Inspector Escalante when they met the first thing Tuesday morning. "That's less than a week away. Two things: first, find Esther Fuentes's friends, especially her best friend."

"What's her name?" Escalante asked.

"I don't know," Mackay answered, "but every sixteen-year-old girl has a best friend. Find her and interview her."

"Okay, what else?"

"Contact Esther Fuentes's mother. Arrange for her to testify."

"That may not be so easy," Escalante said.

"Why? What's the problem? We're investigating her daughter's death. She'll want to cooperate."

"Not necessarily. Her mother's a farm worker. If she doesn't have a green card, she'll be afraid to testify, afraid she'll bring herself to the attention of the Immigration and Naturalization Service. And she may have encouraged her daughter's relationship with Miranda. She may not be so eager to testify against him."

"Well, I can't take a chance that she won't cooperate," Mackay said, "but I don't want to scare her away, either. Do you think she might return to Mexico?"

"Absolutely."

"I can't risk that. I've got to find out everything she knows about her daughter and Miranda."

Kathryn considered her options. "Okay, here's what let's do. Take today to locate and interview Fuentes's friends. Meanwhile, I'll have Mary Elizabeth draw up a subpoena for Mrs. Fuentes. You can contact her tomorrow and serve it."

"What if she refuses?"

"Take her into custody and I'll bring her before a judge."

The phone buzzed. Kathryn picked it up, held her hand over the mouthpiece, and said to Escalante, "Keep me posted."

When Escalante had left, Kathryn removed her hand from the mouthpiece. "Yes."

"Ms. Mackay," Nancy Torres said, "Doctor Simmons just dropped off a package for you."

"A package?"

"Yes, ma'am. He said he had a meeting on the fifth floor in a few minutes and couldn't wait, but that you were expecting it."

Kathryn frowned, knowing she wasn't expecting anything from Robert. "Would you bring it in, please?"

Kathryn opened the brown manilla envelope and a small, square gift-wrapped package fell out, along with a card. The card read, "Sweets for the sweet. Thanks for the weekend . . . Robert."

When Kathryn opened the package, she found a fancy chocolate truffle with a heart on top, which she savored slowly.

Inspector Escalante talked to a half dozen students and all of Esther Fuentes's teachers at Española High School. They told her nothing she hadn't expected: Esther was a straight-A student, a nice girl, quiet, shy, and respectful. She and Raymondo Miranda were inseparable. Mr. Spencer, her homeroom advisor, suggested she talk to a girl named Josefina Valenzuela.

Escalante located Josefina in the library. She was short and slightly overweight, but extremely pretty. Her baggy overalls and sweatshirt did nothing to conceal large breasts and a voluptuous figure uncommon for such a young girl. She had blue designer braces on her teeth and, except for her extraordinary beauty, looked like half the girls on campus.

Escalante showed her ID. "Josefina, I understand you and Esther Fuentes were friends. Could I talk to you for a minute?"

The girl looked around to be sure no one was watching. "Call me Josie, okay?"

"Sure, but why? Josefina is beautiful. It's my grandmother's name. She still lives in Guadalajara."

"Because 'Josie' sounds Anglo."

"I understand, Josie," Escalante said. She was thinking it was a pity that this girl was ashamed of her ethnicity. "How old are you?"

"Sixteen, why?"

"Really? I would have guessed seventeen. How well did you know Esther?"

"Pretty good. We had three classes and study hall with each other. We both lived on Center Street, so we walked to school together. And we hung out sometimes."

"Were you her best friend?"

"I guess so, but she spent most of her time out of school with Ray."

"Raymondo Miranda? How well do you know him?"

"Not very good, but he's really cute. And he's got a cool car and goes to college. When I graduate I'm going to San Jose State. I'm going to try for a scholarship, only my parents . . ."

"Your parents what?"

Josefina looked around to be sure no one was paying attention. "Nothin'. Look, I've gotta study, there's a test next period. Are we finished?"

"Almost. Did you and Esther ever talk about personal things? Really personal things?"

"Sometimes. Like what?"

"Did she tell you she was pregnant?"

Suddenly, the girl slammed her book closed, stuffed it into a backpack, and started to rise, but Escalante held her arm. "Josie, what's wrong? Please sit down."

The girl complied, but said, "I can't talk to you anymore, I've gotta go."

"Josie, this is very important. We know Esther was pregnant when she died."

"I can't talk about it. I promised!"

"Josie, listen. My boss is going to ask you to testify in front of the grand jury. She'll ask you the same question, and you'll have to answer truthfully. It would be easier if you could talk to me about it now, before you testify."

The girl's brown eyes grew huge and round. "I can't, Ms. Escalante. Please! You don't understand. I'll get in so much trouble."

Escalante rose and walked around the table and put her arm over the girl's shoulders. "I know it's hard, Josie, and I'll make it as easy as possible for you. My boss is a really nice lady named Kathryn. She'll make sure nothing bad happens to you."

"I won't do it. I don't care what you do to me, I won't tell on her." Josefina stood up and slung her backpack over her shoulder angrily and stormed out of study hall.

Escalante walked to her car, which she had parked in a red zone with her business card on the dashboard so she wouldn't be ticketed. She climbed in and punched in the DA's number on her cell phone.

Kathryn answered. "Inspector, I'm going to put you on the speaker phone. Mary Elizabeth and I were just talking about the investigation." Mackay punched the speaker button, then hung up the receiver. "Can you hear me?"

"Yes. I'm in my car at Española High. I just talked with a girl named Josefina Valenzuela. She was Esther Fuentes's best friend."

"Good work," Kathryn said. "What did she tell you?"

"Nothing. She refuses to talk to me."

"Will she cooperate with the grand jury?" Mary Elizabeth asked.

There was a brief silence while Escalante considered the question. "Probably not without a subpoena, maybe not even then. She's scared of something, but I don't know what."

"How old is she?" Skinner asked.

"Sixteen."

"Okay," Kathryn said. "Come on in. We'll have a subpoena ready."

Kathryn punched the speaker button and the phone disconnected. "Mary Elizabeth, can you handle the subpoena? Then get it to Escalante when she comes in."

"Sure. Kate, you look awful. Are you okay?"

"Yeah, just a splitting headache, and my stomach's upset. I'll be fine."

"You sure? What's wrong, the flu?"

"Maybe. If it doesn't go away pretty soon, I'll ask Doc Nelson."

"Kate, it's none of my business, but maybe you should go to the doctor. A real one, not Nelson."

Kathryn laughed. "I'll bet he'd appreciate your saying that he's not a real doctor."

"I meant—"

"I know. Don't worry, everything's fine."

"I don't believe you, Kate. You don't look good."

And I feel even worse, Kathryn thought.

20

──

Robert Simmons and Kathryn Mackay were having coffee in her office Thursday morning when Morgan Nelson stuck his head in the door. "Can I come in? I can come back if you're tied up."

"Come on in, Morgan," Kathryn said. "Doctor Simmons and I were just having coffee. Would you like one? I could ask Nancy to send down."

"No, thanks. Morning, Bob. Actually, I'm glad to catch the two of you. I want to run something by you, Kathryn, and I don't often have the chance to consult with another doctor."

"Good morning, Morgan. What's on your mind?" Simmons asked.

Nelson pulled a lab report from the inside pocket of his coat and slid it across the desk to Mackay. She looked at it, then handed it to Simmons.

"Lab report on that drowned girl. Amelia Salazar," Nelson told him.

"Nothing unusual about it," Simmons said. "Tox screen shows chlorpromazine, but not enough to kill her. It's not uncommon for people to sedate themselves before committing suicide, assuming that's what it was. Or it could have been an accident. That much Thorazine would have made her pretty woozy. Maybe she lost her balance and fell in the water."

"That's what I thought, too," Nelson replied. "But the Fuentes girl's blood also contained a high but nonlethal concentration of chlorpromazine. Both pregnant, and both were teenagers."

"You said her name was Salazar?" Kathryn asked.

Nelson looked confused. "Granz caught a match in DMV just like Escalante suggested. One of his detectives brought the girl's father in to ID the body. Didn't he tell you?"

Kathryn was perturbed but let it drop, not wanting to discuss her relationship with Dave Granz in front of Robert Simmons. "You think the Fuentes and Salazar deaths could be connected?"

"Just a hunch. Medically, there's nothing to support such a conclusion."

"Granz is still investigating the Salazar death," Mackay told him. "Fields says so far there's no evidence of foul play."

"Well, if she killed herself, there's another similarity between her and Fuentes. And that's not all, either. Both of them went to Española High School. They were both very pretty, and both were excellent students."

Nelson and Simmons stood up to leave at the same time. Nelson said, "There's something going on. I don't know what it is, but there are way too many similarities to be coincidences. There's a connection between those two deaths. You need to look into it."

21

——

"When it's put that way, they could be connected," James Fields said after Kathryn Mackay told him what Morgan Nelson had said about the deaths of Esther Fuentes and Amelia Salazar. "But how?"

"I don't know, but I want you to look into Salazar's death."

"S.O.'s working it."

"I know, but if there's a bigger picture I need to know before I convene the grand jury."

Fields sat forward in his chair and unbuttoned his beige suit coat. "Why don't you call Granz and ask him to step up his investigation?" It was more a suggestion than a question.

"Normally I would, but he's not very responsive to my requests these days. Maybe you could swing by the Salazar home and interview her parents."

Fields checked his notebook. "They live at one-fourteen Via Mirada. That's in The Flats. I'll get right on it."

* * *

The Flats covered fifty square blocks near where the Santa Lucia River flowed into the Pacific. Adjacent to the county's prettiest beaches, it comprised Santa Rita's ugliest slum, where hookers sold their bodies and drug dealers sold their poison. Teams of bureaucrats, spending millions of redevelopment dollars, had failed spectacularly to eliminate the blight, poverty, and crime. Locals knew it as a place to hurry past, with car doors locked, on their way to the exclusive restaurants and boutiques along the Pacific Esplanade. Cops knew it as a crime-infested ghetto.

Some knew it as an opportunity. The one place in Santa Rita with affordable property prices, the working poor saw it as their only hope for home ownership. As a result, islands of beauty and pride sat amid the sea of squalor and shame.

Fields idled his Mercury Cougar slowly along Via Mirada and pulled up to the curb in front of a tiny white bungalow behind a white picket fence and a perfectly manicured postage-stamp-size lawn. He picked up the mike and logged out with County Comm, locked the car doors, opened a small hinged gate, walked up the brick path, and rang the bell. He could hear the Giants-Padres baseball game through the front door.

A tall, slender Hispanic man wearing blue jeans, a pinstriped Big Ben work shirt, and high-top work boots answered the door. He had a neatly trimmed mustache, and a shiny bald head. "Yes?"

Fields held his badge and ID to the screen door and introduced himself. "Are you Mr. Salazar?"

"Yes."

"I'd like to talk to you about your daughter Amelia, if you have a few minutes. May I come in?"

Salazar pushed the screen open and stepped aside, but didn't answer, and led Fields into a small living room where an upright vacuum was still running. He switched it off and motioned the inspector to sit on the sofa, then sat in an easy chair across from them. "I usually clean house before I go to work."

"I won't take long," Fields said. "Where do you work?"

"I'm a welder at a company in San Jose that makes food processing machinery. I've got to leave in half an hour, so I'm not late."

"Sir, is your wife home? If I could talk to you together, I wouldn't need to bother you again."

"My wife Marguerite died from cancer more than a year ago."

"I'm sorry, I didn't know," Fields said.

Salazar clasped his hands together on his lap. "No reason for you to be sorry."

"Mr. Salazar, you knew Amelia was pregnant?"

"I found out four or five months ago. She got real big. The loose clothes she wore couldn't hide it, so I asked her. She told me to mind my own business, that she'd take care of it." He shook his head sadly. "She was only seventeen years old. How was she gonna take care of something like that by herself? But she said if I asked again, she'd leave, so I didn't ask after that."

"Did she tell you who the baby's father was?"

"No. I would've killed him if I found out."

"Do you know if she saw a doctor?"

"She said he told her everything was okay."

"Do you know her doctor's name?"

"No, she wouldn't let me go with her. We don't have insurance, my company is small and won't pay for it. So we go to the county clinic. They don't charge us much because I don't make much."

Fields watched Gustavo Salazar wring his big, callused hands together like he was washing them. "Her mother wanted Amelia to be better than us. She was going to college after she finished high school. After her mother died, Amelia cried all the time and wouldn't talk about it. I asked her to see a counselor at the clinic."

"Do you know if the counselor prescribed Thorazine for Amelia?"

Salazar glanced at his watch. "I've gotta leave soon. No, I don't know. She never told me whether she saw a counselor. She was private and kept things mostly to herself."

He paused and drew in a deep breath that quivered slightly. "The day before she . . . before she left, she told me she had figured out how to make things all right. I asked her what she meant, but she wouldn't say, she just told me her mother would understand. That night she cooked dinner and made a chocolate cake. The next day she packed me a big sandwich and a piece of cake in my lunch pail. She kissed me goodbye when I left for work and told me not to worry. That was the last time I . . ." Salazar started to cry.

22

Kathryn didn't eat lunch Thursday after Robert Simmons and Morgan Nelson left her office, choosing instead to lie on the sofa in her office to ease her upset stomach.

At one-thirty Inspector Escalante called to advise that she had just served a grand jury subpoena on Josie Valenzuela. She was satisfied that while reluctant, Josie would appear as directed the following Monday.

"What about Mrs. Fuentes?" Mackay asked.

"Headed to her house right now," Escalante said.

Mackay lay her aching head on the arm of the sofa. The next thing she knew, the ringing phone awakened her. When she looked at the clock, it read 2:45. "Yes?" she answered.

"Kathryn? Escalante. I'm on my cell phone headed to the jail. I have Fuentes in custody."

"Damn. What happened?"

"She refuses to appear before the grand jury. She destroyed the subpoena, so I took her into custody."

Kathryn moved to her desk and began scribbling

notes on a legal pad. "All right, take her directly to court. I'll contact Judge Tucker and request she convene a hearing immediately."

"Okay, it'll be a little while, traffic's backed up on the freeway. Cal Trans is repaving the northbound lanes."

"Do we need an interpreter?"

"No, Mrs. Fuentes speaks English. See you in about half an hour."

Although she wore her judicial robe, Judge Tucker convened court in her chambers. She sat behind her desk with everyone else in chairs in a semicircle before her. The court reporter sat to the judge's left.

Judge Tucker nodded to indicate that the court reporter should begin transcribing and announced, "The record shall indicate that present in chambers are District Attorney Kathryn Mackay, Inspector Donna Escalante, and Helena Fuentes. Please proceed, Ms. Mackay."

"Your Honor, I have asked the court to convene in camera pursuant to Penal Code Section 1332, to assure Helena Fuentes's appearance as a material witness before the grand jury. If the court please, I ask that Inspector Escalante be sworn at this time."

Tucker swore Escalante, then Mackay asked, "Inspector Escalante, were you directed this afternoon to serve a subpoena on Helena Fuentes compelling her to appear and testify regarding the death of her daughter before the Santa Rita County criminal grand jury on September fifteenth of this year?"

"I was."

"And did you serve that subpoena on Helena Fuentes?"

"I contacted Mrs. Fuentes at her home in Española

at approximately two o'clock this afternoon, but she refused service."

"By 'refused service,' what do you mean?"

"After I asked if she was Helena Fuentes and she answered in the affirmative, I handed her the subpoena. She asked me what it was and I told her it was a subpoena that required her to appear and give sworn testimony. She stated she would not appear."

"Did she do anything else to indicate that she would not honor the subpoena?"

"Yes, she tore it into three pieces and placed them on the table beside us, then asked me to leave her home." Escalante pulled the bits of paper from her briefcase and handed them to Mackay, who asked that they be marked as a court exhibit, and passed them to the clerk.

"Did you advise her that compliance with a subpoena is mandatory and that refusal is a criminal offense?"

"Yes, but she said she would do whatever was necessary to avoid appearing."

"By that statement, did you believe she meant she might leave the area to avoid testifying?"

"Yes."

"No further questions."

"Mrs. Fuentes, if you promise me that you will appear as District Attorney Mackay has requested, I will allow you to go home. Can you assure me that you will do so?" Judge Tucker asked.

"I mean no disrespect, Your Honor, but I won't testify."

"You understand the District Attorney is looking into the death of your daughter. Don't you want to help?"

"No, she is investigating Raymondo. I won't help her do that."

Judge Tucker thought momentarily, then said, "Then I have no choice but to order you to post bail in an amount sufficient to assure your appearance before the grand jury." Tucker turned to Mackay. "Does the District Attorney have a bail recommendation?"

"Your Honor, I'm afraid that any bail amount which Mrs. Fuentes is able to post would be insufficient to assure her appearance. I request that she be held in the county jail until six o'clock next Monday without bail," Mackay said.

Tucker motioned for the court reporter to suspend transcription, then indicated to Kathryn that she wished to talk out of earshot. They walked to the corner of the office. "Can I do that? Order her held without bail just on the basis of her verbal refusal to testify?" she asked.

"Absolutely," Kathryn answered. "P.C. 1332(b) says that if a witness refuses, she may be committed to the custody of the Sheriff until she complies."

"Can we hold her that long? This is only Thursday afternoon, and the grand jury doesn't meet until Monday evening."

"We can. But she's entitled to a hearing before another judge two days after you order her held. With the weekend coming, that means late Monday afternoon."

Tucker contemplated. "Okay, I'll order her held, but I want that grand jury convened during the daytime, no later than—" She checked the clock. "—2 P.M. Monday. I won't allow this to extend beyond the statutory two-day automatic review and have my order overturned."

"Judge—"

"No 'buts,' Kathryn. Either agree or I'll cut her loose right now. What's it going to be?"

"I'll convene the grand jury at one o'clock Monday afternoon."

Tucker turned without another word, sat at her desk, and instructed the court reporter they were back on the record.

"The court finds there is substantial risk the witness will refuse to honor the District Attorney's subpoena and that her testimony is critical to the grand jury's proceedings. I order the witness held without bail until 1 P.M. Monday, September fifteenth. The District Attorney will arrange for Mrs. Fuentes to be placed in protective custody. She is remanded to the custody of Inspector Escalante for delivery to the women's facility."

23

By one o'clock Monday afternoon, Nancy Torres had contacted seventeen of the nineteen criminal grand jurors. Superior Court room 6 was vacated for the afternoon by presiding judge Jesse Woods, and when Kathryn arrived, the jurors stood in small groups chatting. Escalante arrived outside the courtroom shortly after Mackay, with Helena Fuentes in custody, followed by the court reporter. Mackay stepped into the hall and spoke with her inspector quietly.

"Only myself, the grand jurors, and the court reporter may be present during testimony, but there is an exception for an officer having custody of a prisoner witness. As soon as I've made my opening remarks, I'll have you bring Mrs. Fuentes in and I'll ask you to remain until her testimony is concluded. Then you can take her home."

"Okay," Escalante answered, then sat beside Helena Fuentes on the bench.

When the jury had been sworn a few months before, carry-over jurors Sherry Scruggs and Ed McGuirk had been appointed foreperson and secretary. The foreperson presided over each session similar to a judge in a courtroom proceeding, while Secretary McGuirk's additional duties included taking roll, marking exhibits, and recording minutes of the proceeding.

"The jurors will be seated," Scruggs ordered from the bench where a judge would normally sit. Twelve members sat in the jury box, three on chairs in front, and McGuirk sat at the court clerk's table. When they were in place, the foreperson said, "The secretary will take the roll, please."

After McGuirk had called all nineteen names and announced two absences, Kathryn rose and walked to the podium in front of the jury. She wore a jet black suit, white shirt, and medium black leather heels. She always dressed conservatively before the grand jury, and invariably stood throughout the proceedings.

"Good afternoon," she said. "And thank you for appearing on such short notice. I assure you it was absolutely necessary. I've asked you to convene for the purpose of conducting an investigation into the death of Esther Fuentes. Specifically, I would like you to investigate the conduct of Raymondo Miranda as it relates to the death of Miss Fuentes, and in doing so advise me on the following matters: Did Raymondo Miranda commit statutory rape on Esther Fuentes? Did Raymondo Miranda assist in the suicide of Miss Fuentes? And finally, did Raymondo Miranda murder Esther Fuentes and her unborn child?"

Mackay paused before continuing. "Statutory rape is unlawful sexual intercourse with a female under the age of eighteen. The state is not required to prove the female didn't consent to intercourse, because she is presumed incapable of consenting by reason of her age. Therefore, it is necessary only to establish that intercourse occurred; the female was under eighteen years of age and the male over eighteen; and the intercourse was unlawful."

Kathryn paused while jurors wrote notes. "Assisting a suicide occurs when one person aids, abets, or encourages another person to kill him- or herself. A mutual suicide pact, where two people independently decide to kill themselves and simply act together does not constitute the crime of assisting a suicide. This is true even where one person supplies the instrumentality by which they attempt to kill themselves, for example, where one person supplies and drives a car over a cliff after they have both independently decided to do so. The key is 'active' versus 'passive' involvement in the death of the other person."

Kathryn sipped her ice water. "Murder," she continued, pausing to allow the force of the word to impact the jurors, "is the unlawful killing of a human being or a fetus with malice aforethought. A fetus is defined as an unborn offspring in the post-embryonic period, after major bodily structures have been outlined, which occurs seven or eight weeks after conception."

"A murder occurs, for instance, when a person willfully, deliberately, and intentionally drives a person over a cliff to her death without her acquiescence. It is murder despite the fact that the driver, by some quirk of fate, survives the crash, though he originally intended to take his own life in the crash as well."

Kathryn allowed time for the jurors to complete their notes, then addressed the foreperson. "The People call Helena Fuentes to the stand."

After swearing to tell the truth, Fuentes settled uncomfortably into the witness chair and stared contemptuously at Mackay. She was short and heavy-set, with piercing brown eyes, and wore a maroon jail jumpsuit.

"Mrs. Fuentes," Kathryn began, "do you understand that you are here today to provide testimony before the grand jury and that you have sworn to tell the truth?"

The witness glared at Mackay. "I do."

"If you don't hear or understand my questions, please let me know and I'll repeat them. Would you state your name, please, and spell your last name for the court reporter."

"Helena Fuentes. F-U-E-N-T-E-S."

"Are you married?"

"You know I am," Fuentes responded. "Do I have to answer questions when you already know the answer?"

"Yes, you must answer the questions for the jurors," Mackay directed, then repeated the question.

"You know I am married," Fuentes replied.

"Do you have any children?"

"You already know that," Fuentes answered defiantly.

Mackay stopped and thought for a moment, then decided to treat Fuentes as a hostile witness, an examination technique that permitted her to ask leading questions that were easily answered by a yes or a no.

Mackay returned her attention to the witness. "You had one child, a daughter named Esther, is that correct, Mrs. Fuentes?"

"Yes."

"And Esther was killed in an automobile accident on September first of this year?"

"That's right."

"You know Raymondo Miranda?"

"Yes. He is a nice boy. He and Esther were friends."

"How old is Raymondo Miranda?"

"Ask him."

"I'm asking you."

"Twenty."

"How do you know?"

"I went to his birthday party every year since he was four or five years old. Our families are friends."

"And Esther was sixteen, is that right?"

"Yes."

"Was Esther married?"

"That's crazy. She was a child."

"The question requires a yes or no answer, Mrs Fuentes. Was Esther married?"

"No."

Kathryn nodded, knowing that she would explain in her closing remarks to the jurors that if Esther and Raymondo had been married to each other, their intercourse would not have been unlawful and therefore not statutory rape.

"Okay. Now, when you said earlier that Esther and Raymondo were friends, you didn't mean regular friends, did you? You meant they were closer than that, that they were sweethearts, is that correct?"

Fuentes reluctantly answered, "Yes."

"And you knew the nature of their relationship before Esther was killed in the car accident?"

"Yes."

"You and your husband encouraged Esther's romantic relationship with Raymondo Miranda, didn't you?"

"What do you mean?"

"You knew that Raymondo and Esther were sexually intimate?"

Fuentes glared at Mackay for several seconds before answering. "They were to be married after Esther graduated from college."

"Did Esther ever tell you that she and Raymondo engaged in sexual intercourse?"

"No."

"But you knew your daughter was four months pregnant?"

Fuentes answered so softly that Kathryn asked her to repeat her answer. "No, I didn't know."

Mackay's eyebrows arched but that was the only outward indication of her surprise at the answer. "Esther never complained to you of morning sickness or other symptoms women experience when they're pregnant?"

The witness stared wide-eyed at Mackay as if she had just discovered a long-lost secret. "No, but she . . . she had complained of pain each month. She went to the doctor, but she said it was because of her period."

"Do you know if she received any medication to help with her painful periods, Mrs. Fuentes?"

"She didn't say. But she said she had to keep seeing the doctor, that he needed to take some tests."

"Do you know the name of her doctor?"

"No."

"Do you have a family doctor?"

"No."

"What do you do when someone in your family needs medical care or medicine?" Kathryn asked.

"We go to the county health clinic."

"Is it possible that your daughter went to the county clinic for prenatal care?"

"If she saw a doctor, it must have been there."

"Mrs. Fuentes, would it be possible for your daughter to have been sexually intimate with anyone besides Raymondo, in your opinion?"

Fuentes's eyes narrowed. "Damn you! Esther spent her spare time with Raymondo. We knew where she went and who she was with all the time. Damn you!"

Mackay overlooked the outburst. "One more thing, Mrs. Fuentes. To your knowledge, has anyone in your family ever taken Thorazine?"

"What is that?"

"It's a tranquilizer. Doctors prescribe it for patients who are nervous, to help them be more calm."

"My husband and I work in the fields and have no time to be nervous."

"So Esther could not have found Thorazine at home?"

"No."

"To your knowledge, was Thorazine ever prescribed for your daughter, maybe on a visit to the clinic?"

"No."

Kathryn was almost finished. "Let me ask you again, Mrs. Fuentes. Given that Esther was pregnant, is it possible that anyone besides Raymondo Miranda was the baby's father?"

Fuentes waited long enough that Kathryn was about to admonish her of her legal obligation to answer the question, then whispered, "No, it is not possible. Esther was a good girl."

24

<hr/>

At four-thirty Tuesday morning, Kathryn awoke from a dream in which Helena Fuentes refused to testify before the grand jury and Judge Tucker revoked Mackay's law license on the grounds that it was illegal to waste the jurors' time.

When she was fully conscious, Kathryn realized she was sick and rushed to the bathroom to throw up Monday night's dinner. She swallowed a tablespoon of Pepto-Bismol to settle her stomach, plus four Advil for her headache, and lay back down.

When she woke up again, it was seven-thirty. For the first time since her appointment as District Attorney, Kathryn got to work later than her secretary.

"Doctor Nelson called at eight o'clock," Nancy told her. "He asked you to call him right away."

Kathryn identified herself to the receptionist, then Nelson answered. "Morning, Katie, banker's hours, huh?"

"I don't have to be here at seven o'clock every damn morning. I have another life, you know," she responded.

The line was quiet for a moment, then Nelson said, "Of course, Kate, I'm sorry. I called because Roselba Menendez is faxing the Fuentes DNA test results to me this morning. I'll interoffice it to you as soon as I get it."

"I don't have time for that; the grand jury's already been convened. I'll call her and see if she can walk me through it at DOJ. Can you go to the lab if she's available?"

"Sure. Shall I meet you there?"

Kathryn hesitated. "Could you come by and pick me up? I don't feel like driving."

"Be glad to." Nelson answered tentatively. He knew Kathryn usually drove her own car to avoid being tied to other people's schedules.

Normally unpretentious, Nelson's sole indulgence was a new luxury car every three or four years. When Kathryn climbed into Nelson's new white BMW 740i in front of the government building, she slammed the door, but he didn't say anything.

They were on the freeway headed to South County in heavy traffic when she said, "It's about time DOJ got the DNA results. It's been two weeks."

Nelson shot her a quizzical look. "Menendez did a hell of a job, Kate. It could have taken months. She moved it to the top of her list as a favor. We ought to thank her; she worked on her own time."

Kathryn nodded. "Are the results good or bad? Did she say?"

"They're good, you'll be—" He was interrupted by a red pickup with fat tires, exaggerated suspension, and a gun rack in the rear window, whose horn blasted as it cut in front of his car. The driver was a young guy with long hair and a baseball cap turned backwards. He flipped them the finger.

"What did I do?" Nelson asked rhetorically.

"You weren't going fast enough."

"Fifty-five's the speed limit. I was doing sixty."

"I know, but he was doing at least eighty. Damn redneck, I ought to get his license number and have him cited."

"Lighten up, Katie, you're going to blow a fuse," Nelson admonished. "You've got plenty to do without taking on relatively harmless speeders."

"Harmless, my foot. That's the kind of stupid behavior they call 'road rage.' A guy was shot and killed not long ago for doing something exactly like that to another idiot. You think I should just ignore it?"

They rode in silence until Nelson pulled into the parking lot at the DOJ facility on Research Drive, where Menendez met them in the reception area.

A security guard directed them to sign a visitor log, then the criminalist led them to a huge, open office jammed with computers, desks and chairs, and filing cabinets. They threaded their way to the opposite side and pushed through a swinging gate into a long, narrow hallway. Office and workroom doors lined both sides of the corridor. Most of the doors were closed and locked, but a few stood ajar, exposing an array of scientific equipment.

Menendez punched her ID code into a keypad by one of the doors. "DNA lab's in here. Are you sure you wouldn't rather go over this later, after you've had time to review my report?" she asked Mackay.

"We don't have time," Kathryn answered. "I'll prep you for testifying as you walk me through the procedures. Remember, some of the jurors will be starting from scratch when it comes to DNA, so your testimony will need to educate them. You can refresh my memory at the same time. I've done one admissibility hearing back in '86. Damn waste of time—three weeks long. Then the judge wouldn't let the results in."

"Kathryn, that was before DNA evidence was admitted in evidence in California courts," said Nelson.

Menendez glanced at Nelson, who then shrugged. "DNA stands for deoxyribonucleic acid," the criminalist began. She slid three metal stools to the stainless-steel bench and motioned them to sit. "We call it the chemical 'blueprint of life' because it carries the hereditary instructions for every structure and function of the body.

"DNA is submolecular, which means it's only visible through an electron microscope. There's one in front of each of you. Turn them on; I put slides in them already."

When they had complied, she asked, "What do you see?"

"Looks like a tightly twisted zipper," Mackay said.

"Right, they're called strands. Each 'tooth' of the zipper is actually a pair of chemical elements bonded together. We call them base pairs. There are only four chemicals: adenine, cytosine, guanine, and thymine. We abbreviate them A, C, G, and T.

"Base pairs are combinations of the chemical elements: A-G, C-T, T-A, and so forth. Base pairs occur in a repetitive pattern, or sequence, that we call 'genetic markers.' Each strand contains more than three billion base pairs, but the markers are identical for every DNA strand in the body, and the strands are identical in every cell, regardless of the part of the body it's obtained from."

"Except reproductive cells," Nelson added.

"Right," Menendez answered. "In addition, the sequence of ninety-nine-point-nine percent of the base pairs is identical for every human being because they carry codes for characteristics like two eyes, head hair, stomach acids, fingernails, air-breathing lungs, and other biological functions common to humans."

"So how do you identify a single individual?" Mackay asked.

"By working with the remaining one-out-of-a-thousand markers that are unique to each person, the ones that define our individual physical and biological makeup."

"How?" Mackay asked.

"I used restriction fragment length polymorphism, or RFLP, testing because it's by far the most discriminating technique. Polymerase chain reaction method, or PCR is a molecular copying technique that can generate reliable data from extremely small amounts of DNA. It wasn't necessary to use PCR in this case because Doctor Nelson provided plenty of tissue in perfect condition."

"You'll have to explain the RFLP procedure to the jurors," Kathryn said.

"Okay. On your slide you see only a tiny segment of a DNA strand. A whole strand is too large to work with, so we place it in an enzyme that cuts it into pieces. Then we transfer the severed fragments to a special gel and subject the resulting mixture to a low-level electrical charge. The electrical charge sets up magnetic fields that interact with the DNA fragments and sorts them by size. Then we mix in a chemical, called a 'genetic tracer,' that locks on to certain parts of the DNA. Finally we x-ray the traced fragments with an autoradiograph and photograph the X ray. Here."

She handed each of them three pieces of photographic paper that looked like supermarket bar codes. "One is the fetus's marker pattern, the other two are Miranda and Esther Fuentes's. The photographs simply display the base pair banding patterns, which can be compared visually to each other. It's similar to ballistics, where you place two items side by side and try to line up grooves, scratches, and other marks. If they align perfectly, you've got a match."

Mackay knew she must answer the next question for the jurors to prove Raymondo Miranda was the father of Esther Fuentes's unborn child. "You can identify a single individual, but how do you connect a person to his or her parents?"

"As Doctor Nelson said, ova and sperm cells differ from every other cell in the body in that they contain exactly one-half of a person's DNA markers. When fertilization occurs, the embryo receives half its DNA from each parent. By identifying the parents' markers we can predict the child's."

Kathryn nodded. "The DNA case I prosecuted didn't involve paternity issues. What's the level of certainty when you obtain a match?"

Menendez uncharacteristically smiled and glanced at Nelson, who smiled back. Nelson said, "Depends whether you mean scientifically or legally. You know that courts disagree over which statistical method should be used to establish probabilities.

"But scientists agree DNA results are virtually

conclusive, on the order of one in twenty-four billion. Great enough to conclude that no two individuals have identical genetic markers.

"If you get a match," Nelson continued, placing his three photos alongside each other and sliding them back and forth, "or, in this case, you fail to obtain a match, it's indisputable. Miranda didn't impregnate Esther Fuentes."

Kathryn swallowed hard and stared at Nelson, then at the criminalist, then at the three photographs she held. "You can positively exclude Miranda as the father of Esther Fuentes's unborn child based on RFLP DNA typing methodology?"

Roselba looked first at Morgan, then at Kathryn. "Absolutely. Didn't Doctor Nelson tell you what my report said? I thought it was strange you were in such a hurry to go over my testimony, or that you'd need me to testify at all, at least on the stat rape charge."

"I don't! Son of a bitch! Let's go, Morgan."

25

They were halfway back to the government center before Kathryn spoke. "Damn it, Nelson, why didn't you tell me Miranda wasn't the father when I called you? It would've saved me a lot of time. I just wasted two hours."

"You didn't ask me."

"I asked. You said the result was good."

He kept his eyes glued to the road. "I meant it was forensically conclusive."

"It wipes out the stat rape charge. I don't think it's so good."

"You should," he answered. "If you care about the truth, you'd find the result very good. I'm surprised at you, Katie."

Nelson slid his BMW into a visitor parking space at the government center and shut the engine off.

"Thanks for the ride," she said. "I'll—"

"I'd like to come up for a few minutes, if you don't mind," he told her, opening the driver's door to forestall any protest.

They walked silently up the stairs and into Kathryn's office. Nelson closed the door and flopped into a leather chair. He leaned back and clasped his hands behind his head, then locked eyes with Kathryn.

"What's going on?" he asked.

"Nothing, why?"

"Because you've been angry all morning. If I've done something, tell me so I can either explain or apologize."

"You haven't done anything."

"Then why have you been so disagreeable?"

Kathryn didn't reply, and after a long silence Morgan said, "Is something more happening here at work? Tell me about it. Maybe I can help."

"It's nothing like that. I hesitate to say anything."

"I'm a good listener," Morgan said.

"I know." Kathryn contemplated her answer. "I haven't felt well for a couple of weeks. In fact, I can't remember ever feeling so bad for so long."

"You feel bad today?"

"Terrible. I woke up sick this morning. That's why I asked you to drive, I wasn't sure I could do it."

"Have you seen your doctor?"

"I don't really have one. I'm rarely sick. Except for my gynecologist, I never see a doctor. Anyway, I didn't think it was that serious."

Morgan nodded. "It probably isn't, but tell me about it anyway. What do you mean, you haven't been feeling well?"

"My stomach is upset all the time, especially in the mornings. And before you ask, I'm not pregnant." She managed a weak smile.

"How upset?"

"Enough to throw up, sometimes two or three times a day."

"What else?"

"Headaches—bad ones—and diarrhea."

"You've been under a lot of stress these last two weeks, Katie. Probably started about the time Hal died and you were appointed DA. Stress and emotional trauma often cause the symptoms you describe. Sounds like you're due for a doctor visit anyway. Get a thorough physical, blood tests, urinalysis, ECG, the works."

"I can't afford the time."

"You can't afford not to. It wouldn't take more than a couple of hours. If it's just stress, you can learn some methods for coping with it. If it's something more serious, better to diagnose and treat it right away. Make an appointment."

"I'll see someone as soon as I can."

Nelson looked at her and shook his head. "All right, I know what that means. At least keep a log. Jot down when the symptoms appear, how severe they are, and how long they last. Note what you're doing at the time or just before the onset. Maybe there's a pattern that'll confirm it's just stress. Will you do that?"

"Sure, that I can do," she said.

Nelson nodded and stood to leave.

"Doc, it sounds to me like we've got a motive for murder."

"How so, Kate?"

"Miranda's not the father of his girlfriend's baby."

26

At six o'clock Wednesday evening, foreperson Scruggs convened the grand jury and turned the proceedings over to Kathryn Mackay, who called Josefina Valenzuela to the witness stand.

"How old are you, Josefina?" Kathryn asked.

"Sixteen."

"Where do you live?"

"At four-twenty-two Center Street in Española, with my brothers and sisters."

"Are your sisters older or younger than you?"

"I'm the oldest."

"Where do you go to school?"

"Española High School. I'm a junior."

"Esther Fuentes was also a junior at Española High School. Did you know her?"

"Yes. She was my best friend."

"I know, and I'm sorry for your loss. Did you and Esther ever exchange personal information?"

"What do you mean?" the witness asked.

"Well, as best friends, did you tell each other secrets?"

"Yes, we told each other everything."

Kathryn paused. "Did Esther tell you she was pregnant?"

The witness glanced around the courtroom. "Do I have to answer?" she asked.

"Yes, you must answer my questions."

"Yes, she told me."

"Did she tell you who her baby's father was?"

She averted her eyes. "No," she said softly.

Kathryn suspected the answer wasn't truthful, but decided to revisit the subject later. "Okay, how long after Esther became pregnant did she tell you about it?"

"Right after she . . . missed her first period, maybe three or four weeks."

"Do you know if Esther saw a doctor?"

Josefina slumped in her chair. "I can't say."

"You don't know, or you won't tell me?"

"I promised I wouldn't tell anyone."

"Everything you say here is secret, Josefina," Kathryn said. "But you have to answer the question."

"Esther went to the clinic."

"Which clinic?"

"The free county clinic in Santa Rita."

"How do you know? Did you go with her?"

"I can't tell you."

"Josefina, you must tell me. If you don't, you will get in very serious trouble. Have you ever gone to the Santa Rita County Health Clinic?"

"Yes," she whispered.

"When was the first time?"

"About a year ago."

Kathryn was surprised. "A year ago? Did you go with Esther?"

"I can't talk about it."

"Josie, if you don't cooperate, I'll bring you before a judge, who will make you answer my questions."

"What will he do to me if I won't?"

"The judge will put you in juvenile hall."

"For how long?"

"Until you agree to answer my questions."

Josefina's chin quivered and she started to cry.

Kathryn continued. "Let's start again. When did you first go to the county health clinic?"

"Last January."

"Why did you go to the county clinic instead of a private doctor?"

"My parents work in the strawberry fields. They can't afford a regular doctor."

"Why did you go to the doctor in January?"

"I had a cold."

"When was the next time you went to the clinic?"

"I . . ." The witness did not continue.

"Josie, you must answer my questions. Let me put it a different way. Now, have you been to the county health clinic, either with or without Esther Fuentes, since January?"

"I . . . yes."

"How many times?"

"Twelve."

"Twelve visits over nine months? Why so many?" Kathryn asked. "How many times did you go with Esther Fuentes?"

"A couple of times I went with Esther. The other times I went without her."

"Were you sick?"

"Not always."

"Then, why did you go to the clinic so many times?"

She lowered her eyes and whispered, "He made me."

"Who made you?"

"The doctor."

"I'm confused. What doctor? How did he make you go to the clinic if you weren't sick?"

"He made the appointments. He told me I had to come or he would . . ."

"He would what?"

Josefina's huge brown eyes shifted from juror to juror imploring them for help, but none came.

"Answer the question, please," Kathryn instructed.

"Turn my parents in to the INS. The doctor said if I didn't do what he wanted, they would arrest my parents and deport them to Mexico. I had to let him do it, didn't I?"

A knot formed in the pit of Kathryn's stomach, momentarily displacing the continual nausea of the past two weeks. She feared what she might be doing to Robert, but pressed on. "What did the doctor make you do?" she asked.

Josefina pulled a tissue from the box and blew her nose. She sat up straight and seemed to find a momentary source of strength. "When I first went to the clinic in January, I had a bad cold and wanted some medicine for my cough and sore throat. The doctor had me come back for a checkup. He gave me a dressing gown and asked me to undress so he could see if I was better."

"Then what happened?"

"He took my blood pressure."

"Go on, Josie," Kathryn urged.

"He listened to my heart with a stethoscope, then he told me to lay down."

A wave of despair and foreboding washed over Kathryn as she realized what Josefina would say. She asked, "And did you lie down?"

"Yes, he told me to."

"Then what happened?"

"He listened to my heart again. Then he moved it to my lungs and listened, then down to my stomach."

Kathryn sensed the girl was holding back. "How did he do that, Josie, listen to your heart and lungs?"

"He pulled my gown up, all the way to my neck. I couldn't see what he was doing, then I felt him press down on my stomach. He said he was checking for enlargements and I think he said abnormalities. Then, I felt his fingers on my neck and armpits. Then he . . ."

"Go ahead," Kathryn encouraged her, dreading the answer.

"He put his fingers on my breast. I told him I felt fine, but he told me to be quiet, that he had to examine my breasts."

"And did he examine your breasts?"

"Yes, no, I mean . . ."

"Take your time, Josie," Kathryn said in a gentle, calming tone.

"He put his mouth on my breast. I could feel his tongue. I didn't know what to do, I was scared."

Kathryn stared silently at Josefina. *My God, Robert will be devastated.*

"I understand," Kathryn said. "You're being very brave to tell us this. Are you okay to continue?"

"I . . . I'm okay," she answered. "When he finished,

he let me get dressed. Before I left, he made another appointment for me to come back. I didn't want to, but he said he could only protect my parents from the INS if I came back. I knew what he meant."

"Did you keep that appointment?"

"Yes, I kept all of them. There were twelve, I kept track."

"And each time you returned, did you see the same doctor?"

"Yes."

"And each time you saw the doctor, did he do the things to you which you just described?"

"The first couple of times he just touched me and kissed me, like I told you. Later, he made me touch him."

"Where did he make you touch him?" Kathryn asked gently.

"On his private parts," she answered in a whisper.

Kathryn wasn't sure she wanted to know the answer to her next question, but knew she must ask it.

"Josie, did the doctor make you have sexual intercourse with him?"

The witness didn't answer.

"It's best if we know everything he did to you, Josie. Did the doctor force you to have sexual intercourse with him?"

She gazed at her lap but still did not respond.

"Okay, let me ask you a different question," Kathryn said. "Can you tell me the doctor's name?"

"I can't tell you that," Josefina said. "And I won't answer any more questions, either. I don't care what you or the judge do to me."

Kathryn feared serious emotional damage would

result if Josefina were forced to continue. There was another way to identify the doctor and, although it might destroy Kathryn's relationship with Robert Simmons, it was her only choice.

Kathryn walked to the witness stand and placed her hand on the girl's arm. "That's all right, Josie. You don't need to answer any more questions tonight."

27

―――

Robert Simmons answered the bell wearing blue jeans, a T-shirt, and Fila thongs. He smiled broadly when he saw Kathryn Mackay at the door of his town house.

"What a nice surprise," he said, kissing her on the cheek. He stood aside for her to enter, then took her hand and led her to the living room.

They sat on a leather loveseat. "What brings you here at—" He glanced at the walnut burl grandfather clock beside the white marble fireplace. "—almost ten o'clock at night?" Then he added hastily, "Not that I'm complaining, you understand."

Kathryn clasped her hands in her lap. "I just adjourned the grand jury. I need to talk with you."

"Something's wrong, Kate. It's written all over your face. Tell me."

"Robert, I . . ." She paused. "I don't feel well. I need to use your bathroom."

"You don't look good, either. What's the problem?"

"I don't know. I feel nauseous, and I have a splitting headache. Do you have anything to settle my stomach? Whatever you gave me on the ferry to Victoria helped."

"I'll get something. Go ahead and use the bathroom."

When Kathryn returned to the living room, Robert gave her two tablets and a glass of water. "Take these," he told her.

"What are they?"

"Sulcrafate, in medical terms. It coats and protects the lining of the stomach, like Pepto-Bismol, only these are prescription strength, so they'll work very quickly. It's probably just nerves—you look completely stressed. What's going on?"

Before Kathryn could answer, a teakettle whistled in the kitchen. "Hold that thought, I'll be right back," he told her.

After a minute, he carried in a steaming mug and handed it to her. "Chamomile tea. Sip it slowly. It doesn't taste very good, but it's soothing. Now, tell me what's so important that you drove over here late at night, feeling sick, to talk to me."

Kathryn sipped her tea and made a face. "Bitter." She paused, then continued. "Something came out during grand jury testimony that I need to tell you about, before tomorrow morning."

"Sounds serious."

"It is. You know I'm investigating the death of Esther Fuentes either as a murder or an assisted suicide. Fuentes was a patient at your clinic."

Robert nodded. "You told me her mother thought she might have been, but wasn't sure."

"Her best friend testified before the grand jury tonight that she accompanied Fuentes to the clinic on several occasions. She was a patient there, too."

"It's not unusual for young girls to come in with a friend rather than a parent. Most clinic patients are from low-income families, so I'm not surprised they'd both use our clinic."

"Her friend saw a doctor twelve times in the past nine months."

Robert raised his eyebrows. "Did she tell you why?"

"Yes, that's what I needed to tell you. She was molested by one of your doctors. He made her return repeatedly."

"She was what? Impossible, not at my clinic. Are you certain?"

"Absolutely. Sixteen-year-old girls don't make up stories like she told the grand jury. I'm sorry, I know how you must feel. I came to tell you that I intend to initiate an investigation."

"I . . . I don't doubt what you say, Kate. I'm just in shock. What's the girl's name?"

Kathryn contemplated. "Josefina Valenzuela."

"Kate, a criminal investigation will devastate the clinic, wipe out ten years' hard work, even if the charges aren't true. The allegations will be front-page news, but the exoneration will be on the back page. Can't you wait before starting your investigation?"

"I can't cover this up."

"I'm not asking for a cover-up, just a little time to figure things out. What's the doctor's name?"

"She refused to tell me."

"Well, you see? Maybe she made this up, or maybe she just made a mistake, or . . ."

"I can't sit on this, I need Fuentes's and Valenzuela's medical records. A subpoena will be served on the clinic tomorrow morning."

"Don't subpoena them, Kate, please. I'll pull both

sets of records first thing tomorrow morning and deliver them to you."

"I can't do that, this has to be done by the book. I have to subpoena the records."

"God, my clinic will be ruined. I'll be ruined." Robert whispered.

Kathryn lay her hand on his arm. "Robert, we can't be together until this is resolved. It would be a conflict for me to see you socially while my office investigates the clinic. I had to tell you in person."

"Of course, I understand, Kathryn, but . . . can I call you? To talk?"

Kathryn kissed him on the cheek, then stood. "I'm so sorry, Robert. Please don't make it hard for both of us. I can't talk to you until this is resolved."

He started to stand, but Kathryn gently held his shoulder. "I'll let myself out," she said. When she had closed the door, Kathryn was not surprised to feel a tear trickle down her cheek.

28

At eight-fifteen the next morning, Kathryn Mackay sat in an ancient, cracked leather chair in Judge Jesse A. Woods's chambers. Woods was tall and stocky, with gray hair and a full beard. He wore black suit pants, a white shirt and a red tie, not yet having donned his judicial robe. Kathryn had never observed Woods with any expression on his face except a scowl, and this morning was no exception.

"What's so important that it couldn't wait, Ms. Mackay?" the judge asked.

Kathryn placed a legal document on his desk, which he ignored. Taking his cue, she explained. "Your Honor, I am requesting that you order the county health clinic to turn over two sets of patient records to my office. The records are crucial to a grand jury criminal investigation."

"Whose records?"

"Esther Fuentes and Josefina Valenzuela, Your Honor."

"Fuentes was the girl killed in the automobile accident about three weeks ago."

"Correct. We haven't ruled out foul play, and our witnesses are reluctant to testify."

"I see no problem releasing her records. The doctor-patient confidentiality privilege doesn't apply in a criminal investigation. What about Valenzuela?"

"Fuentes's best friend. She accompanied Fuentes to the clinic several times and was also a clinic patient."

"Not enough reason to violate the privilege," Woods answered.

"Your Honor, last night Valenzuela testified she was molested on numerous occasions by a doctor who was treating her at the clinic. I need to identify the doctor."

"Ask her."

"She refused to identify him."

"Then you need her written consent."

Mackay shook her head. "Penal Code Section 1543 permits a judge to release medical records to law enforcement for good cause. In finding good cause, the public interest must be weighed against any possible damage to the doctor-patient relationship, the treatment services, and even injury to the patient herself. In my opinion, the public interest is overriding if a young girl is being molested at a public health clinic."

Woods plucked a West's Penal Code from a shelf behind his desk, flipped it open, and read briefly.

"It also requires me to establish a reasonable likelihood that the records will disclose evidence of substantial value to the investigation," he said. "I can't make such a finding for Valenzuela's records relative to the Fuentes investigation."

"I have already initiated a criminal investigation into the activities of the county health clinic. Valenzuela's records are crucial to investigate her allegations of sexual abuse."

Woods thought briefly, then picked up the document Mackay had placed on his desk. "This is a subpoena duces tecum for both sets of medical records?"

"Correct," Mackay answered.

Woods signed the subpoena and slid it across the desk. "Have someone besides yourself serve this. It is now eight-forty-five. Be in my court in an hour and fifteen minutes," he ordered.

"I have nothing on your calendar of which I'm aware," Kathryn said.

"You do now," Woods said. He pulled a legal document from a file folder and placed it in front of him, but didn't offer it to Mackay, and she didn't ask to see it.

"Frederick Fouts filed a motion to suppress evidence seized from Raymondo Miranda."

"On what basis?" Mackay asked.

"Read the motion. Your office was served at eight o'clock."

"I haven't been to my office yet this morning."

"Then I suggest you go there and prepare yourself to answer the motion. Bring the officer who seized Mr. Miranda's backpack with you at ten o'clock, prepared to testify as to the legality of the search and seizure."

When Kathryn arrived at her office, Mary Elizabeth Skinner was waiting with the case file and motion.

"What's the basis for Fouts's suppression motion?" Mackay asked.

"That Sterling seized the backpack illegally, without a search warrant."

"He didn't need a warrant, he seized the backpack from Miranda's car at the accident scene. It says so right on the E and PR. Let me see that," Mackay said, and read the motion. "The motion doesn't tell us a damned thing, just says the backpack was illegally seized. Call Sterling. Have him in my office by five minutes before ten."

Kathryn was headed out the door when Sterling charged breathlessly up the stairs of the government building. Before she could brief him, they rounded the corner of the court building's oak-paneled corridor and encountered a throng of reporters, TV cameras, and a contingent of young people milling about outside Superior Court 6. Except for the press, most were in their late teens or early twenties and wore Portola Community College T-shirts and backpacks. When they spotted the District Attorney, everyone fell silent.

"What's this?" Sterling asked.

"A show of support for Miranda, I suppose," Mackay speculated.

"Wouldn't Fouts want this heard in private?" Sterling asked.

"Not necessarily," Mackay answered. "In his position, publicity's exactly what I'd want. If we try Miranda for murder, Fouts won't request a change of venue; he'll prefer to select jurors from the local community. Meanwhile, he's creating a sympathetic jury pool. What's more, when I move to close the hearing to the public, Fouts will accuse me of manipulating the judicial process behind closed doors.

You've heard the old saying that a prosecutor could get a grand jury to indict a ham sandwich. Nevertheless, grand jury investigations must be kept confidential. Fouts can accuse me of whatever he likes. The public and press are going to be excluded from his dog and pony show."

They pushed through the crowd into the courtroom and sat at the prosecution table. The crowd followed and filled the spectator section behind the defense table, where Fred Fouts and Raymondo Miranda were already seated.

Fouts was in his late sixties or early seventies, with a shaggy gray fringe hanging from his liver-spotted bald head and a pair of glasses resting low on his nose. He wore a cheap, rumpled brown suit with black wing tips that needed polishing, and looked like everyone's eccentric uncle. He spotted Mackay, whispered something to his client, and approached.

"Ms. Mackay, what a pleasure to see you. Congratulations on your recent well-earned appointment." He bowed slightly and shook hands with Kathryn.

"Thank you," Kathryn responded cautiously, knowing Fouts to be a consummate gentleman personally, but a cunning and formidable opponent in court. "Why are we here, Mr. Fouts?"

Fouts pointed to the defense table. "An hour ago, my client was lying in a hospital bed with grievous injuries he suffered in a terrible automobile accident. I fear his recovery will be set back immeasurably by the trauma of this proceeding, which he is forced to endure merely to recover the personal belongings which were illegally taken from him. If you return his possessions, I shall withdraw my motion, and we can all set about our legitimate business. If not, you are going to be embarrassed. You can see my client has considerable spontaneous support in the community."

Kathryn glanced at Miranda. He was short and muscular, with jet black hair, fine features, and full, expressive lips. He wore a freshly pressed open-neck shirt with tan Dockers. Even with angry red scars marring his face and with his left arm in a sling, he was startlingly handsome.

"I know your reputation, Mr. Fouts, so I doubt the show of support for Mr. Miranda is spontaneous. And I have no intention of returning property seized during a homicide investigation."

At exactly ten o'clock, Judge Jesse A. Woods swept into the room. The bailiff instructed everyone to sit, and Woods rapped his gavel.

"This hearing is convened at the request of Raymondo Miranda, who is represented by his attorney, Frederick Fouts." He looked at both counsel tables. "Mr. Fouts. Ms. Mackay."

Kathryn rose. "Good morning, Your Honor, Kathryn Mackay appearing for the People. I ask the court to close this hearing in order to preserve the integrity of an ongoing grand jury investigation. As Your Honor knows, neither the public nor Mr. Miranda and his attorney have the right to be present during grand jury proceedings."

"The grand jury isn't convened here today, Ms. Mackay."

"No, but if the court is to hear Mr. Miranda's motion, certain matters pending before the grand jury will be disclosed, and the confidentiality of the grand jury proceeding will be compromised."

The judge looked at Fouts and scowled.

"Your Honor, my client seeks only the return of certain private property, which was stolen from his home by the police. He—"

"The court will hear your argument on the motion later, Counselor," Woods interrupted. "For now, I only want your response to the District Attorney's motion to close the hearing."

Fouts nodded. "The District Attorney isn't conducting an investigation, she's conducting a fishing expedition. The law doesn't extend confidentiality to such activities. If it did, we'd need to lower the 'cone of silence' over the Santa Rita waterfront, the fishing pier, and the beach. My client is entitled to a public hearing, not a private witch hunt conducted in some smoke-filled back room."

Judge Woods thought briefly and stroked his beard. "The court may grant the District Attorney's motion to close this hearing if it finds that closure is essential to preserve higher values, including preservation of the integrity of a grand jury investigation," he stated.

"Furthermore, the court cannot presume, as Mr. Fouts suggests, that a legitimately convened grand jury is operating outside the law. To do so would establish improper judicial oversight of the grand jury clearly unintended by the legislature when it afforded grand juries the utmost confidentiality. The District Attorney's motion to close the hearing is granted."

The judge waved his arms expansively toward the murmuring crowd. "Bailiff, clear the courtroom of everyone except the attorneys, the witness, and, of course, the court reporter."

When the room was empty, Woods turned to

Mackay. "Proceed, but be brief," he told her. "The court's morning calendar is full."

Kathryn called CHP Officer Sterling, who was sworn, and settled into the witness chair. She opened a file, removed a single-page document, and passed it to Sterling. "Can you identify that document for the court, please?" she asked.

Sterling read it briefly, then looked at Mackay. "It is a Sheriff's Office Evidence and Property Report, dated September first of this year. It shows Raymondo Miranda's name, the sheriff's case number, and the CHP case number that I assigned to the automobile accident in which Mr. Miranda was involved on that date."

"The E and PR lists various articles of personal property belonging to Raymondo Miranda, which you inventoried?"

"That's correct."

"Read the list aloud, please."

Sterling consulted the E and PR. "One black leather man's wallet containing a California driver's license in the name of Raymondo Miranda; Social Security card in the same name; various personal papers; photographs; thirteen dollars in currency; a black Swiss army pocket knife; Bucci sunglasses; an Outdoor World backpack; an accounting principles textbook; a spiral-bound notebook; and a pill bottle containing a small number of pills."

"The notebook and pill bottle were removed from the backpack?"

"Yes."

"Now, the E and PR states that you removed the above personal items from Mr. Miranda's automobile at the scene of the accident on Mount Cabrillo Grade

Road the morning of September first, is that correct?"

Sterling looked confused, and read the evidence report again. "This is wrong," he stated simply.

Kathryn stepped back, away from the witness. "Wrong how?"

"I retrieved the wallet, the pocket knife, and the sunglasses from the car, but that's not where I found the backpack."

"Where did you find it?" she asked incredulously.

"At his house. I went there to notify his parents, but they had already left for the hospital."

"At his house? Was it on the front step, or what?"

"No, it was in a bedroom."

"A bedroom! What were you doing in the bedroom?"

"Trying to notify his family about the accident. Nobody answered the door when I knocked, but I could hear a television inside. It was so loud I figured someone was home but didn't hear me, so I tried the door."

"Was the door open or closed?"

"It was closed, but unlocked."

Kathryn paused and drew in a deep breath, fighting off a wave of nausea. She didn't know whether she felt sick because of the sudden turn of events or because of her ongoing health problems. "What did you do after you discovered the door was unlocked?"

"I opened the door and stuck my head in but didn't see anyone. So I checked inside the house. I picked up the backpack off the bed and headed for the hospital."

"No one gave you permission to enter the house?"

"No, the house was empty."

Kathryn stared at the witness in disbelief. "Okay, then what?"

Sterling continued, "I located Mr. and Mrs. Miranda at the hospital, waiting while their son was in surgery. They asked me to wait with them, so I looked through the backpack and found the note in his notebook."

Kathryn struggled to keep her voice even and her demeanor restrained. "Officer Sterling, can you explain why the Evidence and Property Report states that the backpack and its contents were removed from Mr. Miranda's car?"

"No. Lieutenant Earheart took custody of all the evidence I had in my possession at the morgue."

"You told him where you found it?"

"No, Lieutenant Earheart advised me the S.O. property clerk would contact me later."

"What did you tell the property clerk when she contacted you?"

"She never did."

"I've heard everything I need to hear from this witness," Judge Woods interrupted, leaning forward impatiently with his elbows on the bench.

Kathryn knew property could be legally seized from a private home only with a search warrant, with the occupant's permission, or under exigent circumstances: an emergency that makes it impossible, unreasonable, or dangerous to wait for a warrant. None of those criteria applied in this case, and she did not attempt to continue her direct examination of Sterling.

"Mr. Fouts, I don't need to hear any cross-examination. I'll hear your argument now," the judge said, looking at the defense table.

Fouts stood. "Your Honor, on September first my client, Raymondo Miranda, was in a serious car accident that killed a young woman named Esther Fuentes. Miss Fuentes and Mr. Miranda were sweethearts. He is still mourning her loss.

"While my client lay in critical condition at the hospital, Officer Sterling entered his home and illegally seized his backpack. What's more, rather than turning the backpack over to my client's parents at the hospital, Officer Sterling saw fit to illegally search it until he found a note in a school notebook, to which he has since managed to attach a false meaning.

"That illegally obtained note is now at the heart of an investigation being conducted by the Santa Rita County criminal grand jury.

"I demand the immediate return of Raymondo Miranda's back pack and its contents, Your Honor. It contained nothing more than his college schoolbooks and notes, which he needs to stay current with his studies while he recuperates at home."

Judge Woods looked toward Kathryn, who stood.

"Federal law provides that the exclusionary rule is not applicable to grand juries, and since the passage of Proposition 8, federal law determines the application of the exclusionary rule in California. Regardless of whether the backpack was obtained as the result of an illegal search and seizure, as a matter of law it cannot be suppressed from a grand jury proceeding. I ask the court to deny Raymondo Miranda's motion."

Woods frowned at Kathryn and said, "I find the police officer's violation of Mr. Miranda's rights extremely unreasonable, and reprehensible. However, I agree with the District Attorney's conclusion as to the evidence itself. This court lacks the authority to exclude the evidence in question from a grand jury proceeding or to order its return."

Woods sighed audibly. "The motion is therefore denied. However, should the grand jury indict Mr. Miranda for murder based on the illegally seized property, Mr. Miranda shall have the right to bring this motion at trial, where the exclusionary rule does apply and where this court does have authority to act."

29

═

Morgan Nelson set a paper bag and two cups of coffee on Kathryn's desk.

"What's the occasion?" she asked.

"Thought we could have lunch before the Child Death Review Team meets at one o'clock," he answered.

"I'm glad you came by, I forgot all about it. Can't get my mind off Miranda's suppression hearing. What's in the bag?"

"Egg salad sandwiches and chips," he told her. "Cafeteria food, but it's better than nothing."

Kathryn picked up the coffee and took a sip, but pushed the sandwich away. "Just the thought of egg salad makes me sick," she said.

"You look sick."

"Thanks for the compliment, Doc. But you're probably right. Last night I felt so sick I thought I was going to die."

"Did you take anything?"

"Advil and sulcrafate."

Nelson arched his eyebrows. "Sulcrafate's a prescription medication, at least in dosages high enough to do much good. So you finally took my advice and saw a doctor?"

"Well, yes and no. Robert Simmons gave me the sulcrafate."

"Uh-huh," Nelson looked at Kathryn inquisitively. When she didn't expand on her answer, he shrugged his shoulders and added, "I see. What's this about a suppression hearing?"

While he ate, Kathryn summarized that morning's hearing. When she finished, Nelson leaned back in his chair and clasped his hands behind his head. "What a screwup. Did Woods believe you didn't know?"

"Hell, no. I could hardly believe it myself when Sterling testified that he seized the backpack from Miranda's bedroom."

"I thought Sterling was more competent than that."

"He's an accident reconstruction specialist, not a criminal investigator."

Nelson shrugged. "What do you do now?"

"Woods denied Miranda's motion because evidence can't be suppressed at a grand jury proceeding whether it's illegally obtained or not. So, I keep investigating."

"What's the point? Evidence illegally seized during an unreasonable search is automatically tossed out at trial."

"Not necessarily. To exclude evidence at trial, a court must go through a two-step process. First, without considering what the officer was personally or 'subjectively' thinking, what we call an objective test, determine whether the search was reasonable or unreasonable. Then—"

"Then your goose is cooked," Nelson interjected, "because that was an unreasonable search if there ever was one."

Kathryn frowned. "I agree, and so did Judge Woods. But even if the search was unreasonable, the court must next decide whether the evidence should be suppressed, that is, ruled inadmissible or excluded at trial. Usually, it's excluded as a sort of penalty for the illegality, but not always."

"But the Constitution protects against unreasonable search and seizure . . ."

"The Constitution doesn't say illegally seized evidence must be suppressed. The Supreme Court created that rule to encourage proper police conduct. They left a few holes in the rule, and I'll try to squeeze my evidence—the note and pills—through one of them."

"What hole?"

"The 'good faith' exception."

"What's that?"

"In deciding whether to exclude evidence, the court can look at the officer's intent, or state of mind, at the time he conducted the unreasonable search. If he didn't intentionally violate the law, the court can allow the illegally seized evidence into evidence."

"What are your chances?"

"Better than nothing, but slim. The good faith exception is generally limited to searches conducted with a warrant, where a mistake is made by someone other than the police officer."

"Such as?"

"Oh, maybe a judge issued a flawed search warrant, or a clerk failed to notify a police officer that the warrant he is serving has been recalled. We prosecutors have been making slow but steady progress toward expanding the good faith exception to warrantless searches where the police officer acted in good faith. Sterling thought he was doing the right thing trying to help out Miranda's family. I'm going to argue that fits within the good faith exception."

"And if you aren't successful?"

"Then there's no way I can convict Miranda of murder. He may be guilty as hell, but without the note and pills he'll walk because of illegal police conduct."

"What a crock! The law's so screwed up that common sense doesn't apply anymore," Nelson said.

"It gets worse. It won't matter that I had nothing to do with the bad search, if Miranda walks. McCaskill will jam it down my throat right before the election."

Kathryn finished her coffee and slid two thin manila folders across the desk to Nelson. "Take a look at these and tell me what you think. I just got them."

Nelson picked them up and read the tabs. "County health clinic medical records. Esther Fuentes and . . . Josefina Valenzuela."

"Read them."

Nelson glanced at his watch. "I don't have time to read two sets of medical records, Katie. We have to be in the County administrator's conference room in ten minutes."

"I know. Just give me your first impression."

He opened one folder and flipped through a few handwritten pages, frowned, then repeated the process with the second. "Where's the rest?"

"That's it," Mackay said. "Why, what's the problem?"

"Let's start with Fuentes's file. There's no reference to a pelvic exam, blood tests, urinalysis, or ultrasound. Nothing to indicate the doctor attempted to diagnose primary or secondary dysmenorrhea."

"Dysmenorrhea?"

"Painful menses. You told me her mother said she complained of painful periods. It's not unusual, especially in teenage girls, but the doctor didn't test for it."

"What about Valenzuela's file?"

"No patient or family history. The pages aren't in chronological sequence. Looks like someone removed part of them."

"Anything else?"

"They were prepared by the same person. The handwriting's the same in both files, but there's no way to tell who the physician was. These medical records are a joke." He handed the folders back to Kathryn.

Kathryn slipped them into her desk drawer and locked it, then stood up and put on her jacket.

"Who's Josefina Valenzuela?" Nelson asked.

"I'll tell you all about it after the CDRT meeting. We'd better head up to the fifth floor now, so we aren't late."

30

The fifth-floor conference room sat between the Board of Supervisors' offices and those of the County Administrator. Unlike other county meeting rooms with their institutional green metal walls and utilitarian furnishings, it boasted subdued artwork, plush beige carpeting and oak paneling. The centerpiece was a magnificent satin-finished redwood conference table, eighteen feet long and half as wide, encircled by fourteen overstuffed dark leather chairs. American and California flags on ornate brass poles stood at the head of the table. Exterior windows were framed with off-white drapes, and commanded a breathtaking view of the river that bisected downtown Santa Rita and the adjacent park, where a seniors' outdoor art exhibition and wine tasting was under way.

The one person present looked up and smiled when Mackay and Nelson entered. "Hi, Kate. Morgan. Glad you could make it."

Diane Tipton was in her late thirties, petite, pretty, with straight short brown hair and striking green eyes. Soft-spoken and elegant in a crisp gray Anne Klein suit, her unpretentious demeanor belied an influential position as executive director of the county's Interagency Council on Child Abuse and Neglect, commonly called ICAN.

The Child Death Review Team, operating under the auspices of ICAN, comprised six members: the ICAN director and one representative each from the Sheriff-Coroner's office, law enforcement, the District Attorney's office, the County Human Resources Agency, and the County Health Services Agency.

Following the lead of Los Angeles County, Kathryn Mackay and Diane Tipton formed the team in the mid-eighties to address the growing problem of unexplained child deaths, which numbered in the thousands each year nationally. The team brought a multiagency perspective to the problem, coordinating information and resources that previously hadn't been exchanged across jurisdictional lines.

As a direct result of the team's timely intervention, many tragedies had been prevented that previously would have eluded everyone's attention until after a death occurred. More than a dozen caregivers had been convicted of murdering children in their custody, including one whose crime had gone unsolved for more than ten years. The CDRT also actively lobbied for accident prevention measures such as child-proof packaging and swimming pool fence ordinances.

Kathryn sat across the table from Morgan Nelson. "These meetings are supposed to start promptly at one o'clock. Where is everyone?" she asked bluntly. Realizing her irritability resulted from feeling so sick, she smiled at Tipton and added, "Usually I'm the last to get here."

If Diane was offended, it didn't show. She laughed and said, "True. Everyone's on the way, they're just running a little late."

Dave Granz rushed in at five minutes after one and sat beside Nelson, acknowledging the women with a nod of his head. Peggy Blair and Frederika Guererro arrived together moments later. Blair was a registered nurse, chief of Public Health and Nursing, who worked directly under the supervision of Dr. Robert Simmons. Guererro headed the Child Protective Services Division of the County Human Resources Agency.

When everyone was seated and the door closed, Diane Tipton opened the meeting with the usual formality.

"The September nineteenth meeting of the Child Death Review Team is called to order. All matters discussed here today are strictly confidential and stay in this room. No information or evidence obtained from this session shall be used by any agency in a subsequent case action without separate investigation or subpoena. Each member will please indicate his or her understanding of these instructions by saying 'aye.'"

All five team members responded, and Tipton continued. "The Sheriff-Coroner has provided a list of every death involving a person under age eighteen that has occurred in our county since we last met. All but two occurred in the presence of an attending physician, three during childbirth, one by automobile accident, and one by drowning. Two cases are notated as justifying review by this team."

Two manila folders were distributed to each member, who reviewed them briefly, then waited for Nelson to open a discussion of his autopsy findings.

"Case one," he began. "Esther Fuentes. Sixteen years of age. Hispanic. Española High School student. Fuentes was the passenger in a car driven by her twenty-year-old boyfriend, Raymondo Miranda, when the car went over the edge of Mount Cabrillo Grade Road and landed in a creekbed fifty feet below. Fuentes was dead when the paramedics arrived. Miranda survived. Cause of death craniocerebral trauma."

Nelson made eye contact with each team member, and continued. "There are two remarkable autopsy findings. First, Fuentes was approximately sixteen weeks pregnant. Second, toxicology screen showed a very high level of chlorpromazine in her blood at the time of death."

Peggy Blair interrupted. "High enough to have caused death eventually?"

"No."

"If it wasn't enough to kill her, what was its role in her death?"

"That's what we're investigating."

"Do we know where she got the Thorazine?"

"We believe the boyfriend provided it," Kathryn interjected.

"And, it wasn't Thorazine," Nelson clarified.

"Chlorpromazine is generally sold under the Thorazine brand name," Blair responded.

"This chlorpromazine wasn't sold here," Nelson answered. "It came from Mexico."

Blair persisted, ignoring Nelson's clarification of the generic drug name. "If he's her boyfriend, why would he give her Thorazine?"

"She was pregnant with another guy's baby," Granz told her. "He drugged her so he could take her out, and himself with her."

"Let's go on," Nelson said. "Case two. Amelia Salazar. Hispanic female. Seventeen years of age. Her body washed up on a county beach and was discovered by a jogger early morning, September third. Cause of death drowning.

"There are two remarkable autopsy findings. First, Salazar was approximately eight and a half months pregnant. Second, like Fuentes, tox screen showed a very high level of chlorpromazine in her blood at the time of death."

"I know it's an obvious question," Blair said, "but was it high enough to be fatal?"

"Again, no."

Guererro looked at Granz. "What has your investigation turned up so far?"

"No evidence of foul play. Looks like an accident or suicide."

"Do you know where she got the chlorpromazine?"

"No."

Frederika Guererro was short and heavyset, with dark skin and piercing brown eyes. She was known as a vocal proponent of Hispanic rights. Although unpolished and blunt, she was smart and as tenacious as a pit bull. "Thorazine, chlorpromazine, or whatever you call it isn't the drug of choice on the streets."

"True," Blair added, "and it hasn't been prescribed as a tranquilizer for years except for seriously mentally disturbed patients. It certainly wouldn't be prescribed for teenagers with anxiety problems, especially a pregnant teenager."

"So what's your point?" Granz asked.

"Feels to me like too many similarities to be coincidental. Both girls are Hispanic, same age, students at the same high school, pregnant, and both found dead as a result of accident or suicide with massive amounts of chlorpromazine in their blood."

Dave Granz leaned forward, placing his elbows on the redwood table. "A few months ago we reviewed the death of a pregnant teenager who committed suicide in Española. Her name was Escobedo, I think. The police recovered a suicide note."

"Do you recall how she killed herself?" Kathryn asked.

"A drug overdose. That's what made me think of it," Granz answered, "but I don't remember what drug she took."

"That's easy enough to find out. I'll pull my autopsy protocol. The tox report will tell us what drug she OD'd on," Nelson volunteered.

"It's a stretch to say it's connected in some way to these two deaths," Peggy Blair said.

Guererro pulled on an earlobe. "I disagree. I remember that death, too. She was Hispanic, fifteen or sixteen years old, and I think she was a student at Española High School."

Diane Tipton gazed at the ceiling, thinking aloud. "I wonder . . ."

"Something else related to these three deaths?" Kathryn asked.

"Probably not, but maybe it's worth mentioning. You may recall about three months ago we reviewed the death of a young girl who apparently hemorrhaged to death following a D and C to terminate her pregnancy. She was Hispanic and was a student at Española High."

"If I'm thinking of the same one, her tox screen showed a high level of chlorpromazine," Nelson added.

The room fell totally silent, and the six team members exchanged alarmed looks. Kathryn reacted first.

"Dave, can you contact Española and Santa Rita Police Departments and get copies of their reports on those two deaths?"

Granz nodded and scribbled notes in his spiral notebook.

"I'll pull both autopsy protocols," Nelson said.

"Freddie?" Kathryn said, looking at Guererro.

"I'll search Human Resource files and pull whatever we have on both girls," she said.

"Peggy, can you check Health Service records and see if you have anything on those two girls?"

"Will do," she answered.

"All right," Kathryn said. "We need to schedule an emergency meeting as soon as possible. I know it's a weekend, but how about Saturday at 6 P.M.? This can't wait until Monday."

31

"I need to talk to you right away," Inspector Donna Escalante said when Kathryn returned from the Child Death Review Team meeting.

"In my office," Kathryn directed with a hooked index finger. She dropped her briefcase on the desk and sat down, then popped the tab on a can of Diet Coke.

Escalante sat across from her boss in a leather chair and crossed her right leg over her left, then started bouncing the dangling foot up and down nervously. She waited silently while Kathryn swallowed four Advil capsules and a sulcrafate pill that Robert Simmons had given her the night before.

"What's on your mind?" Kathryn asked.

The tempo of Escalante's bouncing foot increased. "I got a call from WeTip at one-thirty," she began, referring to the privately operated nationwide anonymous crime tip hotline. People with information about a crime could call a toll-free number, where an operator would obtain enough information to forward the tip to the appropriate law enforcement agency.

WeTip often yielded information helpful to on-going investigations, although it occasionally simply consumed investigative resources chasing down bad leads. Yet, in twenty-four years, it accounted for more than six thousand felony convictions and three million dollars' worth of illegal drug seizures. No tip was summarily discounted or taken lightly.

"Concerning what?" Kathryn asked.

"Esther Fuentes."

Kathryn sat forward, her interest piqued. "What did the caller say?"

"Not very much. The operator said the caller was female, sounded pretty young. Said she could tell us all about what happened to Esther Fuentes, and why. She insists on talking to you personally because she says she wants to be sure she gets the thousand-dollar reward from WeTip."

"The reward is only payable on conviction as a direct result of her tip, not if the information is merely helpful. Did they tell her that?"

"Yes."

"Okay, when is she going to call back?" Mackay asked.

Escalante handed Mackay a note. "She wants you to call her this afternoon. Her name's Gabriela Hernandez. The number is in Ixtapa, Mexico, on the Pacific coast north of Acapulco."

"Very unusual," Kathryn mused. "Callers usually insist on anonymity, and receive a secret code and number. Even payment of reward money is handled at a secret postal location so there's never any direct contact with the informant. I've never heard of anyone doing this before."

"Me neither, but what do we have to lose by calling?"

Kathryn thought for a moment. "Get Skinner in here. I'll put the call on speaker phone. I want you here, too, in case she only speaks Spanish. And bring a tape recorder."

Ten minutes later, Mary Elizabeth Skinner, Donna Escalante, and Kathryn Mackay gathered around the conference table in the district attorney's office. A Radio Shack minicassette recorder with a new sixty-minute tape sat on the table beside the speaker phone.

"Ready?" Kathryn pressed the speaker button and when the dial tone came on adjusted the volume, then punched in 5-2, Mexico's country code, and 7-4, Acapulco's city code, then 3-0-3-3-3, the number provided by the WeTip operator.

"Buenas tardes," a man's voice answered, "Hotele Krystal, Ixtapa."

"Buenas tardes, señor. ¿Puedo hablar a Gabriela Hernandez, por favor?" Kathryn inquired, calling on the Spanish lessons she had taken for the past several months from a private tutor.

"Uno momento," he replied, then the line clicked and elevator music played for several seconds before the line was picked up.

"Actividades Sociales y Recreación. Gabriela Hernandez."

"Buenas tardes, Señorita Hernandez. Yo soy Kathryn Mackay."

"Hello, Ms. Mackay," the woman replied. "Can we

speak English, please? Most of my coworkers speak only Spanish."

"Certainly. How may I help you?"

A long silence on the other end was followed by what sounded like a door closing. "I have just gone into a separate room," Hernandez said, "so we may speak privately."

She cleared her throat. "I lived with my aunt and uncle and attended Española High School until three months ago," she began. "But I moved back to Zihuatanejo to be with my parents when . . . when my baby was born."

Kathryn didn't answer, and Hernandez continued.

"My aunt still lives in Española. She called to tell me about Esther Fuentes's death, and that you may arrest Ray Miranda for her murder."

Kathryn checked the minicassette and assured herself it was running.

"Esther was one of my best friends," she continued.

"How old are you?" Kathryn asked.

"Seventeen."

"You had other close friends in Española besides Esther Fuentes?"

"I won't tell you any more until I have something in writing that you will pay me the reward. I know all about the WeTip program. It was advertised a lot in Española to encourage people to report drug dealers."

"You haven't told me anything that might help us convict someone of a crime, or that WeTip will pay a reward for."

"Josefina Valenzuela was my other best friend. All three of us were patients at the county health clinic."

Another long pause followed. Then, "And I know who the father of Esther's baby was."

Kathryn and Escalante exchanged looks. "Gabriela, I want my inspector to fly to Ixtapa and accompany you back to the United States immediately."

"That is not possible, Ms. Mackay. I have a child to care for, and I cannot be away from my job. Jobs are difficult to get. You must come here to speak with me."

"Gabriela, wouldn't it be better if—"

"No, you must come here. This weekend. You can fly into the Zihuatanejo airport. There are several flights each day, and it is only a few miles from Ixtapa. We will go to a *notario publico* who is also a lawyer. We will sign a paper saying I get the reward, then I will tell you everything you need to know."

Kathryn shrugged. "All right, I can arrange that."

"Come to the hotel Saturday afternoon as soon as you arrive. I will be working."

As soon as she hung up the phone, Kathryn said, "Mary, call the airlines. Book me on whatever flight gets me into the Zihuatanejo airport the earliest on Saturday. Reserve a room at Hotel Krystal. Inspector Escalante, round up everything you can locate on Ixtapa and Zihuatanejo—maps, tourist brochures, whatever."

Half an hour later, Escalante dropped off an Owens English language guide to Zihuatanejo and Ixtapa. It contained beautiful color photographs of the area and reasonably detailed maps of both cities.

Skinner booked air reservations on an Alaska Airlines flight departing San Francisco Saturday morning and arriving at Zihuatanejo in the early afternoon. Hotel Krystal offered an excellent room rate, since high season didn't begin for another two months.

Satisfied with the arrangements, Kathryn checked her clock and was surprised to see that it was almost 6 P.M. She smiled ruefully at the realization that she would be required to pay another late fee when she picked Emma up from school. As she rushed down the steps of the government building, she imagined that she could single-handedly finance an entire private grammar school with her late fees alone, never mind the tuition.

32

When Kathryn told her about her trip to Mexico, and that they would lose another weekend together, Emma was unhappy but stoic. She was accustomed to being disappointed when it came to weekend plans with her mother.

Just before the seven o'clock news began, Emma curled up beside Kathryn on the sofa to eat a peanut butter and jelly sandwich. Kathryn forced down a glass of milk, then promptly dashed to the bathroom and threw up violently. She tasted bile, and saw blood in the toilet. She was shivering uncontrollably when she returned to the sofa and covered herself with a blanket. She washed down more Advil and sulcrafate with ginger ale, and lay down with her feet on Emma's lap.

The medication no longer seemed to work. For nearly a week, she had eaten no solid food, subsisting on coffee, Cokes, and milk, which now refused to stay down. She had lost five pounds. Today, the slightest exertion left her exhausted. Besides the debilitating nausea, her head throbbed unmercifully, her heart palpitated wildly, and she could barely function mentally.

"Mommy, what's wrong?" Emma asked.

"Nothing, sweetie, just an upset tummy. I'll be fine."

"You've been sick all week, Mommy. Maybe you should go to the doctor. I'll bet you need a shot."

"You're probably right, honey. I'll try to come home from work early tomorrow. That'll make me better. If it doesn't, I promise I'll go see a doctor next Monday, right after I get back from Mexico."

Kathryn didn't make the promise lightly. She could no longer pretend her health problem wasn't serious, or ignore it without risking hospitalization. Or worse.

The Channel 7 News logo was followed by Steve Wallace and Arliss Kraft on a dais, smiling. Arliss presented an overview of the news: a sailboat fire at the small craft harbor; a bomb threat at a local post office; an up-close-and-personal interview with Gary Plummer about the 49ers' loss to the Green Bay Packers the previous Sunday. Then Kraft turned to her partner.

"Good evening, ladies and gentlemen," Steve Wallace said, shifting from a side cam view to a frontal shot.

"Controversy, dissension, and charges of cover-up at the Santa Rita District Attorney's office. Let's go to an interview filmed earlier this afternoon."

The screen faded, then reappeared on the steps of the courthouse. Wallace's back was to the camera, which focused on Neil McCaskill's face.

Wallace introduced McCaskill, emphasizing his position as former Chief Deputy District Attorney, then said, "A hearing was held this morning in Judge Jesse Woods's court to consider a motion to exclude evidence in the investigation into the death of Esther Fuentes, the sixteen-year-old girl who was killed in a tragic automobile accident three weeks ago. Can you explain why District Attorney Mackay had the media and public excluded from that hearing?"

McCaskill appeared to contemplate his answer. "I can't comment on Mackay's secret investigation, but I can tell you that, had Channel 7 not been excluded, you would have learned about illegal police conduct which occurred during the investigation of the death of Esther Fuentes. The District Attorney didn't want you there because you would have told your viewers about it."

"Could the illegal police conduct affect the investigation?"

"Absolutely. Evidence illegally seized during an investigation is not admissible at trial. Where the evidence is crucial to the case and is excluded, as it is in this case, Esther Fuentes's murderer will walk free."

"As a candidate for District Attorney in the upcoming election, do you have anything more to say about District Attorney Mackay and the Fuentes investigation?"

"When I am elected District Attorney, I promise the citizens of Santa Rita County that I will not hide behind the secrecy of the grand jury. If and when I initiate grand jury proceedings, I will request that

their sessions be held in public, subject to the scruti-
ny of the media."

"You son of a bitch," Kathryn said under her
breath.

"What, Mommy?" Emma asked.

"Nothing, honey. I didn't say anything."

33

When Kathryn arrived at her office Friday morning, she called Peggy Blair to say she couldn't attend Saturday evening's Child Death Review Team meeting.

"What happened? We agreed it's important to meet immediately," Blair said.

"I have to go out of town to meet with an informant in the Fuentes investigation."

"On Saturday?"

"It can't be avoided. That's why I called. I need you to pull the medical records on someone who was a patient at your clinic."

"What's the name?"

"Gabriela Hernandez." Kathryn spelled the name so there would be no mix-up.

"Can I do that without a subpoena?" Blair asked.

"Not for me, you can't, but you can for the team. Her records are integral to the team's review of the Fuentes and Salazar deaths, and possibly the other two girls we discussed yesterday."

"What do I do with the records?"

"Take them to the CDRT meeting Saturday evening."

"All right. Anything else?"

"Make sure Hernandez's records gets into Dr. Nelson's hands."

"Okay. Good luck," Blair answered, and hung up.

Kathryn immediately called Morgan Nelson. "If you're going to be at the morgue this morning, I'd like to stop by."

"Sure, what for?"

"Tell you when I get there. Eleven o'clock okay?"

"Make it twelve and I'll spring for lunch," he offered.

Kathryn rubbed her stomach. "Thanks for the offer, but I feel terrible. I can't eat anything. How 'bout a rain check?"

"Any time. See you in a couple of hours."

Kathryn spent an hour and a half clearing her calendar and returning urgent phone calls, then stuffed a stack of manila folders in her briefcase and grabbed Fuentes's and Valenzuela's medical records from her desk drawer.

When she left, Kathryn told her secretary, "I'll be at the morgue until about two o'clock. Then I'm going by the travel agent. After that I'll be at home. Call if you need me."

"Okay," Torres said. "Is there anyplace I can contact you in Mexico over the weekend, if necessary?"

"No, I'll be there just a day or so, and I have no idea where I'll be most of the time. See you Monday morning."

When she parked her car at County General Hospital, Kathryn closed her eyes, leaned her head against the headrest, and fought off a wave of nausea and heart palpitations. After they passed, she locked the car doors, walked to the hospital elevator, and punched the down button. When the elevator started its descent, Kathryn's stomach churned, and as soon as she stepped into the basement where the morgue was situated, she rushed to the women's room and threw up.

Nelson looked up when Mackay entered, and immediately said, "You're white as a sheet."

"I just threw up."

"Describe your symptoms."

"Headaches, nausea, vomiting, and diarrhea. Sometimes I have heart palpitations. And . . . no, it's not related."

"Tell me."

"Blurred vision, but I'm overdue for an eye exam. My contact lens prescription needs to be updated."

"Do you have trouble concentrating? Confusion, inability to think clearly at times?"

"When the headaches are really bad."

"Kathryn, I'm worried about you. I won't lecture you about going to the doctor, it doesn't do any good. Will you at least let me help?"

Kathryn changed the subject. "Did you see McCaskill's interview on the news last night? That son of a bitch."

"I saw it. What are you going to do about him? You can't let him run around disclosing confidential information."

"I know. As soon as I get back from Mexico, I intend to discipline him."

"Mexico?"

"That's what I need to see you about," she said. She

handed him Fuentes's and Valenzuela's medical records, then briefed him on Gabriela Hernandez's call.

"Too many similarities to be coincidental," he said. "Factor Hernandez into the mix, and there may be five related victims."

Nelson rubbed the day-old stubble on his chin. Kathryn knew Nelson typically worked at night, often thirty-six straight hours. "Except," he speculated, "Hernandez is alive while the other four . . ."

Nelson's desk phone chirped and he picked it up, listened briefly, and said, "Yes she's here." He covered the mouthpiece with his hand. "Robert Simmons. Would you like some privacy?"

"No, stay," she said, motioning him to sit, and accepting the proffered handset.

"Hello, Robert," she said.

"Good morning, Kate. Peggy Blair told me you requested Gabriela Hernandez's medical record for CDRT review. I'll pull whatever we have and give it to her."

"You and I agreed we wouldn't talk until my investigation is completed. How did you know where to find me?"

"I figured it couldn't hurt to talk on the phone for a minute, so I called your office. Your secretary told me where you were. I really called to ask how you're feeling."

"Not very good."

"I'm sorry to hear that. Nancy said you're going out of town for the weekend. Do you feel up to it?"

"Not really, but I have no choice. The medical records I asked Peggy to pull belong to a young woman who may be crucial to my investigation."

"Investigation into Fuentes's death, or my clinic?"

Kathryn contemplated. "Both."

"I see." He was silent several seconds, then asked. "Where are you going?"

"Ixtapa, Mexico. I leave tomorrow morning and return Sunday."

"Traveling's the worst thing you can do when you're sick. Can't you send someone else from your office?"

"No, I have to go personally."

"Can I drive you to San Francisco tomorrow?"

"That's not a good idea. I'll take the shuttle to the airport."

"I understand. Take care of yourself. And, Kate . . . I miss our time together."

Kathryn glanced at Nelson, who was studying a piece of paper in what Kathryn realized was an unsuccessful attempt to not overhear in the tiny office. "Me, too," she said softly.

Kathryn handed Nelson the phone. He replaced it gently in the cradle. "Katie, I have to tell you that—"

"Please don't, Doc. I can't handle it right now. I'm on the verge of tears and I don't want to cry."

"Anything I can do?"

"You said you want to help. What do you need to do?"

"I need to draw some blood."

"Why? What are you looking for?"

"Any one or two of the symptoms you describe could indicate anything from acute anxiety to a serious stomach disorder. Taken together, they're confusing. I'm hoping the blood tests will clear it up."

"Clear what up?"

"I don't want to speculate and scare you unnecessarily. But I wish you'd admit yourself to the hospital for tests. Send Escalante to Mexico."

"I can't. Hernandez refuses to talk with anyone but me. If I lose her, we may never get to the bottom of Fuentes's and those other deaths."

"Then at least wait and leave tomorrow afternoon. I can have the blood test results by then."

"I can't, but go ahead and draw some blood. I hate needles, so let's get it over with."

After Nelson extracted two vials of blood, Kathryn picked up her airline tickets and itinerary at the travel agency, made reservations on the Airporter, and picked Emma up from school. When they got home, she fed Emma a quick dinner.

While Emma ate, Kathryn asked, "Honey, would you mind if I took you to Ruth's to spend the night? That way, I won't need to wake you up early when I leave for the airport."

Tears filled Emma's eyes. "It's okay, Mommy, I know you have to work. But I'll miss you. Will you be too busy working in Mexico to call me tomorrow?"

Kathryn's eyes watered, too, and she hugged Emma tight. "Of course I'll call you, sweetie. I'm never too busy. Now, finish your dinner and put plenty of food and water in Sam's dish. I'll go pack your pajamas and toothbrush. You and Ruth can check on Sam tomorrow, okay?"

Later that night, Kathryn gathered the strength to pack a small overnight bag. She changed the message on her answering machine, then went to bed just before nine but barely slept.

34

"Cold, isn't it?" the driver said when Kathryn climbed into the airport shuttle van outside the Holiday Inn at 5:30 A.M.

She handed him twenty dollars and accepted the receipt. "Sure is. Summer fog is worse than winter. The damp goes right through you, but at least I dressed for it," She wore chino trousers and a cardigan sweater.

As soon as the van dropped her outside the San Francisco airport, Kathryn checked the status board and was relieved to see that Alaska Airlines' flight to Zihuatanejo would not be delayed due to fog.

The terminal was almost deserted, and she walked directly to the ticket counter. "Are there any first-class seats available on this flight?" she asked, handing the agent her ticket.

He punched the computer terminal and nodded. "Yes, ma'am. Would you like to upgrade?"

"How much would it cost?" Kathryn asked.

"A hundred and fifty dollars."

Kathryn handed her American Express card to the

agent and sighed. "Yes, thank you." She spent her own money on the luxury because her queasy stomach demanded quick access to a lavatory, and she hoped the more comfortable seats and extra legroom would permit her to sleep.

She passed quickly through security, carrying a single carry-on bag and briefcase. By the time the plane broke through the fog cover at fifteen hundred feet, Kathryn had curled up with a blanket and pillow, and closed her eyes.

"Ma'am . . . ma'am?" The flight attendant nudged Kathryn awake.

"Wha . . . yes?"

"We are descending into Zihuatanejo."

Kathryn was still half asleep. "Zihuatanejo? I thought we stopped in Los Angeles."

"We did, ma'am." He smiled. "You slept through it, and the entire flight, too. I didn't have the heart to wake you for breakfast. I hope you don't mind."

"I'm grateful," she told him. "I needed the sleep."

The plane overflew Zihuatanejo's lone runway, turned south along Costa Grande for several miles, then banked left and aligned itself for final approach.

The pristine narrow beach, clear turquoise water, and dense jungle slipped beneath the wing, then succumbed to swampy estuaries and an industrial zone. The plane skimmed over the rooftops, touched down, and taxied to a gate outside the terminal. At an adjacent gate, suntanned tourists were boarding an Aero Mexico jet.

Kathryn was the first passenger to deplane. She unbuttoned her sweater and pushed up the sleeves, then stepped onto the portable boarding platform, where she was greeted by a blast of superheated air and a blazing tropical sun. Suddenly, she lost her footing and stumbled.

"Are you all right?" A Mexican man in a business suit grasped her arm. "You almost fell."

She leaned against the plane's fuselage and touched her right fingertips to her forehead and held onto the handrail.

"I think I'm okay. I felt dizzy for a minute, I guess it was the sudden heat and humidity. Thanks, you go ahead."

A dozen passengers filed past before Kathryn felt strong enough to follow them onto the sweltering tarmac. They trailed single file toward the bright pink building and pushed through a swinging glass door beneath a huge turquoise sign that read "Welcome to Zihuatanejo." Red block letters on the door spelled out "Oficina de la Aduana y Immigración."

Having no checked luggage, Kathryn bypassed the baggage carousel and proceeded to the immigration kiosk, where a uniformed officer inspected and stamped her passport and temporary visa, then motioned her to the customs station.

The officer accepted the customs declaration and pointed to a large round stainless-steel button. "Push the button, please," she said.

Kathryn complied, and a bright red light flashed.

"Step to the inspection counter, *por favor*," the officer instructed. "Your luggage must be inspected."

"I only have a carry-on and my purse," Kathryn protested.

"Step to the inspection counter, please," the woman repeated.

"Buenos días, Señora," the inspector greeted her with a smile. "Welcome to Mexico. It will take only a moment to inspect your possessions, then you may enjoy your vacation. What is in your bag?"

"Just personal items, clothing, and . . ." The last thing Kathryn remembered was feeling nauseous and faint, and her knees buckling.

She awoke scared and confused and looked around quickly, trying to orient herself. She lay on a folding cot in a large, white, cold office, covered by a blanket.

"What happened . . . Where am I?" she asked.

"You collapsed while awaiting your baggage inspection," a woman answered.

"I . . . I collapsed? Who are you?"

"The airport nurse."

Kathryn tried to sit up, but the woman gently pushed her back onto the cot. "Please relax, Señora."

"Where am I?"

"In the office of the airport manager."

"How did I get here?"

"The customs officer and inspector brought you so you would be cool, then they called me. How do you feel now?"

"A little light-headed. I must have fainted. It was so hot in the terminal."

The nurse smiled. "Yes, the heat sometimes affects people that way. Unfortunately, the terminal's air conditioning is not working."

The nurse helped Kathryn sit up on the cot with her feet on the floor. Kathryn felt woozy, but remained erect. "I think I'll be all right. Can you arrange a taxi for me, please? Where . . ." she looked around the room and spotted her bags on a desk.

A distinguished-looking man in his sixties, short

and slight with beautiful white hair and a fatherly smile, sat behind the desk. He wore a handsome tailored beige suit.

"Of course, I will be honored to assist you," he said. "I am Señor Miguel Jorge Zuniga, the airport manager. What is your destination?"

"Hotel Krystal in Ixtapa," Kathryn answered.

"If I may suggest it, Señora, perhaps you should ask the driver to first drop you at Medica Ixtapa to be seen by a doctor."

"That isn't necessary," Kathryn assured him. She stood shakily, and reached for her bags. "It's just the heat. I can cool off and rest in my hotel room. May I have something cold to drink?"

"As you wish." He stood, bowed slightly at the waist, then said something in Spanish to a young boy who watched silently from a corner. The boy dashed from the room and returned momentarily with a frosty Diet Coke.

"My grandson," Zuniga said with a smile. "Please permit me, Señora." He picked up the carry-on bag and handed the purse to Kathryn. "This way, please."

The taxi driver tossed the bag in the trunk and turned to Zuniga.

"¿Cincuenta y seis pesos, a Hoteles Krystal Ixtapa, es verdad?" the airport manager asked.

"Sí," the driver answered.

The airport manager scribbled on a slip of paper and handed it to the driver. "Aeropuerto recibo."

Zuniga stuck his head in the rear window. "The driver will drop you at your hotel. It is only a few kilometers. You will be there within fifteen minutes."

"How much is the fare? I have no Mexican currency."

"It shall be paid by the airport. And, it is not customary to tip taxi drivers in Mexico, so do not feel you must do so."

"It isn't necessary to . . ."

"It is our pleasure, Señora. Enjoy your stay in Ixtapa. I hope you feel better soon."

"Me, too," she said under her breath.

The taxi roared off in a cloud of swirling blue exhaust fumes. Men wearing work clothes and straw sombreros worked along the shoulder of the road. They halfheartedly swung machetes at the vines whose tentacles penetrated the perimeter cyclone fence, in a futile effort to hold the encroaching jungle at bay.

The road from the airport was heavily congested, and the taxi bounced its way over dusty construction zones, past gigantic commercial coconut groves, and through small commercial districts, until it finally crested the hill above Ixtapa.

Kathryn spotted Playa El Palmar, the main beach, which swept in a graceful arch from the golf course on the east to the mouth of Marina Ixtapa on the west, past four kilometers of ocean-front hotels, resorts, and condominium complexes.

Descending the grade, the taxi gained speed alarmingly, but when Kathryn checked the speedometer, she discovered it didn't work. Suddenly, the driver slammed on the brakes and skidded to a crawl just in time to avoid tearing out the Nissan Sentra's undercarriage on a series of speed bumps.

Entering the hotel zone, the driver weaved his car through heavy traffic on Paseo de Ixtapa, a broad boulevard divided by a grassy median planted with coconut palms and tropical shrubs.

Open-air *mercados*, restaurants, real estate offices, *farmacias*, and shopping centers lined the right side of the street. Luxury hotels and beach clubs rolled past on the left: Sheraton Ixtapa, Royal Holiday Beach Club, Presidente Internacionale, and Dorado Pacífico.

Bogart's, a Casablanca theme restaurant, and Christine's Disco flanked Hotel Krystal's entry, which terminated at a huge, pastel marble open-air lobby. Kathryn thanked the taxi driver and tipped him two dollars, despite Señor Zuniga's admonition, and carried her bag to the registration counter.

After completing the paperwork, she placed her passport and excess cash in a security lockbox, dropped the key in her purse, and rode the elevator to the eighth floor. She located her room and let herself in.

Unlike the muggy lobby, room 801 emitted a blast of cold air as soon as she opened the door. She stepped inside and encountered a faint moldy smell, which she assumed was unavoidable in the damp tropical climate. The room was spacious, well furnished, and impeccably clean.

Kathryn tossed her purse on the king-size bed, pulled a bottle of purified water from her overnight bag, and went into the bathroom. She stripped naked, brushed her teeth, and stood under a cool shower for ten minutes. Finally, she swallowed four Advil and a sulcrafate tablet, lay on the bed, and closed her eyes.

A wave of nausea swept over her. She fought it back, but her heart began to palpitate and she felt light-headed. She swung her legs over the side of the bed and sat up, drew in several deep breaths of cold air, then walked to the bathroom and threw up the Diet Coke.

She wiped her face with a damp cloth, sat at the table beside the minibar, and flipped open the hotel directory.

"Let's see," she muttered, "room service, lobby bar, security, ah, here it is, social activities." She picked up the phone and dialed.

"Actividades Sociales y Recreación. Gabriela Hernandez."

"Buenas tardes, Señorita Hernandez. Yo soy Kathryn Mackay."

"Where are you, Ms. Mackay?"

"Room eight-oh-one."

"Come to the social activities cabaña between the lobby bar and the swimming pool. We can speak there."

"All right, five minutes."

Kathryn put on shorts and a light blouse. She stepped off the elevator across from the El Mortero Restaurant, and walked past the lobby bar, where a group of men sat drinking beer and watching a football game on a big-screen TV.

The cabaña was a small square building with a palm-thatched roof. It sat across from the swimming pool, beside a grassy area where children were playing croquet. Two signs hung from the front. One said "Departamento de Actividades Sociales y Recreación" and the other "Toallas de Playa."

A Mexican man in swimming trunks stood at the open service window talking to a young woman. When he left, Kathryn stepped to the counter.

"Buenas tardes," the woman said. She wore tan shorts and a matching short-sleeved shirt with "Gabriela Hernandez" embroidered over the left pocket. "Did you wish to reserve a beach palapa for tomorrow?"

"Buenas tardes, Gabriela, I'm Kathryn Mackay," Kathryn said, extending her hand.

Gabriela was tall, perhaps five-eight, and buxom. Her long, shiny black hair hung over her shoulders, and she wore no makeup except for lipstick. She did not smile, but she grasped Kathryn's hand firmly. "I'm not sure I'm happy to see you, Ms. Mackay, but it is very important that we talk."

"I understand. Where should we go?"

Gabriela glanced at her watch. "We can meet at six o'clock." She wrote several lines of information in Spanish on a slip of paper and handed it to Kathryn.

"What is 'La Sirena Gorda'?" she asked.

"My parents' restaurant in Zihuatanejo. Give this to the taxi driver. He will drop you off at the end of Paseo del Pescador, near the basketball court."

"The basketball court?"

"Zihua's version of a town plaza," she replied. "Playa Principal, the main beach, will be on your right, restaurants and shops on your left. Walk about a block and the restaurant will be on your left, across from the large tree. The restaurant will be closed, but the door will be open. My parents are expecting you."

"Can't the taxi drop me off closer to the restaurant?"

"The Paseo is only accessible from each end. But don't worry, you'll be safe."

Kathryn glanced at the note again, and put it in her shirt pocket. "What does 'La Sirena Gorda' mean?"

When Gabriela smiled, she was stunningly beautiful. "The Fat Mermaid."

Kathryn returned the smile. "You'll be there when I arrive at six o'clock?"

"Yes, or shortly after, depending on the traffic. Now, I must help the children finish their croquet game. It is part of my job to award each child a prize for participation and to put away the equipment. I'll see you at six."

35

"¿Cuantos pesos?"

"Veinte."

Kathryn handed the taxi driver four five-peso coins. "Recibo, por favor."

She folded the receipt and slipped it into an inside pocket of her purse along with her airline and hotel receipts. She had violated the county's advance-approval policy for out-of-state travel, but hoped the County Controller would reimburse her.

The sun hung above the basketball court at the west end of Bahía Zihuatanejo, but the early evening air was comfortable. Several groups of boys were engaged in pickup games, so Kathryn walked around the court to the entrance of Paseo del Pescador.

The Paseo was a narrow, shady path, lined on the landward side by storefronts that housed small restaurants and shops. Many of the shops were closed, but the restaurants provided open-air dining and enjoyed a brisk business.

Opposite, along the beach, a few fishermen displayed the bug-eyed remains of their day's catch at the edge of the concrete walk. Their boats were dragged onto the sand and turned upside down. Outdoor kiosks, food booths, and merchandise displays reduced the walkway to only a few feet in width, but no one seemed to mind.

Several couples, most of whom appeared to be Mexican tourists or local residents, strolled hand in hand, chatting and browsing store displays and restaurant menus. Kathryn wished she had come for a more pleasant purpose.

A block down the Paseo, she located an adobe brick–walled, circular plaza, built partially into the walkway and partially over the beach. A gigantic tree grew in the center, encircled by an adobe bench. Several old men sat on the bench smoking and talking. The tree's huge, low, hanging limbs shaded the sand, the walkway, and the adjacent building.

La Sirena Gorda sat nestled in the building opposite the tree, the only restaurant on the Paseo not open for business. The building facade displayed the restaurant's name and a chubby, stylized green mermaid. The seating area, comprising a dozen brightly decorated tables already set for the next meal, was visible behind the security screen.

Kathryn pushed a small swinging door open, and a buzzer sounded. Momentarily, Gabriela Hernandez appeared, accompanied by a tall woman who looked to be in her mid-forties. She bore a striking resemblance to Gabriela and wore navy blue shorts and white blouse with a green mermaid logo over the left breast.

"Hola, Señoras," Kathryn said.

"We are quite fluent in English, Ms. Mackay, although I appreciate that you make the effort. I am

Christina Hernandez, Gabriela's mother. Would you like something to eat, or a cold drink?"

"A Diet Coke would be fine, thank you."

Señora Hernandez nodded to Gabriela, who disappeared for a minute, and returned with two cans, gave one to Kathryn, and kept one for herself.

Señora Hernandez motioned them to sit at a dining table. "My husband and I will be in the kitchen if you require anything. We closed the restaurant early so you and Gabriela could speak privately."

"I'm sorry if I interfered with your business."

"It is not a problem. Stay as long as you wish," she said, then disappeared into the kitchen.

"Gabriela," Kathryn began, "I am very sorry about the loss of your friend. I know how awful it is to lose someone close to you."

"Yes?"

"Three weeks ago, a man I knew died very suddenly."

"Who was he?"

"His name was Harold Benton. I worked for him for more than twelve years."

"But he was your boss. Esther was my best friend."

"He was much more than my boss. He was also one of my closest friends."

"Do you miss him?"

"Yes. I think of him almost every day."

"Me, too. I knew Esther ever since my parents sent me and my brother to live with my aunt. It is so hard to believe she is dead."

"Of course," Kathryn said. "Your brother still lives in Española?"

She made eye contact with Kathryn. "Yes. Can we

discuss the reward? I probably sound greedy, but the reward money is important. I have a son to support."

"I understand, but you need to tell me about Esther before I can promise anything."

"Then I should tell you about myself, first."

Kathryn pulled her Radio Shack minicassette recorder from her purse and set it on the table between them. "Is this all right?"

"I don't mind." She took a deep breath.

"My parents wanted me and my brother to receive good educations, and sent us to live with our aunt and uncle, so we could attend high school in the United States."

"How old is your brother?"

"Three years older than me. He goes to Portola Community College."

"Go on."

"I was a junior last year, and I was on the girls' volleyball team. Right after the semester started, I fell during practice and hurt my ankle. The coach gave me a school medical slip and told me to go to the county health clinic in Santa Rita."

"Did you go?"

"Yes."

"Had you ever been to the clinic before?"

"No, it was the first time."

"Please continue."

"The doctor asked lots of questions about my family and me, then he x-rayed my ankle and gave me some pain medicine."

"Was your ankle broken?"

"No, just sprained. He told me to put an ice pack on it when I got home. Then he made an appointment for me to come back the next week."

"Why?"

"The coach told me I needed a doctor's okay before I could play again."

"Did you go back the next week?"

"Of course. I wanted to play volleyball."

"Did you see the same doctor?"

"Yes."

"Tell me what happened."

"He gave me a gown and told me to undress. He said I should have a complete physical examination, especially since I was playing competitive sports. He left the room while I undressed. When he returned, he asked about my family, especially my brother."

"Your brother?

"The first time I saw him, I told him my brother's F-1 visa had expired, and he was having trouble renewing it. The doctor asked how he was doing."

Kathryn didn't answer, and Gabriela continued. "He made me lie down on the examination table. Then he pushed my gown up and began pressing on my stomach as if he were examining me. But then I felt something wet on my breast. I raised my head and looked. His mouth was on my nipple."

Kathryn recalled Josefina Valenzuela's testimony. "What did you do?"

"I started to pull away, but he held me down. He told me his brother was an INS enforcement officer, but that as long as I did what he wanted, my brother could stay and finish school, even though his visa expired."

She drew in a deep breath. "He put his hand between my legs."

"Then what?"

"I stayed still, and he put his finger inside me.

Them he unzipped his pants and made me touch him. After he . . . when he finished, he made an appointment for me to go back and see him again."

"You went back?"

"I had to."

"What happened the next time?"

"He gave me a dressing gown and told me to undress again. Except this time he locked the door and watched while I took off my clothes. He told me to lie on the table, then he pushed my gown up like before. He took off his pants and lay on the table and started kissing me. After a while, he got on top of me. He raped me. When he finished, he made another appointment for me to return."

"Did you?"

"My brother was only one semester from graduating from college. I couldn't let him be deported to Mexico."

"How many times did you go back?" Kathryn asked.

"I don't know exactly. Almost every week. In December, I missed my period. In January, when I missed it again, I told the doctor. He ran a blood test and told me I was pregnant."

"It was the doctor's baby?"

"Yes. I had never been with a man before. I was a virgin."

"Did you tell him he was the father?"

"Yes. He wanted to do an abortion. But I refused, and we argued. That's when he gave me the pills."

Kathryn's head snapped up. "The pills?"

"Tranquilizantes."

"Tranquilizers?"

"He said they would calm me. He told me they were very strong, that they would kill me if I took too many."

"What kind of tranquilizers were they?"

"Thorazine, he said, but the label was from a Mexican farmacia."

"Do you still have the pills?"

"No, I threw them away. I didn't want to hurt my baby."

"Did you go back to the clinic after that?"

"No, I decided to come home and have my baby here."

"When was your baby born?"

"July twenty-eighth. I named him Ricardo, after my grandfather."

"Do your parents know all this?" Kathryn asked.

"My parents are very traditional. For them to know I was raped would bring them great shame. So I made up a boyfriend and told them we were intimate. It is easier for them to accept that I made a mistake."

"I see. Did—" Kathryn was interrupted by the recorder clicking off with a full tape. She glanced at her watch, surprised to find that an hour had elapsed. She retrieved a new tape from her purse.

"You're sweating. Would you like to sit outside where it is cool?" Gabriela asked.

"Yes, I would," Kathryn said gratefully.

They walked to the plaza across from the restaurant. Gabriela sat on the bench and leaned against the tree, and Kathryn sat beside her.

"I sat under this tree often when I was a child," Gabriela said. "I walked to the restaurant after school and my parents would ask how my day was. I was always so excited to tell them what I learned that day. They would give me something to eat, then I would spend the afternoon studying under the tree."

She stared wistfully, her eyes miles away.

"Sometimes I spent the afternoon talking with the old men, the fishermen. They gave me candy and told me heroic stories about how they sailed through terrible storms in their tiny, open boats. I think they exaggerated, but I didn't know it then."

Kathryn restarted the recorder and placed it on the back of the bench. "Let's back up, what did you do after you learned you were pregnant?"

"I didn't tell anyone for a long time. I wore loose overalls, so it was easy to hide for a while. Eventually, Esther asked me. That was in May. I didn't mind, I planned to tell her before I came back home."

"What did she say when you told her?"

Gabriela paused. "That she was pregnant, too."

Kathryn nodded. "Did she say who the father of her baby was?"

"Yes, Eduardo Berroa."

"Who was he?"

"The doctor at the clinic. My baby's father."

Kathryn felt like she had just been punched in the stomach. "Gabriela, I need you to return to the United States and testify to what you just told me."

"I can't. If I go away, my job will be gone when I return. And everyone will know who my baby's father really is. I can't allow that to happen."

"If you don't, Dr. Berroa won't be punished for what he did to you and Esther."

Kathryn thought. "Would you submit your baby to blood tests to prove Dr. Berroa is the father?"

"No. My baby will not suffer for this."

"Gabriela—"

"Talk to Josefina Valenzuela," Gabriela said simply.

"About what?"

"Tell her I said it's okay for her to tell you everything now. She'll know what you mean."

Kathryn clicked off the recorder, put it in her purse, and removed her checkbook.

Gabriela looked at Kathryn. "What is that?"

"Your reward."

Gabriela carefully accepted the check and placed it in her shirt pocket. "Thank you." She glanced at her watch. "I'll call a taxi to take you back to your hotel. It's ten after eight."

36

<hr>

"It's ten after eight in Mexico," Morgan Nelson announced, checking the wall clock in the conference room. "They're two hours ahead of us."

Diane Tipton convened the emergency Saturday evening Child Death Review Team meeting by asking Nelson why Kathryn Mackay was absent.

"She flew to Mexico to talk to an informant in the Fuentes death investigation. All I know is it was important, or she wouldn't have missed this meeting."

Peggy Blair from Health Services distributed copies of four sets of papers. "Medical records of Gabriela Hernandez, Amelia Salazar, Carlotta Escobedo, and Rita Rios."

Nelson placed his set atop Josefina Valenzuela's and Esther Fuentes's records without looking inside.

"I brought the PD reports on Escobedo and Rios," Dave Granz said. "They were both patients at the county health clinic?"

"That's right."

"Salazar was the girl who drowned. Who are Hernandez, Escobedo, and Rios?" Freddie Guererro asked.

Nelson pulled two autopsy protocols from his briefcase. Not knowing whether he should disclose Hernandez as Mackay's informant, he started with Escobedo.

"Carlotta Escobedo died last May eighteenth," he said. "Drug overdose."

"Thorazine?" Guererro speculated.

"Correct."

"She and her mother, Anita, rented an apartment in Española," Granz added. "The mother told police Carlotta was sick that morning and stayed home from school. She found Carlotta's body on the bed when she got home from work at five-thirty."

"Don't tell me, let me guess." Guererro said.

"Right again," Granz answered. "According to the Española PD report, she was finishing her junior year at Española High School. Good student, popular, no trouble at home. It was investigated as a suicide and closed. She left a note."

"Did it say why she killed herself?" Tipton asked.

"No."

"Are you sure Anita Escobedo was Carlotta's mother?" Blair asked. "Our medical records indicate she lived with a sister named Anita Escobedo, a thirty-six-year-old registered nurse in the U.S. on an H-1B visa."

"Would that make a difference in her eligibility for medical treatment at the clinic?" Granz asked.

"No." Blair answered.

"Under an H-1B visa, a person can bring a child into the U.S., but not a sister." Guererro interjected,

"If Carlotta was Anita's sister, not her daughter, then Carlotta was here illegally."

"There were two remarkable autopsy findings," Nelson interrupted, to keep things moving. Everyone's attention shifted to him.

"One, tox screen showed a massive level of chlorpromazine in her blood, which, as I said, was the cause of death. Two, she was approximately twelve weeks pregnant."

"Son of a bitch," Guererro said. "What about Rios?"

"Rita Rios. Hispanic, sixteen years old. Hemorrhaged to death in her bedroom following a dilation and curettage to terminate her pregnancy."

"D and C used to be the standard method for early abortion," Blair commented. "But for the most part, clinics have replaced it with vacuum aspiration."

"That's true," Nelson said, "but a D and C can be performed in a physician's office under a local anesthetic."

"According to her family, that's how it was done," Granz said, reading from the police report. "But if a doctor performed the abortion, why did she hemorrhage to death?"

"I couldn't tell until I got the results of the tox screen. It . . ."

"Thorazine," Guererro suggested.

"Enough to reduce her anxiety before the procedure, yes, but much more significant was the DDAVP."

"Desmopressin! She was a hemophiliac?" Blair asked.

"That's right. Her blood was lacking Factor IX. She suffered from hemophilia B."

"Hemophilia is usually passed from grandfather to

grandson. Girls who inherit the gene are usually symptomless carriers."

"True, it's rare but not unheard-of in women. My guess is she self-infused DDAVP just before the procedure. It's possible the doctor administered it, but he or she wouldn't have suspected she had hemophilia unless she'd been treated by that same doctor before."

Nelson flipped quickly through Gabriela Hernandez's medical record, then those of Amelia Salazar, Carlotta Escobedo, and Rita Rios. He opened Josefina Valenzuela's record and looked through it. Finally, he pulled Esther Fuentes's record from the bottom of the pile and studied each page carefully. None of the other team members spoke while he did so. Finally, he looked at Peggy Blair.

"Did you look through these files?"

"Yes, except for Valenzuela's. Why?"

"The physician notes all appear to be written by the same doctor, but I can't make out who wrote them."

Blair scanned them quickly. "You're right. Clinic procedures require physician notes to be signed or initialed after each patient contact. None of these are."

Tipton spoke for the first time since opening the meeting. "Let's summarize the situation. Fuentes, Salazar, Escobedo, and Rios. All Hispanic, all teenagers, all Española High School students, all pregnant, all with Thorazine in their blood. All dead. Too many coincidences among these four girls."

"Six," Nelson corrected, pointing to two additional files. "County health clinic medical records of Gabriela Hernandez and Josefina Valenzuela. Also written by the same doctor, also unsigned."

"Why weren't they presented to the CDRT for review?" Tipton demanded.

"They aren't dead yet."

Nelson's beeper chirped. He checked the number and suddenly scooped the autopsy protocols and medical records into his briefcase. Although he didn't want to tell the other team members, his lab assistant had been instructed to page him as soon as Kathryn's tox screen was completed.

"I have to get back to the morgue," he told them. "As soon as I've taken care of the emergency, I plan to spend however long it takes finding out exactly how the deaths of those four girls are connected to one another, and to the two who are still alive. I sure as hell don't intend for there to be another death."

37

═══

When Morgan Nelson returned to the morgue, he sat at his desk and opened the pizza box he picked up at Pizza Amore on his way back from the CDRT meeting and stuffed half a slice in his mouth. He ran his fingers through his hair in frustration, then, as an afterthought, checked his fingers. Satisfied he hadn't transferred pizza topping to his head, he picked up the toxicology report his lab technician had left on his desk for review.

The report was labeled "MACKAY, K., blood draw 13:30 hours, 09/19." He read it quickly, frowned, and read it again, then pulled a small hardcover volume from a bookshelf entitled *Poisoning: Diagnosis and Treatment.*

He opened the back cover to the index, ran his finger down the page until he located the section he was looking for, flipped to the page, and read:

Drugs, cardiovascular: Digitalis Preparations.

Cardiac glycosides and digitalis increase the force of contraction of the myocardium. In excess doses they cause extrasystole, ventricular tachycardia and, eventually, ventricular fibrillation. Potassium loss by vomiting, diarrhea, or diuresis increase the drugs' toxicity.

Digitalis poisoning can result from injection or ingestion. Principal manifestations of digitalis poisoning are nausea, vomiting, irregular pulse, diarrhea, headache, mild to severe delirium or mental confusion, blurred vision, aberrant color vision, slow or irregular pulse leading to ventricular fibrillation and death.

Acute poisoning induces symptoms very similar to myocardial infarction, and is sometimes misdiagnosed as such.

Chronic poisoning. The above symptoms will come on gradually when smaller overdoses are taken. Nausea and vomiting tend to limit overdoses, but continued overdose by injection or ingestion results in an accumulation of the drug, leading to the same result as acute poisoning; ventricular fibrillation and death from apparent myocardial infarction.

Realizing he had not asked Kathryn if she had experienced excessive urination or distorted color vision, Nelson pounded his fist on the desk, knocking the pizza box onto the floor. Then he picked a piece of pizza from the box and absently took a bite.

Suddenly, he dropped the book on his desk, composed an urgent note to his lab tech directing him to run another tox screen immediately, on a blood sample collected almost three weeks before.

Reluctantly he accepted the conclusion, which was inescapable: if he didn't contact her immediately, Kathryn Mackay would die soon.

Nelson returned to his office and called Donna Escalante and James Fields's home telephones. No answer. Next, he called County Communications, but was advised that neither Escalante nor Fields was on call that weekend. He had them try Dave Granz and Mary Elizabeth Skinner's pagers and home phones, with the same results. As a last resort, he called Nancy Torres, who answered on the first ring.

"Nancy, this is Dr. Nelson from the coroner's office. I need to contact District Attorney Mackay immediately. I think her life may be in danger."

The voice on the other end of the line sounded alarmed. "Her life is in danger? How?"

"I don't have time to explain," Nelson said. "I must talk to her immediately. Do you know where she's staying in Mexico?"

"No, Chief Deputy Skinner made all the arrangements. Have you tried—"

"Yes, I tried, but she wasn't home. What travel agency did she go through?"

"I'm sorry, I don't know."

Nelson slammed the phone down, thought for a minute, then picked up the telephone directory. He searched for and found Mexico's country code, and dialed the Mexican operator for Ixtapa. A lengthy conversation in both English and Spanish yielded the telephone numbers of six tourist hotels. He called five with no results.

The sixth was Hotel Krystal.

He asked the same question he had asked the others.

"Good evening. I am Dr. Morgan Nelson calling from the United States. I am the Santa Rita County Coroner. I need to know whether a woman named Kathryn Mackay is registered at your hotel."

"I'm sorry, sir, the hotel's policy does not permit me to reveal the name of any guest."

"This is extremely urgent, a matter of life and death."

"I'm sorry, but for the security of our guests, Hotel Krystal does not divulge the names of its guests. I'm sure you understand."

"No, goddamn it, I do not understand! Hello, hello." He clicked the receiver repeatedly, but heard only the dial tone.

Frustrated, Nelson dialed Kathryn Mackay's home phone. When her answering machine answered, he left a message.

"Kathryn, this is Morgan Nelson. It's about . . . about ten o'clock Saturday night. If you check your messages from Mexico, call me right away. It's a matter of life and death. You need medical help, now!"

Nelson paused, gathering his thoughts. "Katie, if you get this message Sunday night after you get home, call me immediately, no matter what time it is."

38

===

Unable to sleep after interviewing Gabriela Hernandez, Kathryn rolled over in bed and checked the clock: ten minutes before midnight.

She switched on the lamp and picked up the phone. When room service answered, she asked, "Can you deliver a glass of milk and some cookies to my room, please?"

"Galletas, of course. What kind do you prefer?"

"What do you have?"

"Galletas azucar."

"What are those?"

"Sugar cookies."

"What else do you have?"

"We have only sugar cookies."

Kathryn resisted the urge to inquire why he asked what she preferred if they had only sugar cookies, and ordered a plateful.

She contemplated calling Morgan Nelson, decided it was too late, then realized it was 10 P.M., not midnight, in California.

The international operator spoke only Spanish.

After a painfully laborious discussion, she established a connection with Nelson's private line at the morgue.

The line was busy.

By the time Kathryn consumed the three biggest and best sugar cookies she had ever tasted and drank a glass of icy cold milk, she was too tired to try another call.

She drew the heavy blackout drapes over the sliding glass veranda door, doused the table lamp, tucked a blanket under her chin to ward off the cold, air-conditioned air, and fell immediately asleep.

She awoke to a pitch-black room, rolled onto her back, and pressed the button on her Timex Indiglo. It was eight-thirty.

Confused, she got out of bed and drew open the drapes. Dazzlingly bright sunshine flooded the room, blinding her briefly, but her eyes quickly adjusted, and she saw several dozen people strolling on the beach and others already lying under palapas, their bodies shiny with sun lotion.

Still disoriented, she located CNN on TV channel 13. The overlay at the bottom of the screen said "CNN Sunday Morning Newswatch. 9:32 AM."

Fumbling through her purse, she located her return ticket and, assured the flight didn't depart Zihuatanejo for seven hours, replaced it in her leather passport case.

After a long shower, Kathryn put on panties, shorts, a T-shirt without a bra, and leather sandals, then rode the elevator to the lobby and strolled to the adjacent open-air restaurant.

Encouraged by the fact that she hadn't thrown up the previous night's cookies and milk, she requested a table by the pool and ordered a banana-strawberry-melon smoothie, coffee, and a bagel.

A long queue had already formed outside the social and recreation activities cabaña, waiting to reserve beach palapas for Monday. A woman whose facial features Kathryn couldn't quite discern handed out huge blue beach towels.

She gulped down the smoothie, then slowly savored her bagel and drank two cups of strong, steaming coffee that, she mused, would probably grow hair on a bowling ball. It tasted wonderful.

The roaring El Palmar surf stimulated Kathryn to imagine herself lounging on the beach in a bikini, sipping a coco frio, holding hands with Robert Simmons, and making plans for dinner and long, leisurely sessions of passionate lovemaking. She promised herself that when her investigation of the clinic was concluded, she would suggest it, and smiled inwardly.

A young boy screamed, flew down the stone waterfall, crashed into the deep end of the swimming pool, and startled Kathryn from her reverie. She glanced once again at the social activities cabaña, recalling Gabriela Hernandez's story, and her fantasy slipped away as quickly as it had appeared.

Kathryn called the waiter to the table and signed a receipt, which she assumed charged breakfast to her room, and checked her watch. Ten o'clock, plenty of time to stroll along the beach and get some exercise.

She walked past the snack bar, slipped off her sandals, and stepped onto the velvety sand, then stood at the water's edge for several minutes, allowing the warm surf to wash over her feet and legs.

She checked the beach in both directions, decided

the less heavily developed westerly direction would be more relaxing, and set off at a brisk, heart-rate-elevating pace.

Beach activities at the Double Tree Hotel were in full swing, and Carlos-n-Charlie's ocean-front restaurant was packed for breakfast. She and Robert would eat breakfast here, she decided, looking out over the water.

A few meters past the hotel, bright orange plastic tape demarcated a sand runway where a fleet of Volkswagen-powered, fabric-winged airplanes roared in and out, ferrying sightseers on fifteen-minute junkets over Ixtapa.

Boats towing parasailers enjoyed a land-office business, as did the jet ski and surf runner rentals, and massage parlors.

Farther down the beach, signs sprouted from vacant lots like weeds, advertising real estate sales and condo time-shares.

The beach terminated at a riprap jetty, which Kathryn climbed, to find herself overlooking the hundred-meter-wide channel connecting Marina Ixtapa to the open ocean. Although the marina was new and mostly vacant, several dozen yachts rocked placidly in their slips. Their transoms read like a travelogue: Windsong, San Diego; DoBeGone, Los Angeles; SailAway, Sausalito; Callisto, San Francisco.

Stacked like stairs up the hill across the inlet, pricey condominium complexes hovered over the harbor. One, the stark white Isla Alegre, especially caught Kathryn's eye. Dense bougainvillea vines tumbled from each of its four roof levels, the bright red flowers cascading down the building like a tropical firefall.

Reluctantly, Kathryn turned and headed slowly back to the hotel to pack for the trip home. She stopped first at the social activities cabaña, where she located Gabriela Hernandez and another young woman instructing a group of children on the rules of beach volleyball.

When Gabriela spotted Kathryn, she excused herself. "Good morning, Ms. Mackay."

"Good morning, Gabriela," Kathryn said. "I'm going to my room to pack, then take a taxi to the airport. But I wanted to say good-bye."

Gabriela extended her hand, but before Kathryn could accept, she changed her mind and put her arms around Kathryn. "Thank you so much. Will you let me know what happens?"

Kathryn felt a surge of affection that surprised her. She returned the hug, and said, "Of course. I'll keep in touch by phone. You have been very helpful, and very courageous."

"If you ever return to Zihuatanejo, please let me know," Gabriela said. "My family would be honored to have you as a guest at our restaurant."

Past a lump in her throat, Kathryn promised she would, gave Gabriela a last squeeze, and returned to her room. She checked out of the hotel at one o'clock and took a taxi to the airport. When she arrived, she was pleased to learn that the air-conditioning system had been repaired.

At three-thirty the Alaska Airlines DC-9 lifted off the Zihuatanejo runway and climbed into a cloudless Mexican sky. From her window seat, Kathryn watched the coastline recede into tropical jungle, then over the state of Michoacán surrender to a geometric checkerboard of irrigated farmland.

Briefly, the coastline reappeared when the captain announced Puerto Vallarta off the port wing, but gave way to the blue, featureless, shimmering Gulf of California.

Kathryn smiled when she realized that, while queasy, her stomach did not induce an overpowering urge to throw up. She ordered a Diet Coke with ice, opened her carry-on, and removed a case file, then reconsidered and asked the flight attendant for a magazine. Settling back in her seat and sipping her drink, she permitted her mind to digest the previous two days' events.

After a brief layover in Los Angeles, the plane touched down at San Francisco International Airport just before six o'clock. Kathryn cleared the deserted customs checkpoint and headed for ground transportation, where the Santa Rita Airport Shuttle was due at six-thirty.

"Kathryn, Kathryn! Over here."

Startled to hear her name, she looked up to see Robert Simmons leaning against the international terminal security gate, waving.

39

———

"Robert, what are you doing here? How did you . . ."

"You said you were returning Sunday evening. Alaska Airlines has one of the few direct evening fights from Mexico. I got lucky."

"But why? We agreed we wouldn't see each other until I completed my investigation."

"I know, but what's the harm? No one will see us here." He put his arm around her, and she didn't resist. "I miss you, Kate. I wanted to see you."

Kathryn leaned against him briefly, then pulled away. "It's not just others seeing us together, it's the appearance of a conflict. You shouldn't have come."

"How did your trip go?" Robert asked, changing the subject abruptly.

Kathryn hesitated, then decided that since she had already told him about Josefina Valenzuela's testimony, she could tell him what she learned from Hernandez.

"I interviewed a young woman in Mexico who was raped by a doctor at your clinic."

"My God, not another one!"

Suddenly, Robert placed his hands on Kathryn's shoulders. "You look terrible, Kate. Let me see your face," he said, turning her toward a light. Then he took her pulse.

"Do you feel all right?" he asked.

His question alarmed her. Her head ached and her stomach was upset, but she hadn't thrown up since Saturday.

"Better than I did a few days ago. Why?"

"Because you're very pale. Your pupils are dilated, and your heart rate is down. When did you eat last?"

"This morning. I had coffee and a bagel. And a fruit smoothie."

"What was in the smoothie?"

"Banana, strawberries, kiwi, and honeydew melon, I think. Does it matter?"

He furrowed his brow and handed her several pills. "It might. I want you to take these."

He took her arm and led her to a bench, then looked around. "I don't see a water fountain. Sit here a minute, I'll go get something to take them with."

"I don't—" she started to protest.

"Kate, this is probably a terrible time to say it, but I'm in love with you. I'm also a doctor. I can't let anything happen to you."

A minute later, he returned with a cup. He removed the lid and handed it to Kathryn. "Diet 7-Up with lots of ice."

Kathryn considered, then popped the pills into her mouth and washed them down. "That tastes good. Now, please don't say anything more," she told him. "I can't handle it now. I'd better go or I'll miss the shuttle."

"Let me take you home."

"I can't, Robert."

"Those pills might induce mild heart palpitations and make you a little light-headed. Nothing to worry about, the effects won't last long, but I should watch you for an hour or so. I promise I won't ask about your investigation. You can sleep all the way home if you want."

"I suppose it couldn't hurt," she agreed. "But let's not talk, okay?"

He raised his hands, palms out, in mock surrender. "Deal. My car's in short-term parking. I'll get it and pick you up outside baggage claim."

"Not necessary, I travel light," she said, pointing to her carry-on bag. "But you can carry that for me so I can finish my 7-Up."

Robert's car was a Mercedes Benz E-320. When he punched the door control and alarm button, the car's interior lit up and the trunk sprang open. "Give me your bag."

He dropped the leather carry-on in the trunk and shut the lid, helped Kathryn into the passenger seat, and fastened her seat belt, brushing her breast suggestively.

Kathryn ignored the overture. "Leather seats smell so good," she said, drawing in a deep breath. "Maybe someday . . ."

He chuckled, started the engine, weaved through traffic to the exit, and headed south toward San Jose on I-280. Neither spoke for fifteen minutes.

"Robert, I need to stop."

"In Palo Alto? Why?"

"I feel sick."

"Can't you wait until you get home?"

"No."

He turned off on Sand Hill Road and swung into a gas station. Kathryn threw the door open and ran to the rest room. Robert tuned the car stereo to a classical music station, adjusted the speaker fader and balance controls, and hummed contentedly to Ravel's *Bolero*.

When Kathryn opened the rest room door, she stumbled to the car, opened the rear door, and sat down behind Robert.

"Wouldn't you rather ride in the front?" he asked softly.

"I . . . I, oh, why am I . . ." She opened the door and walked around the car. "What was I thinking?"

"Don't worry about it. I told you the medicine might make you light-headed. That means it's working. Go to sleep. I'll wake you when we get to your condo."

Kathryn lay her head against the leather head rest. When she awoke, Robert was shaking her by the shoulder.

"Kate, we're here. Wake up."

She opened her eyes and immediately clutched her stomach.

"What's wrong?" Robert asked.

"Cramps," she said.

"Perfectly normal for that medication. Here." He handed her more pills.

"Take these as soon as you get inside. They'll help with the pain. Then go right to sleep. Call your doctor first thing tomorrow morning and make an appointment. Promise?"

She nodded and gave him a peck on the cheek. "Thanks, I don't know what I'd have done if you hadn't met me at the airport and brought me home."

"My pleasure."

"Your car's instrument lights look funny. They have halos around them, and they're yellow," she said. "My car has red ones."

"They aren't yellow, they're red. Now go inside and get in bed."

She kicked off her shoes at the door, and shed everything except her panties as she raced to the bathroom. She fell to her knees and dropped the pills. They rolled under the vanity, but rather than retrieve them, she heaved violently into the toilet.

By the time her stomach emptied, her heart was racing wildly and she felt dizzy. When she stood, she turned and collided with the bathroom door, ripping a gash over her left eye. Pressing a dry washcloth to her forehead, she staggered to the bedroom and collapsed on the bed.

Then she noticed the message light blinking on her answering machine. She wanted to ignore it but couldn't. She had asked Ruth to let Emma sleep over Sunday night, but Ruth had tentative plans. She had agreed to try to break them and promised to leave a message advising whether or not Kathryn needed to pick Emma up.

She groaned, rolled over, and punched the message button. It was Morgan Nelson. She listened to his message and dialed his number. He picked up on the first ring.

"Where are you, Kathryn?"

"At home."

"How do you feel?"

"Worse than ever."

"Describe your symptoms."

"I . . . What? Do what?"

"Describe your symptoms, Kate."

"Okay, let me think. I just threw up everything I ate for the past day and a half. I have terrible stomach cramps, and . . ."

"Is your heart palpitating?"

"Yes."

"How did you get home from the airport?"

"Robert Simmons drove me."

Silence. Then he asked, "Did he give you any medication, or anything to eat or drink?"

"He gave me . . . he gave me some pills at the airport."

"What did you—"

"And more to take after I got home."

"What did you take the pills with at the airport?"

"He bought me a 7-Up."

"Have you taken the others yet?"

"The others?"

"Kathryn, concentrate. Have you taken the other pills yet, the ones he said to take after you got home?"

"No, I dropped them on the floor."

"Good, don't take them. Tell me what color the message light on your telephone is."

"Yellow."

"What color is it supposed to be?"

"Uh, red, I think."

"Damn! Kathryn, I'll be there in five minutes. Do you hear me?"

"Yes. Morgan, I'm frightened. What's wrong with me?"

He had already hung up.

40

Morgan Nelson found the front door unlocked and Kathryn Mackay lying on her bed.

"Kathryn, It's Morgan."

She sat up, fell back, and propped herself up on her elbows. "What's wrong with me? You look all blurry."

"You ingested a digitalis overdose. Are you having trouble breathing?" he asked, taking her pulse.

"I'm a little short of breath. What's digitalis?"

"Heart medicine. You said you threw up after taking the pills at the airport?"

"Yes. I don't take heart medicine."

"I didn't think so. How long after you took the pills did you throw up?"

"About fifteen minutes. And again when I got home."

"Did your stomach empty completely?"

She smiled weakly. "Damn right. I got the dry heaves. How could I have taken heart medicine without knowing it?"

"I'll tell you later."

He pulled a tiny green oxygen bottle from his bag,

adjusted the regulator, and slipped the mask over her nose and mouth. "Breathe normally and lie back."

She complied, and he pulled the blanket over her chest, leaving her right arm exposed.

"I'm going to start an IV, okay?"

She nodded.

He wrapped a heavy rubber band around her upper arm and drew it tight, wiped the inside of her elbow with an alcohol swab, then gently inserted the needle. Kathryn watched, but didn't react or speak. He connected the needle to a clear plastic tube, and slid the opposite end of the tube over the tip of a plastic bag, then hung the bag from the bed's headboard. Clear liquid flowed down the tube into Kathryn's arm.

Kathryn lifted the oxygen mask. "What is that?"

"Normal saline," he said, replacing the mask. "Relax until the paramedics arrive."

Kathryn lifted the mask again. "Paramedics?"

"You're going to the hospital."

"I have to work tomorrow."

"No, you don't." He replaced the mask a second time. "Your doctor needs to monitor your condition."

"Emma has to go to school. She's at Ruth's."

"I'll pick her up tomorrow morning and take her to school."

When the paramedics arrived, Nelson took one of them aside and explained the situation. "I started a potassium chloride five percent dextrose saline drip," he told her. "Monitor her vitals and transport to County General."

"Emergency?"

"Take her to Admitting, I'll meet you there."

After the paramedics left, Nelson rummaged through Kathryn's dresser and closet, pulled out a bra, panties, cotton nightgown and robe, jeans and shirt, and threw them in a Safeway bag, along with the shoes he picked up by the front door. In the bathroom he grabbed a toothbrush, toothpaste, hairbrush, and contact lens case and tossed them in with the clothes. He found her purse on the sofa, placed it in the bag, and headed for the hospital.

Kathryn was sitting in a wheelchair, IV connected, talking with the admitting officer.

"Is there a problem?" he asked.

"She doesn't have an insurance card."

Nelson dropped the purse on Kathryn's lap. "It's probably in your wallet," he said.

"I think I'm feeling better. I'll come see you tomorrow," she told him.

"Listen to me, Kathryn, you're very sick. And, if your doctor doesn't run some tests and monitor your condition, you might get a hell of a lot sicker."

"How much sicker could I get?" she asked rhetorically.

"You could die. Find your insurance card and tell her the name of your personal physician."

"I told you I don't have a doctor except my gynecologist." She thought about it, then compromised. "I'll admit myself if you'll be my doctor."

"Katie, you need . . ."

"You still have privileges at the hospital, right?"

"Of course, but . . ."

Kathryn handed the admitting officer her insurance card. "Doctor Nelson is my doctor. I must have a private room."

When the paperwork was completed and an identification bracelet fastened on her wrist, the admitting officer buzzed an orderly, but Nelson dismissed him and pushed the wheelchair to the elevator himself. "Now I remember why I quit practicing medicine on live patients. You're going to be a pain in the ass. Why do you need a private room?"

"So I can work. How long are you going to keep me locked up?"

"A day or two," he said, helping her into bed.

"How could I take an overdose of heart medicine that I don't use? I haven't taken any medicine except . . ."

"Give me your arm."

"Robert?"

He looked at her and nodded, then began to draw blood. "I need to evaluate your blood electrolyte levels. Digitalis induces diuresis, which leeches potassium from your system and increases the drug's toxicity."

Nelson swapped blood vials and began to draw another. "I'll draw more tomorrow after you've fasted for twenty-four hours, for kidney functions testing. I'm almost done. Are you okay?"

"How could he give me heart medicine by mistake?"

"You need an electrocardiogram. Interpreting an ECG is a science in itself, so I'm going to contact the on-call cardiologist as soon as I finish labeling the blood vials."

"Morgan, answer me. How could Robert give me heart medicine by mistake?"

Nelson removed his wire-frame glasses and sat on the edge of the bed. "I'm pretty sure Dr. Simmons gave you a massive overdose of digitalis intentionally."

"It had to be a mistake."

"I don't think so."

"But, why would Robert think he needed to treat me for a heart problem?"

"He wasn't treating you for a heart problem, Kathryn. I think he was trying to cause one."

"He was what?"

"I think he was poisoning you."

Kathryn sat upright. "Why would he—"

"I think he was trying to kill you."

She sank back onto the bed. "I don't believe you."

"Let's not talk about this now while you aren't feeling well," he said. "I'm going to ask Granz to arrange for a couple of sheriff's deputies to be posted outside your room. I'll stay until they arrive, then I'll come back in the morning. We can talk then."

"I can't wait until tomorrow, for God's sake! Why do you think Robert is poisoning me?"

"The tox results on the blood samples I drew before you left for Mexico. You had a very high digitalis level in your system. I think you've been ingesting small incremental overdoses of digitalis for the past couple of weeks. It accumulates."

"What if it continued to accumulate?"

"You'd die of an apparent heart attack. If it happened in the presence of a physician, no autopsy would be required."

Kathryn stared at him in disbelief. "You're saying that . . ."

"We'll talk about it tomorrow."

41

Dave Granz rode by on a black Harley-Davidson and waved, but didn't stop.

"Help! Please help me," Kathryn screamed, but only an inaudible squeak escaped her lips.

The drugs had turned her legs to jelly. Unable to climb off the examining table and run, she kicked as hard as she could, but the faceless man in the lab coat was impervious to her ineffectual attempt at self-defense. She clamped her jaws tight, but he pried them open.

"You're pathetic," he sneered, and stuffed a handful of vile-tasting pills in her mouth. She gagged. He laughed and stuck a dagger through the back of her hand, pinning it to the table.

"Kathryn, wake up."

"Oh, God . . . he was . . ." She took a deep, terrified breath, but it caught in her throat as a sob.

"Morgan?"

"You were having a nightmare."

"What are you doing?"

"Removing the IV needle from your hand."

"I feel drugged."

"I added a mild sedative to the IV last night to help you sleep, and moved the needle from your arm to your hand."

"What time is it?"

"Eight-fifteen Monday morning."

She sat up. "I have to take Emma to school."

He pushed her gently back onto the hospital bed. "I picked her up half an hour ago."

"You did?"

"Yep. We went to Winchell's for chocolate donuts, then I dropped her off at school. Right now I need to run down to the lab, but I won't be gone more than a half hour. I brought you a newspaper."

She opened the *Santa Rita Courier* to the front page.

DA HOSPITALIZED
Near Fatal Drug Reaction

SANTA RITA: Paramedics rushed District Attorney Kathryn Mackay to County General Hospital last night. An unconfirmed source says she suffered a near-fatal reaction to her heart medication.

Contacted at his Santa Rita home, ex-Chief Deputy District Attorney Neal McCaskill told the Courier Mackay had apparently been keeping her heart problems secret. He stated that when he is elected District Attorney, the citizens can count on his excellent health. Meanwhile, he will assume responsibility for the grand jury investigation into the death of teenager Esther Fuentes.

"That son of a bitch!" Kathryn slammed the paper on the bed. When Nelson returned, she was fuming.

"How the hell did this leak out?" she asked, handing him the newspaper, folded so the article was on top.

"The reporter was probably listening on a scanner when they brought you to the hospital last night."

"How could they print this crap?"

"What do you mean?"

"It sounds like I'm about to die. And McCaskill's such a jerk. Where does he get off saying he'll take over my investigation? Skinner runs the office when I'm away. They should've called her."

"Doesn't make good press to quote her, she hasn't filed to run against you in the next election."

"I've got to get out of here."

He pulled a chair beside the bed. "Let's talk first."

"What about?"

"You. Dr. Anthony was the on-call cardiologist last night. She arrived right after you went to sleep, and hooked you up for a twelve-lead ECG and—"

"A what?"

"A full twelve-lead ECG recording. In addition to your chest, leads are attached to both ankles and wrists. She switches among the electrodes to view the heart's electrical activity throughout the body, records the results on paper strips, then interprets the strips."

"Looking for what?"

"Damage or irregularities, in your case caused by a digitalis overdose. Your ECG was normal."

"What about the blood tests?"

"Digitalis preparations induce diuresis and leech potassium from your system, so I ran blood electrolytes screens and kidney function tests to verify that—"

"Morgan, you don't need to explain how the clock works every time I ask what time it is. What's the bottom line?"

He smiled sheepishly. "Your heart and renal functions test normal; you've suffered no permanent damage. Your blood potassium is low, and you still test positive for digitalis, although at a low level. Recovery is a matter of light medication and diet. I prescribed cholestramine powder, which you take with fruit juice to prevent absorption of any more digitalis until it's metabolized. Eat lots of bananas, strawberries, kiwis, and pistachios for a while; they're high in potassium. You'll experience no after-effects or other problems."

"Thanks, Doc."

He nodded. "For the past two weeks you complained of headaches and nausea, which could be anything, but the symptoms you described Friday were textbook-typical of drug toxicity. My technician paged me out of the CDRT meeting Saturday evening to read your tox screen. As soon as I saw it, I recognized the symptoms. Digitalis causes unique vision problems: blurred and double vision, altered color perception, increased light sensitivity, and halos. I should have asked about vision problems. That was my first mistake."

Kathryn laid her hand on his arm. "You'd have to be a walking encyclopedia to remember every symptom of every medical problem someone could have. Besides, when did you last diagnose a live patient?"

He dismissed her attempt at humor with a flip of

his hand. "A fatal digitalis level can't accumulate gradually unless it's ingested incrementally by mistake. You'd never make that mistake. That means someone overdosed you without your knowledge."

"How does that implicate Robert?"

"Acute digitalis poisoning induces ventricular fibrillation and heart failure, like a heart attack. Benton was in his mid-fifties, practiced a high-stress profession, lived in a pressure cooker every day. He has a heart attack in the presence of the head of Public Health. Simmons unsuccessfully administers CPR, but Hal's dead when paramedics arrive."

"I talked to Robert right after," Kathryn protested. "He was devastated."

"You'd be devastated, too, if you just murdered the District Attorney."

"Morgan!"

"Let me finish. If a doctor's present when someone dies, no autopsy is required. Simmons knew that. He signs off on the death certificate. Cause of death—heart attack. I don't do an autopsy. The body is released to the family and cremated within days."

"But you took tissue and fluid samples before releasing Hal's body," Kathryn speculated.

"Correct. After I read your tox results Saturday night I put two and two together and had Benton's tested. Enough digitalis to stop his heart almost instantly."

"How?"

"You told me you saw Simmons carrying coffee to Hal's office that morning."

"Wouldn't Hal have tasted it in his coffee?"

"Two or three grams is fatal, less than a tenth of an

ounce. He'd never taste a few ground-up tablets in a cup of coffee."

Kathryn sat silently, then asked, "But why?"

"You figure it out."

She thought for a while. "If you're right about Robert, why didn't he just give me a massive dose and get it over with? Why spread it out over two or three weeks?"

"Too similar, and too soon after Benton's death."

"Assuming you're right, how did he give it to me? He couldn't just hand me a fistful of pills and expect me to take them without question."

"Oh really? What about at the airport?" Before she could comment, he continued. "He probably ground up tablets and fed them to you."

Kathryn contemplated. "Possible. He was always buying me things to eat and drink. Sandwiches, coffee, soft drinks, wine. He even sent candy to my office. Why did he stop?"

"He didn't, you did. Last Wednesday night after the grand jury you told him about Valenzuela, that you planned to open an investigation into the clinic, and you stopped seeing him. Did he give you anything to eat or drink?"

"I was sick during the grand jury hearing. He gave me a cup of chamomile tea and . . ."

"A sulcrafate tablet?"

"Yes." She paused. "Let's say you're right and he gave me digitalis every time we were together. Why didn't it kill me?"

"Because you kept throwing up, which limited the dosage you could accumulate."

"I don't get it. If—"

"You were seeing a lot of Simmons. Who initiated all the contact?"

"He did, now that I think about it."

"Why do you think he saw you?"

"I thought he liked me," she said softly.

"He probably did, but he also needed to be around you as much as possible."

"To keep poisoning me?"

"Yes. And there was another reason. What happened whenever you told him you were nauseous?"

"He gave me sulcrafate."

"To settle your stomach so you wouldn't throw up."

"It worked, too. He gave me extra sulcrafate to take when we weren't together."

"Digitalis is absorbed quickly, but it's also metabolized quickly, so it has to be taken daily. Sulcrafate decreases its toxicity, so he had to give you higher doses to overcome the sulcrafate. Medically, it's a vicious circle. Give you digitalis, it makes you nauseous; give you sulcrafate, it keeps you from throwing up; give you more digitalis, it makes you more nauseous. Like a dog chasing its tail."

"Son of a bitch!"

"He would have got it right eventually. Then, one final dose and you'd have an apparent heart attack just like Hal."

"But he never gave me that final dose."

"Yes, he did, last night at the airport. You just got lucky."

"I don't feel so lucky."

"He gave you too much, and you threw up immediately. If you hadn't, your heart would have stopped. He probably figured to drive your body to Valley Med or some other hospital over the hill, ID himself, and sign you out as a heart attack. No muss, no fuss, and no autopsy. Just like Hal. But you didn't die, so he gave you more when you got home to finish the job. Probably planned to come back in the morning and discover the body."

Kathryn shook her head in amazement. "Why would Robert want to kill either Hal *or* me?"

"Maybe it's related to your job."

"Related how?"

"Beats me, but it's the one thing you and Hal had in common."

Kathryn thought silently. "Damn!"

"What?"

"Hal had a notation in his appointment book the morning he died. I've got to check it out."

"A notation concerning what?"

"A meeting about an R-file."

"A what?"

"R-files were confidential investigations Hal conducted personally, usually because they were politically sensitive. The R-file meeting was scheduled at the time Hal was meeting with Robert."

"Let me play the devil's advocate for a minute. Maybe Simmons was helping Hal on some secret investigation."

"That's not what Robert told me. He said they met to talk about the needle exchange program."

She paused again. "I can't believe how stupid I am. I told Robert about Hal's R-file investigations over coffee just a couple of days after Hal died. I said I planned to continue them."

"You'd better look into this. I'll release you from the hospital so you can get to your office."

"Good, let's go."

"One more thing," Nelson said. "Saturday night after I put all this together, I called every hotel in Ixtapa trying to warn you so you could see a doctor."

"You called the Krystal?"

"Yes. I asked if you were registered, but they refused to divulge their guests' names, so I never knew you were there. Otherwise, I could have referred you to a clinic in Ixtapa for treatment."

"You had no way to know I was there if they wouldn't tell you."

"That was my other mistake. If I had asked the question differently, they would have. Instead of asking if you were registered, I should have said, 'I want to leave a message for Kathryn Mackay.' They'd have put me through to your room—no questions asked."

42

"Thanks." Kathryn dropped her insurance card into her purse and picked up the cholestramine powder off the counter, then pushed open the pharmacy door.

"How do you find anything in there?" Morgan Nelson chided, pointing at the huge shoulder bag.

"It's a secret filing system that only women know."

They walked across the hospital's main lobby, and Nelson punched the elevator down button. "You sure I can't give you a ride?"

"I'll call a taxi."

"Then I suppose I'd better get back to the Hellhole," he said.

Kathryn touched him on the arm. "Thanks for everything, Morgan."

"Forget it." He turned away to check the elevator's progress. "Mix the powder with plenty of fruit juice, but get something to eat, too. Your system's depleted."

"I'll grab juice and a bagel on my way to the office."

"I think that R-file may hold the key to all of this,

Katie," he told her. "Call me as soon as you find out something."

After Nelson disappeared into the elevator, Kathryn watched for a moment, then walked to a pay phone and called a taxi. The driver waited while she ran into the Bagelry, then dropped her at the government building at 12:15 P.M.

She slipped past the vacant reception area, strode quickly to her office, unlocked her bottom left desk drawer, and pulled out a leather Cambridge daily planner. She wiped off the dust with a tissue and unsnapped the clasp, then, using an eraser, flipped the pages until she located Monday, September 1.

In Harold Benton's unmistakable neat block printing, the lone notation read "R-10, 8^{30}."

Kathryn pushed her chair away from the desk and walked to the blond, solid-oak cabinet built into the exterior office wall beneath the windows. Without a private safe, Kathryn figured Benton would secrete sensitive documents in the only secure storage available.

She knelt in front of the double doors and pulled, but they refused to budge, so she peered closely at the round brass locks.

"Yale," she read aloud.

A key chain with a Craftsman key-chain screwdriver hung from an eye hook on the inside of the drawer where the appointment book had been. As if someone might be watching, Kathryn glanced around furtively, then placed a pair of Dr. Dean Edell reading glasses on her nose and checked each key until she located a small, two-edged brass key. It opened the credenza's left door.

"Bingo," she said, but after quickly looking inside, added, "Damn, it's empty."

At one o'clock, her secretary returned from lunch.

"Nancy, do you have any idea where Mr. Benton might have put something he didn't want anyone to see?"

"Like what, Ms. Mackay?"

"Confidential files."

Nancy glanced at the credenza. "If I knew exactly what you're looking for, I'd be happy to help."

"I'm looking for Mr. Benton's R-files."

"Mr. Benton didn't keep his R-file investigations in file folders, Ms. Mackay."

"He was conducting a confidential investigation when he died. Are you saying he didn't keep a written record of that investigation?"

Torres smiled. "Oh, no, he kept records. They're on his computer."

Kathryn looked confused. "There was no computer here when I moved in. I brought the computer from my old office."

Torres dropped to her knees, stuck her head and shoulders into the extreme corner of the credenza, dragged out a black leather Targus computer case, and handed it to Mackay.

Kathryn set the case on her desk, unzipped it, and lifted out a Toshiba Satellite Pro 430CDT laptop computer. She raised her eyebrows and whistled softly.

"Pretty high-tech." When she lifted the cover and pressed the on-off switch, nothing happened.

"The battery's probably dead," Torres suggested. "It doesn't belong to the office; he bought it himself. I don't know why, he knew very little about computers, and it wasn't used very often."

"So, you typed the files for him on his laptop instead of the office computer?" Kathryn asked.

Torres sniffed indignantly. "No, he typed them himself. He was very secretive about it. As far as I know, no one except Mr. Benton saw what's on that computer, not even his private secretary."

"I'm sure that didn't indicate a lack of trust. Thanks, Nancy. Please close my door when you leave, and hold my calls until I tell you otherwise."

Reluctantly, her secretary turned to leave, and sniffed again. "Certainly, Ms. Mackay. Buzz me if you need help."

When the computer's power cord was plugged in and the on-off switch pressed, a green AC power light and a red charging icon flickered on, followed by the Windows95 logo and a password dialogue box. "HAROLD" appeared on the top line, and the cursor blinked on the password line, waiting for input.

"Oh, shit, I need a password."

She typed HAROLD.

The computer answered, "The Windows password you typed is incorrect."

"That figures," she mumbled, and typed HAL.

"The Windows password you typed is incorrect."

ELLIE. Benton's wife's name.

"The Windows password you typed is incorrect."

NAPPY. Benton's dog's name.

"The Windows password you typed is incorrect."

"This could go on forever." Kathryn picked up the phone and buzzed her secretary. "Nancy, do you have any idea what password Mr. Benton used to access his computer?"

"No, Ms. Mackay, as I said, I never used his laptop, but try something really obvious. He wouldn't have used anything he couldn't remember easily."

"Damn, that could be anything," Mackay said to herself.

She typed RFILE and pressed Enter. The password dialogue box disappeared, the screen refreshed, and a Start icon appeared at the bottom left corner.

Kathryn dropped the arrow to Start and pressed the mouse button, then clicked Run.

C:\WP51\WP was highlighted.

The Enter key brought up a blank blue screen.

"Thank God for small favors. At least he used WordPerfect," she muttered.

Pressing the F5 key produced a short list of word processing files from the DATA directory.

"Son of a bitch, there it is," she said, dropping the cursor to a line that said RTEN. When the file appeared, she stared at it in amazement.

```
TY908YT0 Q00584UE

S54VYTU40YQ2 Y4BU90YWQ0Y54 VY2U 8-GP

GL QAW GOON
S5362QY4Q40:              E9S5RUT5, Q4Y0Q
T5R:                     GH ZA2E GOLH
8U2Q0Y54 05 BISOY3:      9Y90U8
BISOY3:                  E9S5RUT5, SQ82500Q
TQOV 5V TUQOX:           GN 3QE GOON
54 QR5VU TQOU, S5362QY4Q40 8U7AU90UT 68YBQ0U
S549A20A0Y54 8UWA8TY4W TUQOX 5V BISOY3
```

"What the hell is that?" Kathryn muttered. "I must've screwed something up."

She shut the computer down and rebooted it, but when she retrieved the RTEN file, the same nonsense appeared.

She picked up her phone and dialed an internal office extension.

"Fields."

"Jim, Kathryn."

"Kathryn, I didn't know you were back. Are you okay?"

"I'm fine. Can you come to my office right away, please."

"Be right there."

Fields sat in Kathryn's chair in front of the computer screen with her looking over his shoulder.

"What did I do?" she asked. "As far as I know, I started the computer up correctly."

"You can't do anything wrong by booting up the computer. This file is encrypted."

"What do you mean, encrypted?"

"It's written in code. Have you ever worked a cryptoquote puzzle in the newspaper or a puzzle book?"

"I don't even know what they are."

"Take a famous quote, for example, 'Ask not what your country can do for you, ask what you can do for your country.'

"The puzzle writer replaces each letter in the quote with a different character, based on a predetermined rule. For, example, 'A' is replaced by '7', 'T' is replaced by a question mark, '9' by 'M,' and so forth.

"You try to decode the quote by figuring out the replacement pattern. Once you do, you simply reverse the process and read the quote. The same technique can be applied to confidential documents."

"Sounds pretty simple."

"Conceptually, it is, but the encryption pattern can get incredibly complicated, and they're damn near impossible to break without a key."

"A key?"

"The replacement pattern is called a key. If you have the key, it's a simple matter to apply it to the encrypted document and convert an unintelligible mess, like what you've got here, to a coherent message."

"Well, I need you to decode it for me."

"Kathryn, remember when we were investigating the Lancaster murder, and we drove to San Jose to check his wife's personal computer? I told you if I encountered encrypted files, we'd need somebody who knows what they're doing. That's who you need now. I can't do this. Call the County Computer Services Department. They can probably do it in a few minutes. It doesn't look like a very complicated encryption scheme."

"I can't call them, Jim. This is one of Hal Benton's confidential R-files. I need you to do it for me."

"It could take a long time, and I can't guarantee I'd ever get it."

"Couldn't we just try every possible combination, and see what we come up with? I'll help. How long could that take?"

"Forever. The difficulty in breaking a key depends on how big it is, measured in bits. All computer characters are represented by combinations of ones and zeros. A single-bit key would have two possible combinations; zero-one, and one-zero. Each additional bit doubles the possible combinations, so an eight-bit key has two hundred fifty-six possible combinations, a forty-bit key has over a trillion possible combinations. Forty-bit keys are the minimum for encryption programs."

"You're sure we couldn't do it manually?"

"You're persistent, I'll give you that," Fields grinned. "But, testing fifty thousand keys per second, it would take a computer two hundred fifty-five days to test all possible combinations. We need the key."

"How do you know all this stuff?"

"I'm a closet computer nerd. I read everything I can get my hands on about computers."

"You're saying Hal sat at his computer and typed this investigation file in code?"

"That's not how it works. First, you type the file in a word processing program like WordPerfect, just as you normally would, and save the file. Then, you use encryption software to convert the original file to encrypted form, making it unreadable by anyone who doesn't have the key. You decrypt it using the same program in reverse, using the same key."

"Where would he get something like that?"

"It's included in most utility software, and you can download freeware encryption programs off the Internet. There are also some terrific inexpensive programs you can buy at any software store."

Fields thought for a minute. "If Hal wanted to keep this file confidential badly enough to encrypt it, he would have done it himself. I wouldn't be surprised if he had an encryption program on the laptop. Let's see."

He exited the word processing program, ran the cursor up the Start dialogue box until 'Programs' was highlighted, and clicked the mouse button.

He read slowly, "Accessories; Cardworks; HP Deskjet Utilities; Microsoft Reference—Encarta—that's an encyclopedia; TRAVROUTE SOFTWARE; EGS PROTECT. That's it."

"That's what?"

"EGS stands for 'Extra Good Security.' Sounds cutesy, but it's a terrific encryption program. It's free for noncommercial use off the Internet, but you have to buy the commercial version. It's not very expensive. I'll start it up."

Kathryn pulled a chair alongside Fields, and watched as he loaded the program. He found a function called EDIT KEY and opened it. The only file was RTENKEY.

"There it is," he said," opening the file.

—START—EGS PROTECT KEY BLOCK—START—

—KEY—RTENKEY—KEY—

—Version: 2.1.2—

AQ0PBR9OCS8NDT7MEU6L STOP

FV5KGW47HX3IIY2HJZ1G STOP

K1ZFL2YEM3XDN4WCO5VB STOP

O5UAP6T0Q7S9R8$#&??= STOP

END END

"More gobbledygook," Kathryn said.

"To us, maybe, but to the computer, it's just a string of ones and zeros representing letters, numbers, and typographical characters. EGS reads this key to encrypt files, and the same key to decrypt them. All I need to do is figure out how to run it."

Fields scrolled through the program's status bar until a FILES drop-down box appeared. One of the choices was "Decrypt." He clicked on the icon and a dialogue box asked,

"Please designate the name of the file to decrypt and the path in DOS format."

He typed C:\WP51\DATA\RTEN and pressed Enter.

"Please designate the decryption key by DOS filename."

He typed RTENKEY.

The computer answered, "Please direct the output: (F)file; (P)printer; (S)Screen."

Fields depressed the S key.

The computer responded, "EGS PROTECT is decrypting file C:\WP51\DATA\RTEN, using RTENKEY. Please wait."

After two or three seconds, the computer screen refreshed and displayed:

DISTRICT ATTORNEY

CONFIDENTIAL INVESTIGATION FILE R-10

16 AUG 1998
COMPLAINANT: ESCOBEDO, ANITA
DOB: 12 JUL 1962
RELATION TO VICTIM: SISTER
VICTIM: ESCOBEDO, CARLOTTA
DATE OF DEATH: 18 MAY 1998

ON ABOVE DATE, COMPLAINANT REQUESTED PRIVATE CONSUL-
TATION REGARDING DEATH OF VICTIM

"You did it Jim," Kathryn said. "Can you print it out?"

"I need to take it to my office."

"Why?"

"Hal's computer is set up for an HP Deskjet printer. That's what I use."

"Don't let anyone see it."

Fields nodded and shut down the computer. He closed the cover, unplugged the power cord, and placed it in the Targus case. "I'll have a copy of that file for you in fifteen minutes."

43

"There it is." James Fields dropped two pages of computer-generated hard copy, stapled in the upper left corner, on Kathryn Mackay's desk and pulled up a leather client chair.

"You read it?" she asked.

"I caught a few passages as it printed out. Enough to see why Hal kept it confidential. This is serious shit."

Kathryn scanned the document quickly. "Will you excuse me, please, Jim."

"Sure." Fields stood and carefully replaced the chair where he found it. When he left, Kathryn picked up the file and read it slowly and thoroughly.

DISTRICT ATTORNEY

CONFIDENTIAL INVESTIGATION FILE R-10

16 AUG 1998
COMPLAINANT: ESCOBEDO, ANITA
DOB: 12 JUL 1962
RELATION TO VICTIM: SISTER

VICTIM: ESCOBEDO, CARLOTTA

DATE OF DEATH: 18 MAY 1998

ON ABOVE DATE, COMPLAINANT REQUESTED PRIVATE CON-SULTATION REGARDING DEATH OF VICTIM. INSISTED SATURDAY AM MEETING ONLY ACCEPTABLE TIME.

AE SISTER OF CE. AE IS REGISTERED NURSE AT ESPANOLA COMMUNITY HOSPITAL. AE STATED CE COMMITTED SUICIDE MAY 18 THORAZINE OD. CE PREGNANT AT TIME OF DEATH.

AE SAYS SHE WAS CONTACTED BY COUNTY HEALTH CLINIC NURSE WHO CLAIMS CE WAS MOLESTED BY A DOCTOR WHILE PATIENT AT CLINIC. NURSE SAYS MOLESTATION AND FORCED SEX WITH HISPANIC TEENAGE GIRLS BY DOCTOR IS COMMON KNOWLEDGE AMONG NURSES.

AE PROVIDED COPY OF CE'S MEDICAL RECORD. SKETCHY. NOT INITIALED OR SIGNED BY PHYSICIAN.

ADVISED COULD NOT INVESTIGATE WITHOUT AE IDENTIFYING NURSE. AE IDENTIFIED MEREDITH MERRILL, RN AT CLINIC.

AE IDENTIFIED AS MOTHER OF CE IN MEDICAL RECORD. AE ADMITTED SHE IDENTIFIED CE AS DAUGHTER IN ORDER TO BRING HER TO THE U.S. UNDER HER H-1B VISA. AE UNDER-STANDS INS COULD PROSECUTE/DEPORT IF THIS BECOMES PUBLIC KNOWLEDGE.

<u>CONCLUSION</u>: AE IS CREDIBLE. SHE HAS CONSIDERABLE TO LOSE BY COMING FORWARD. DETERMINE TO CONTACT ROBERT SIMMONS TO DISCUSS ALLEGATIONS.

18 AUG: MON: MET RS HIS OFFICE. HE IS UNAWARE OF SEXUAL MISCONDUCT AT CLINIC. SIMMONS REQUESTED TIME TO CON-DUCT OWN INTERNAL INVESTIGATION. DENIED. REQUESTED I CONDUCT INITIAL INQUIRIES TO DETERMINE VERACITY OF CHARGES. SIMMONS FEARFUL INVESTIGATION WILL DAMAGE CLINIC IRREPARABLY EVEN IF CHARGES UNTRUE. AGREED TO PERSONALLY HANDLE INITIAL INQUIRIES PROVIDED SIMMONS

ARRANGE FOR IMMEDIATE INTERVIEW WITH MM. INTERVIEW SET FOR MON 8/25 WHEN MM RETURNS FROM VACATION.

25 AUG: MON: INTERVIEW MM MY OFFICE 5:30 PM. MM STATED IT IS COMMON KNOWLEDGE AMONG NURSES THAT CLINIC DOCTOR HAS MOLESTED SEVERAL FEMALE PATIENTS. DOCTOR SEES PATIENTS W/O NURSE PRESENT. LOCKS EXAM ROOM. MAKES OWN FOLLOW-UP APPOINTMENTS. MAINTAINS INADEQUATE RECORDS. VICTIMS ALL YOUNG, HISPANIC, AT-TRACTIVE.

MM FEARS REPRISAL AS SHE BELIEVES DOCTOR'S BEHAV-IOR CONDONED BY HIGH-LEVEL CLINIC MANAGEMENT. MM RELUCTANTLY IDENTIFIED DR EDUARDO BERROA AS PERP.

CONCLUSION: MM CREDIBLE.

27 AUG: WED: SIMMONS AT SEMINAR MON & TUES. CON-TACTED WED. MET MY OFFICE 5:30 PM. ADVISED OF INTENT TO COMMENCE GRAND JURY INVESTIGATION OF HIS CLINIC. RS REQUESTED THRU WEEKEND TO IDENTIFY TOP MANAGEMENT WITH KNOWLEDGE OF CRIMES. AGREED. NEXT APPOINTMENT WITH RS 8:30 MON 9/1.

When she finished reading, Kathryn folded the papers in her lap, pushed away from her desk, leaned her head against the chair back, and closed her eyes.

She sat for several minutes, then picked up the phone.

"Morgue. Nelson."

"You were right, Morgan. Simmons tried to kill me and I can't prove it, but I know he tried to kill Hal, too."

"How do you know, Katie?"

"The R-file. I found it on Hal's computer. The file was encrypted, so I had Fields decipher it."

"Sounds like the CIA. What was in it?"

Mackay picked up the printout.

"On August sixteenth, Hal interviewed a woman who claimed her sister was molested by a doctor at Simmons's clinic, and later committed suicide."

"Hal was investigating the clinic?"

"Sort of. The woman got her information from an RN at the clinic named Merrill. She brought Hal her sister's medical records. Hal described them as, quote, 'Sketchy. Not initialed or signed by physician.' unquote. Sound familiar?"

"Too familiar. What else?"

"Hal interviewed Merrill on the twenty-fifth. She confirmed the woman's story."

"Did she say why she didn't come forward herself?"

"Apparently she didn't actually see him molest anyone, but she did see him examine certain patients with no nurse present and lock the exam room door so no one could interrupt. She also saw him schedule follow-up appointments himself for certain patients."

"Did she give Benton a name?"

"Eduardo Berroa."

"Berroa! He's not at the clinic."

"What do you mean?"

"He left and opened his own practice."

"When?"

"Very recently. I just received the announcement."

"Do you know where?"

"In that new office complex adjacent to Española Community Hospital." He paused, then added, "Berroa. I'm really surprised. He's a good doctor."

"He may be a good doctor, but he's also a rapist."

Nelson paused, then asked, "You said patients."

"Merrill believes Berroa molested several female patients besides Escobedo, all young Hispanics. She was right, Morgan, Berroa molested those women."

"How do you know that? You just said Merrill never saw him in the act."

"Given what I know, it's not necessary."

"What are you talking about?"

"Gabriela Hernandez told me Berroa raped her and fathered her child."

"Unbelievable! What was the woman's name who contacted Hal?"

"Let's see . . . Escobedo. Anita. Her sister's name was Carlotta."

"Jesus Christ! Katie, do you remember at the CDRT meeting, Granz mentioned an Española teenager who killed herself by drug overdose?"

"I remember. What about it?"

"Her name was Carlotta Escobedo. We reviewed her death at the emergency meeting Saturday. Died of a Thorazine overdose. She was pregnant. A patient at the clinic. Sister's name was Anita Escobedo."

"Why didn't you tell me about this sooner?"

"When? You were practically comatose Sunday night, and we didn't have time this morning."

"That's true, sorry."

"No problem. We also reviewed that abortion death Saturday. Rita Rios, sixteen years old, tox showed traces of Thorazine. She was a patient at the clinic, too."

"Valenzuela, Salazar, Hernandez, now Escobedo and Rios. What the hell do we have?"

"What else did Merrill tell Hal?"

"That she's afraid of retaliation. She believed the

doc's behavior was condoned by someone high up in clinic management."

"Simmons," Nelson declared. "There's your motive, Katie."

"What are you saying?" Kathryn asked.

"Berroa is raping his young, pretty Hispanic patients. Merrill says someone high up is covering for Berroa. Simmons is as high up as anyone gets at HSA."

"But, why would Simmons do that?"

"That's your job to find out. Maybe Berroa has some sort of leverage over Simmons. Something that Simmons can't afford for anyone else to know about. Whatever it is, it looks like he killed Hal to protect himself from Berroa."

"The final entry in Hal's R-file says Hal told Simmons on Wednesday the twenty-seventh about his interview with Merrill, and that he intended to commence a grand jury investigation. He gave Simmons until the following Monday, September first."

"To do what?"

"ID the person who was covering it up."

"What time was Hal scheduled to meet with Simmons Monday?"

"Eight-thirty."

"What are you going to do about Simmons, Katie?"

"I dropped the pills Simmons gave me on the floor of my bathroom last night. I'll send Fields over to my condo to get them, and have him deliver them to you. I need you to ID them right away. Call me as soon as you've confirmed they're digitalis. I'll have Simmons arrested for attempted murder."

44

"Would you drive over to my condo and pick up a handful of pills I dropped on my bathroom floor last night. Get all of them and take them to Doc Nelson. Wait while he IDs them." Kathryn handed James Fields her key ring.

"Can do," he said. "What are they?"

"Nelson will explain."

"What about Sam?" he asked, referring to Emma's golden lab.

"He's outside on the deck. He wouldn't bite even if he were in the house, unless you forgot to bring him something to eat."

Fields laughed. "I was worried he might slobber on my new suit."

"Jim, this is really urgent."

"I'll hurry," he promised.

When Fields had left, Mackay rang Donna Escalante, Mary Elizabeth Skinner, and Dave Granz and asked them to meet with her in her office immediately. When everyone was assembled, she filled them in on the situation.

"Those deaths are related to the Fuentes investigation?" Escalante asked.

"Absolutely," Mackay answered. She rummaged around the top of her desk but couldn't find what she was looking for. "Inspector, do you have the Fuentes file?"

"You had it before you left for Mexico."

"That's what I thought." Mackay buzzed her secretary.

"Yes, ma'am?"

"What happened to the Fuentes file? It was on my desk last Friday."

"Mr. McCaskill took it."

"When?"

"This morning."

"Did Mr. McCaskill say why he took it?"

"He said he was going to take over the grand jury investigation."

"Damn," Kathryn swore softly. "Thank you."

Kathryn depressed the disconnect button, but didn't remove the phone handset from her ear. She held a hand out, asking everyone to stand by, then dialed another number.

"Chief Deputy McCaskill."

Chief deputy, my ass, Kathryn thought. "This is District Attorney Mackay. I want you in my office now. Bring the Fuentes file with you."

Everyone sat in uncomfortable silence for several minutes, until McCaskill slammed open Mackay's office door. He glared at Skinner and Mackay.

"Lieutenant. Inspector," he said, acknowledging the two officers. He casually tossed a manila folder on his boss's desk, and started to pull up a chair.

"Don't sit down, Mr. McCaskill," Kathryn told him.

"I want you to return to your office and remove all your personal effects. Then you are to leave this office. You're fired."

"Fired! What the hell are you talking about? You can't fire me."

"I can, and I have."

Kathryn turned to Skinner. "Mary, accompany Mr. McCaskill to his office. Allow him to remove any personal items, then escort him out of the office. If he gives you any crap, call for an inspector and have him arrested for trespassing. Rejoin us once he's gone."

McCaskill stalked to the door, followed by Skinner. "I'll sue your ass, Mackay," he said, turning, then walked out.

"Take your best shot," she said softly. She picked up the file, but before she could open it the phone rang.

"Ms. Mackay, Dr. Nelson is on line one," Nancy Torres said.

Kathryn picked up the phone. "Digitalis?" she asked.

"Digitalis. Simmons gave you enough to kill an elephant."

"Doc, can you give Fields a quick verbal statement, and copies of the tox reports on Hal and me?"

"Already done. He's on his way. Should be at your office any minute."

"Thanks, Morgan . . . for everything."

Kathryn sent her secretary to the Starbucks cart for coffee while she, Granz, and Escalante waited for Fields and Skinner. Before the coffee was delivered, Fields rushed in and handed her several sheets of paper.

"Tox results and Nelson's statement," he announced, out of breath.

When Skinner returned, Kathryn brought her up to speed then turned to Fields.

"Jim, you seized the pills and took Nelson's statement. I named you the affiant for a Ramey warrant. Judge Tucker's standing by in chambers."

Fields nodded.

"Mary, you'll take my testimony before Tucker. I'll brief you on the way down."

"We'll need two teams, to hit the clinic and Simmons's home at the same time," Granz said. "I'll head up one team. Fields, you head up the other. I'll send one of my detectives with your team."

"Agreed," Fields answered.

"Mary, you go with Fields in case any legal problems come up," Mackay instructed. "I'll take Inspector Escalante and go with Dave."

Granz stood. "Go get your warrant. I'll grab a detective and meet you outside Tucker's court."

Mackay, Skinner, Fields, and Escalante walked the unsigned arrest warrant to Superior Court 6, where Judge Jemima Tucker waited in chambers.

Tucker had removed her judicial robe for the afternoon, and greeted them in a plain but expensive-looking black suit.

"I hope this is important, Ms. Mackay," she said. "I had an appointment."

"It is, Your Honor. Thank you for staying."

Unceremoniously, Tucker swore Fields, who affirmed the affidavit under oath.

"I understand you're prepared to testify, Ms. Mackay?"

"That's correct."

Tucker arched her eyebrows. "Raise your right hand."

Skinner elicited Kathryn's testimony concerning her relationship with Robert Simmons from its inception through the events of Sunday evening. Mackay testified in detail about their personal involvement, his attempts to kill her, and her belief that he killed Harold Benton.

When Kathryn's testimony was concluded, Tucker sat stunned and silent. "I'm going to make this a no-bail warrant," she declared. "Dr. Simmons is a flight risk and a danger to the public. I don't want him walking the same streets I do."

Dave Granz and Detective Jim "Jazzbo" Miller were waiting outside chambers as promised. Miller was short and heavyset, with red hair, a ruddy complexion, a bushy red beard, and green eyes. His nickname was the result of his weekend avocation as the trombonist in a local jazz band.

Mackay handed the warrant to Granz and a duplicate to Miller. "Okay," she said. "Let's arrest Robert Simmons."

Mackay had established a telephone relationship with Simmons's secretary, so it was agreed that she would speak for the team. It was a few minutes before 5 P.M. when they approached her desk inside the Public Health Department administration offices.

Kathryn smiled. "Good afternoon. I'm Kathryn Mackay from the District Attorney's office. We've spoken on the phone, but we've never met in person."

The secretary, whose name tag said "Hello, I'm Velma" shook the proffered hand firmly.

"I'm so pleased to meet you. How may I be of assistance?"

"This is Lieutenant Granz from the Sheriff's Office, and DA Inspector Escalante. We're here to speak with Dr. Simmons."

"Concerning what, if I may inquire?" Velma asked.

"The Sheriff and I are very grateful for Dr. Simmons's assistance regarding the Board of Supervisors' new needle exchange program. We hoped he might be able to spare a few moments."

"Was he expecting you?"

"No, I'm afraid he wasn't."

"I thought not. You see, Dr. Simmons didn't come to work today."

"Did he call in sick?"

"No, that's the strange thing. He didn't call in at all, he just didn't show up this morning. I called his house several times, but he didn't answer. Even his answering machine isn't on."

"I see," Kathryn said.

"I checked his appointment book," Velma told her, motioning through an open door to Simmons's empty desk in the office behind her, "but he had no appointments outside the office."

"Thank you," Kathryn said, stepping away to where Granz was already on his cell phone.

"Okay," he said into the phone after listening for a minute. "We'll be right there."

Fifteen minutes later, they were standing in the middle of Simmons's bedroom. The bed was unmade, and the drapes were still shut.

"What about the kitchen?" Kathryn asked Miller.

"Dirty cereal bowl in the sink. A half-full Mr. Coffee

was still turned on. Looks like the stuff I used to drink in the navy. He left the TV on in the living room, too."

Granz and Escalante were tossing Simmons's dresser drawers and nightstands.

"Underwear, socks, and shirts are all gone. Simmons split in one hell of a hurry," Escalante said.

"Yep," Kathryn replied, as she rummaged through the closet. "I can't tell what's missing, but there are lots of vacant spaces. Only one empty hanger where he kept his suits, though, and I'll bet that's it," she said, indicating an expensive black suit that lay in a heap on the floor beside the bathroom door. "Looks like he only took casual clothes."

She peered into the bathroom, where Fields was searching the medicine cabinet. The opaque glass shower door stood ajar, a puddle of water on the floor under the corner. Crusty shaving cream and whisker residue ringed the marble sink, and a damp towel hung from the edge of the bathtub.

"Anything?" she asked.

"Nada," Fields answered.

"He packed light and got out of here quick. What tipped him?" Miller asked.

Kathryn picked up a newspaper from the bed. It was folded with the story about her hospitalization on top.

"This," she declared. "He expected me to be dead this morning. My guess is he got up, started coffee, and had breakfast while he read the newspaper. When he found out I was alive, he got scared and took off."

"Where to?" Fields asked.

"Damned if I know."

45

"Miss Valenzuela, District Attorney Mackay informed me that you refused to answer certain questions when you testified before the grand jury last Wednesday evening. Is that correct?"

Josefina looked at Judge Tucker, then the court reporter, whose hands were poised over her transcription machine, and swallowed. "Yes."

"You have taken an oath to answer the District Attorney's questions honestly and completely, to the best of your ability here this morning, and I will tolerate no such behavior from you in my court. Do you understand?"

She nodded.

"Answer aloud, so the court reporter can record your response," Tucker admonished the witness.

"I understand," she replied.

Tucker nodded at Kathryn Mackay. "Proceed."

Inspector Escalante handed Mackay a transcript of Valenzuela's grand jury testimony. Kathryn flipped to the first page, which was tagged with a red sticker, and the critical passages marked with a yellow high-lighter.

"Josefina, last Wednesday at the grand jury, you told me that when you went to the county health clinic, one of the doctors touched you improperly while you were being examined. Do you recall that?"

"Yes."

"I asked you to describe exactly what the doctor did to you. Do you remember what you said?"

"Not exactly."

Mackay read from the transcript. "Did you tell me, 'He put his mouth on my breast. I could feel his tongue'? Was that your testimony?"

Valenzuela looked at her lap. "Yes."

"And was that a truthful statement?"

"Yes, it was the truth."

Kathryn flipped to another page. "Later, you testified that the doctor made you touch him and when I asked where he made you touch him, what was your testimony?"

"I said he made me touch him on his private parts."

"And was that a truthful statement?"

"Yes."

"Okay, Josefina, now when I asked if that doctor made you have sexual intercourse with him, you refused to answer that question. I'm going to ask you again, Josefina, did the doctor at the clinic force you to submit to sexual intercourse with him?"

Valenzuela looked pleadingly at Judge Tucker.

"Answer the question, Miss Valenzuela," Tucker said.

"He raped me," the girl said softly.

"Your Honor, I couldn't hear the witness's response," the court reporter said.

Before Tucker could direct her to speak up, Valenzuela sat up straight in her chair and glared at Mackay. "He raped me," she said forcefully.

Kathryn pursed her lips and sighed. "Thank you, Josefina. One more question. What is the name of the doctor who raped you while you were a patient at the county health clinic?"

Valenzuela looked at the ceiling, then the floor, then fixed her gaze on the oak-paneled wall above the empty jury box. With only Judge Tucker, Mackay, Escalante, the court reporter, and herself in the room, the room was silent, but Valenzuela didn't speak.

Tucker leaned forward and started to admonish the girl, but Mackay furrowed her eyebrows and shook her head, indicating she would handle the girl's reluctance. Tucker nodded and sat back in his chair.

"Josie?" The girl shifted her gaze to the ceiling.

"Josie, look at me, please," Kathryn said kindly.

When the witness had complied, she asked, "Do you know a girl named Gabriela Hernandez, Josie?"

"I . . . How did . . ."

"Gabriela called me, Josie. I traveled to Ixtapa over the weekend and spoke with her. She told me the doctor at the clinic raped her, too, and that he is the father of her baby."

Josefina stared at Mackay in astonishment. "She told you?"

Kathryn nodded. "Gabriela said to tell you it's okay to tell me everything now. Will you tell Judge Tucker the name of the doctor who raped you, so he can never do it to anyone else?"

The witness sat silently long enough that Tucker

told her softly, "Please answer the question, Miss Valenzuela."

"Berroa. Dr. Berroa," she answered quietly.

The court reporter looked at Kathryn and cupped a hand over her ear, and shook her head.

"Repeat the doctor's name so the court reporter can hear," Kathryn told her.

"Dr. Eduardo Berroa raped me."

"Thank you, Miss Valenzuela," Judge Tucker said, handing the signed arrest warrant to Kathryn, who stood with her hand on the girl's arm.

46

At 12:45 P.M. Mackay, Escalante, Granz, and Jazzbo Miller reconnoitered in the parking lot of Los Arboles Medical Center in Española. Like all the other buildings on Adelita Street, it was new, commanded a breathtaking view of the bay, and was within walking distance of the hospital.

Miller stationed himself outside the employee exit in the rear of the building, which later in the afternoon would be shaded by a row of towering eucalyptus trees bordering the parking lot. Escalante crouched beneath a row of office and examining room windows.

Granz and Mackay waited on the front steps for the doors to open after lunch. To the right of the heavy double doors, a free-form black marble directory hung inside a glass case. Affixed to the plaque were two or three dozen shiny brass nameplates. Most were blank, but a few were engraved with physicians' names. On one, someone had written "Eduardo Berroa, MD" with a black felt-tip marker in large block letters.

"You know, Kate, I sorta hope Berroa pulls a scalpel and tries to kill me with it, then runs when it doesn't work out for him."

Kathryn glanced at the white scar on Dave's cheek, inflicted years earlier by a serial killer named Lee Russell, whom the press dubbed the Gingerbread Man. Russell had ambushed Granz in a dark alley, slashed his face and neck with a surgical scalpel, and left him for dead.

"That's not funny."

He smiled. "Sure it is."

Once, Dave's lopsided grin had won Kathryn's heart, but now it awakened melancholy and painful memories.

"Berroa won't think it's funny, though, when I blow his ass into Santa Clara County," he added, patting the Glock nine-millimeter pistol under his jacket.

"Don't get carried away, Granz, this isn't the Wild West and you're not Wyatt Earp."

Dave set his hand on hers. "You know me better than that. It's just talk."

"That's what Mark Furman said."

Kathryn let Dave's hand rest on hers for several seconds, but when he tried to interweave his fingers among hers, she withdrew it.

"I—" she started, but was interrupted by the custodian unlocking the office door from inside.

"You were saying?" Granz asked.

"It was nothing," she said. "Let's go."

Granz shrugged and followed her into the reception area, which smelled of fresh paint, new carpeting, and unused furniture. A nurse at the reception and admitting station, wearing an embossed nameplate that said "Denise Silva, RN," saw them coming.

"Detective Dave, to what do I owe this wonderful surprise?" She smiled at Granz.

Whatever fleeting feeling Kathryn might have entertained dissipated faster than it had appeared. Kathryn knew she could never trust Dave again after he betrayed her by having an affair with Julia Soto. Remarks like Silva's would always create doubt.

"This is District Attorney Kathryn Mackay," he said. We're here to see Dr. Eduardo Berroa. Where is he?"

"I'll call him for you."

"No, that's all right," Granz said. "Just tell us where he is, and we'll find him."

Silva pointed down a hallway. "He's in his office, room one-oh-one, the first door on the right. But, I should call him before you go in." She picked up a phone.

Kathryn shook her head. "Put the phone down, please. This is official police business."

Confused, Silva looked at Granz, then Mackay, but replaced the handset as she had been instructed.

Granz and Mackay skirted the counter and pushed open a half-height swinging gate. It opened into a long, brightly lit hallway lined with blond oak doors and cluttered with computer boxes, unidentifiable medical equipment, and furniture still in its plastic wrap.

The first door on the right bore a white plastic plate on which "Eduardo Berroa, MD" was written in the same block letters as the exterior directory.

Granz looked at Mackay, who nodded, and twisted the knob.

Eduardo Berroa stood behind his desk at the opposite side of the spacious but sparsely furnished office in front of a bay window lined with potted plants. He was bent over a computer monitor with a cable in his right hand and looked up when they entered, but didn't seem surprised.

Berroa was about forty, five-eight and slightly overweight, with thinning hair and dark olive skin. His huge brown eyes and heavy eyebrows were accentuated by plastic horn-rimmed glasses. His brown slacks were wrinkled, and his tie was loose and the top shirt button unfastened. Except for the scowl on his face, he looked like a giant teddy bear.

"Damn it, can't you knock?" he asked.

"Eduardo Berroa?" Granz asked.

"I called you computer people early this morning. You're too late. I've figured out the problem, so I don't need your help. One of the pins in the monitor cable plug was bent."

He turned away and fiddled with the monitor cable, then looked up. "Don't try billing me for a service call, either, because I won't pay it."

"Are you Eduardo Berroa?" Granz repeated.

Berroa removed his glasses, dropped them on the desk, and squinted. "Who the hell are you?"

Granz pulled out a basket-weave leather case, flipped it open, and held it out to show Berroa his badge and photo identification card.

"I'm Lieutenant Granz from the Sheriff's Office. This is District Attorney Kathryn Mackay," he replied, indicating Kathryn.

"Are you Eduardo Berroa?"

"Yes, I'm Dr. Berroa," he said. "What do you want?"

Granz stepped around the desk and placed his hand on Berroa's shoulder.

"Eduardo Berroa, you are under arrest for the rape of Josefina Valenzuela."

"I what!? What are you talking about?" Berroa shouted, jerking away. "Get out of my office! How dare you barge in here and—"

Granz grabbed Berroa's right arm in a powerful grip, spun him around, and twisted with enough force to discourage further resistance. He removed handcuffs from a case under his jacket, and slapped one cuff over Berroa's right wrist, ratcheting it shut.

"Place your left hand behind your back," he ordered.

When Berroa had complied, Granz cuffed the left wrist, then walked the doctor around to the front of the desk.

"You have the right to remain silent," He read. "Anything you say may be used against you in court. You have the right to the presence of an attorney before and during any questioning. If you cannot afford an attorney, one will be appointed for you, free of charge, before any questioning, if you want."

Berroa stared at Granz but didn't respond.

"Do you understand each of these rights, Mr. Berroa?" Granz asked.

"*Doctor* Berroa," he answered.

"Sir, do you understand the rights Lieutenant Granz explained to you?" Mackay asked.

Berroa shifted his intense gaze to Kathryn. "I understand enough to exercise my constitutional right to remain silent."

47

Frederick Fouts sat next to his client in the other leather chair, facing Kathryn Mackay and Donna Escalante.

"Good afternoon, Ms. Mackay. Inspector. I trust this won't take long. My client should be home in bed recuperating."

"Thank you for coming on such short notice, sir. I'll be as brief as possible." Kathryn made eye contact with Fouts, then Raymondo Miranda. She was struck once again by the young man's startling good looks.

"I asked to see you because I believe your client can provide information that is crucial to my investigation into the death of Esther Fuentes. In exchange for his statement and testimony, I am prepared to extend an offer of immunity to Mr. Miranda."

Miranda started to speak, but Fouts placed a hand on his arm.

"My client might be willing to cooperate under certain circumstances, but let me be certain I understand your offer. As you know, prior to 1997, you were permitted to offer only transactional immunity.

Now, under the new 'use immunity' law, you can proffer limited immunity, which still exposes my client to criminal prosecution under certain circumstances. Are you offering my client use immunity or transactional immunity? If your immunity offer is limited in any way, then my client would not be interested."

"I am offering transactional immunity. Your client will be immunized against any inculpatory statement he makes here today, or in his testimony, with regard to any criminal activity whatsoever."

Fouts whispered to his client, and Miranda nodded vigorously, then looked at Mackay.

"My client accepts your immunity offer, Ms. Mackay. Ask your questions."

Escalante switched on a minicassette recorder, placed it on Mackay's desk, and read into the recorder, "It is 3 P.M., Tuesday, September twenty-third. Present are District Attorney Kathryn Mackay, Inspector Escalante, and Raymondo Miranda, who is represented by his attorney, Frederick Fouts, who is also present."

"In exchange for his statement and testimony, Raymondo Miranda has accepted the District Attorney's offer of transactional immunity for all charges which might arise against him up to this time. Is that your understanding, Mr. Fouts?" Kathryn asked.

"That is correct," Fouts answered.

Kathryn turned to Miranda, who looked scared. "Mr. Miranda, can you describe your personal relationship with Esther Fuentes, please?"

"She was my girlfriend." Miranda's voice was soft and well modulated, but shaky.

"How long had you known each other?"

"Ever since we were kids."

"Your families knew you were girlfriend and boy-friend?"

"Yes."

"Did you know Esther was pregnant?"

He waited several seconds before answering. "Yes."

"How?"

"She told me."

"When was that, Mr. Miranda?"

He leaned over and whispered something to Fouts, who nodded.

"Ms. Mackay, my client asks that you refer to him by his first name. He prefers Raymond."

"Of course, I'm sorry." Kathryn smiled. "Raymond, when did Esther tell you she was pregnant?"

"About a week before we . . . before she was killed."

Escalante handed him a box of tissues and patted his shoulder. "Take your time."

"Before that, did you notice any changes in Esther?"

"A couple of months before school was out, March or April, I drove her to the county health clinic. I think she had some sort of infection. When she came out, she was really upset, but when I asked what was wrong, she wouldn't tell me. After that, she wasn't the same."

Kathryn glanced at Escalante, who arched her eyebrows. "Was that the only time you took her to the clinic?" Escalante asked.

"No, I took her quite a few times after that. She didn't have a car."

"Did she tell you why she went to the doctor so often?"

"She said it was female problems. I didn't ask any more questions."

"How did Esther act each time she left the clinic?"

"Mostly she was quiet and wouldn't talk on the way home. Then she just stopped talking to me completely."

"What do you mean?"

"Sometime in August, she said she wanted to break up with me. I called, but she wouldn't talk to me even on the phone. She hung up on me, so I went to her house. That's when she told me she was pregnant. I didn't believe her at first."

"Did she tell you that you weren't the father?"

"She didn't have to. I knew."

"How could you be so sure, Raymond?"

Miranda looked at every person in the room before he answered. "We were waiting until we got married. I thought she was a virgin."

"Were you angry?"

"Sure. Wouldn't you be?"

"What did you do?"

"I got pissed off and started swearing. I drove around in my car all night. I didn't talk to her for almost two days. Then I called and said I had to see her."

Kathryn didn't answer, and he continued.

"I picked her up in my car and drove up through the park to the top of Mount Cabrillo Grade Road. We stopped to talk at this turnoff. It's a driveway that goes onto a dirt road and through a gate into some farmer's pasture. It's kind of secluded; you can't see it from the road unless you look hard. All the kids park there at night on the weekends and make out. Everyone calls it The Farm.

"She was crying really hard, but I wasn't pissed anymore." He sniffed and wiped his eyes and nose with a tissue, then carefully placed it in the wastebasket.

"I asked if she was in love with the other guy, but she said there wasn't another guy, that she loved me. That's when she told me about the doctor."

"Go on."

"She said a doctor at the clinic forced her to have sex with him, and the baby was his. When I asked why she let him, she said she didn't have a choice, that he threatened to have her and her parents deported."

"What did you say?"

"I said we should get married, that I didn't care who the baby's father was."

"Why didn't you get married?"

"She refused. Said she wasn't good enough for me anymore, that she'd screw my life up, too. That's when she started talking about it."

"Talking about what?" Kathryn asked.

"Suicide."

He drew a deep breath and let it out slowly. "I tried to talk her out of it, but the more we talked, the more she decided it was all she could do. I decided if she was going to die, I was too.

"After Esther's folks left for work on Monday morning, she called me. I drove over and picked her up and brought her to my house. She took most of the pills, but left a few of them because she started to get sick. I put the bottle in my backpack."

"What pills, Raymond?"

"The doctor gave her some pills he got in Mexico. She said they calmed her down. After she took the pills, we drove out past the fairgrounds. By the time we drove through the park past the white deer, I thought Esther was dead, but I guess she was just asleep."

Mackay, Escalante, and Fouts all sat silently while Miranda cried softly.

"I stopped my car right in the middle of the road and sat there for a long time with the engine running. I was so scared, I couldn't make myself do it. I thought about leaving her body beside the road and driving away, but I couldn't do that either. Finally, I worked up the guts to drive off the cliff. Funny I could work up the guts to do that, but not to tell my parents or the cops."

"You made a mistake, Raymond, a very serious mistake, and you will never forget what happened," Kathryn told him. "In time most of the pain will go away, and you will go on with your life. But you must learn from this mistake."

Raymond looked out the window and wiped his eyes, but didn't answer.

"Just one more question, Raymond. Did Esther tell you the doctor's name?"

"She said it was Dr. Berroa."

Kathryn stood and shook hands with Fouts, who smiled sadly. "Thank you, Ms. Mackay."

Kathryn nodded and extended her hand to Raymondo Miranda. He accepted it gingerly.

"You are free to go, Raymond," she said. "I wish you well."

After Fouts and Miranda left, Kathryn turned to Escalante, who dabbed at her eyes with a tissue.

"We have work to do," Kathryn said. "Are you all right?"

"I will be," Escalante answered.

"Me too," Kathryn told her.

48

Kathryn shook her watch and checked it to be sure it hadn't stopped with the display reading 4:27 P.M. Exhausted from the day's events, which had culminated in the interview with Raymondo Miranda, she stuffed memos and files in her briefcase and prepared to go home, but was interrupted by the phone just as she picked up her purse.

"Yes, Nancy?"

"There's a call for you on line one."

"Tell whoever it is I'm gone for the day. I'll return the call tomorrow."

"I think you'll want to take this one, ma'am. It's a collect call from Dr. Eduardo Berroa. I already accepted the charges."

"Yes?" Kathryn said into the phone.

"It's Dr. Berroa." The jail's recording equipment, hooked to all outside phone lines, caused a hollow echo, as if the call originated from inside a Campbell soup can.

"It's late, Mr. Berroa. What do you want?"

"First, for you to remember to call me 'Doctor.'"

"You stopped being a doctor the first time you raped one of your patients. Are you going to play games or tell me why you called?"

"I want to talk about a deal."

"I thought you chose to exercise your right to remain silent."

"I changed my mind."

"I don't make deals with rapists."

"What do you have to lose by listening?"

Kathryn didn't answer.

"Are you still there, Madam District Attorney?"

"I'm here. What kind of deal are you talking about?"

"I'll talk to you and Lieutenant Granz, but not here at the jail. I guarantee it'll be worth your while. Well?" he prompted.

"I'll have you over here in fifteen minutes," Kathryn said, hung up, cursed, then placed two calls. The first was to Dave Granz. The second was to James Fields.

"Fields."

"Jim, Kathryn. I have a personal favor to ask. You can say no if you want."

"Fat chance," he laughed. "Name it."

She told him about Berroa's call. "Granz and a couple of detectives are bringing Berroa to the sheriff's interview room. Could you pick Emma up from school and drop her at Ruth's? I can't get there and back in time."

"Have you checked with Ruth yet?" he asked.

"I figured I'd better call you first."

"Why don't I pick her up and take her home with me instead. It's been a while since our kids were that age. We'd love to have her."

"I couldn't ask you to do that. It's—"

"It's settled, then," he said. "I'll pick Em up from school. We'll grab a pizza and a movie at Blockbuster on the way home. That way, if you're late picking her up, nobody'll notice."

"Without checking with your wife first?" Kathryn asked. "Shirley will kill both of us."

"She'll kill me if she finds out I had a chance to bring Emma home for the evening and didn't."

"Okay, thanks, Jim. I'll return the favor. And give her a big hug for me, will you?"

"Several of 'em. See you later, and take your time. Good luck with Berroa."

At a quarter past five, Kathryn took the stairs to the third floor and, once inside the sheriff's office, rapped on the door to the suspect interview room.

Eduardo Berroa sat at the far side of the interview table wearing an orange jumpsuit and eating a sandwich. He nodded at Mackay, who sat opposite him and placed her recorder on the table between them. Granz sat beside Mackay.

"Let's get started," Kathryn said, switching on the recorder.

Berroa stuffed a handful of corn chips into his mouth, set the sandwich on the paper bag, and reached over to switch off the recorder. "No recordings, no Miranda warnings, and no statement until after we've made a deal."

"Sounds like you know your way around the criminal justice system," Kathryn said, "but that doesn't surprise me."

"I know exactly how the system works, Ms. Mackay That's why you can't Mirandize me, and why I don't want a lawyer present. I don't intend for you to be able to use what I have to tell you, that is, not until we reach an agreement."

Kathryn stared at Berroa, and he grinned at her, then at Granz. "Lieutenant, could I get something to wash my sandwich down? Turkey is so dry."

Granz glared, but punched the intercom and asked a deputy to bring three Diet Cokes.

"What sort of deal do you have in mind?" Kathryn asked.

"You may record everything I tell you, but you must make a statement on the tape that you did not Mirandize me before I made my statement. You are to repeat that at the end of my statement. We both know that will ensure that you cannot use my statement in the event we don't reach an understanding."

"And the understanding?"

He grinned again. "You dismiss the Valenzuela rape charges against me, in exchange for my testimony against Simmons. I receive immunity against any incriminating disclosures I make during my statement and testimony against Simmons."

"That's it?" Kathryn asked.

"Yes. If you don't think what I have to say is worth the deal, then neither of us has lost anything except a little time. Do we have an understanding?"

Kathryn glanced at Granz, who shrugged, set the recorder on the table, switched it on, and stated who was present and where. Then Mackay noted that Berroa had not been advised of his constitutional right to remain silent, leaned back in her chair and waited.

Berroa cleared his throat. "A few years ago I conceived a program to revolutionize the delivery of health services to low-income people. I proposed to assign each patient a primary care physician, whom they would see each time they visited the clinic, rather than shuffling them like cattle from one mediocre doctor to another. Patients benefit from a personal relationship with their doctors and receive better health care as a result. In short, my idea was to run the county clinic like a modern HMO."

"Mr. Berroa, what does this have to do with . . ."

"Patience, Ms. Mackay, and it's *Doctor* Berroa. I proposed my plan to Dr. Simmons, who endorsed it enthusiastically. Unfortunately, he lacked vision, and he stole my idea, claiming it as his own. In addition, the way he implemented the program merely perpetuated the racism already ingrained in the health-care delivery system."

Berroa sipped his Coke. "Based on the racist assumption that because I am Mexican, I could best relate to other Mexicans, he assigned all indigent Hispanic patients to me. I am from an affluent Mexican family, Ms. Mackay, and could no more relate to low-income, uneducated Hispanic patients than Dr. Simmons, who himself came from a lower-middle-class background. So, I threatened to file a racial discrimination lawsuit. My charges had merit, so he made me an offer I couldn't refuse."

"Meaning?" Kathryn asked.

"He paid me twenty-five thousand dollars to forget my lawsuit. That's where I got the money to open my new office with state-of-the-art computer and medical equipment. The other part of that agreement permitted me to select all my own patients, on whatever criteria I thought desirable, for as long as I remained at the clinic."

"You can corroborate this?"

"Damn right. I insisted that he sign an agreement to that effect. I have the original in a safe-deposit box. But I made a mistake."

"So did Simmons."

"Mine was bigger, I'm afraid. As you have discovered, I have an affinity, shall we say, for pretty young girls. Before long, my patient list included mostly attractive young women, Hispanics, to be precise, over whom I had considerable influence due to the fact that many of their families, or they themselves, were undocumented. You'd be surprised how many illegal immigrants there are when you look for them.

"Last July, Anita Escobedo visited Dr. Simmons and made a very ugly allegation concerning a doctor's relationship with her sister, who happened to be one of my patients. Simmons threatened to report me to the police under the child abuse reporting law, but I prevailed on him to recall our agreement and implied I might make certain disclosures public. We came to a mutual understanding under which I resigned from the clinic in exchange for his silence. Dr. Simmons, it turns out, isn't a very good poker player."

"Explain," Kathryn said.

"I insisted on a second agreement, which he signed under threat of public disclosure. I was bluffing, of course, but he couldn't take the chance. I suppose he figured I could always return to Mexico, while all he had to look forward to was Flatrock, Arkansas. Anyway, in addition to his silence, he promised in that agreement to remove certain parts of the medical records of a number of clinic patients. You understand I'm not admitting there was anything inappropriate in those files. In fact, I—"

"What happened to the records Simmons removed?" Kathryn asked.

"Simmons wasn't nearly as astute as you, Ms. Mackay. You'd think he would have kept them, a little quid pro quo to level the playing field, but he overlooked the possibility. He gave them to me, and I destroyed them."

"Give me the names of the patients, asshole," Granz snarled.

"Calm down, Lieutenant, anger and hostility will raise your blood pressure. Let's see, on his own volition, Dr. Simmons may have improperly removed certain medical information from the files of Esther Fuentes—I read about her accident, terrible thing— then there were young women named Salazar and Hernandez."

"All of them," Granz insisted.

"Well, you know about Escobedo and Valenzuela. I can't recall any more."

"Rios," Granz prompted.

"Ah yes, Rita Rios, she was also one of my patients. Hemorrhaged to death following an abortion. I understand Dr. Simmons signed the death certificate, but before he did, he removed certain information from her medical records, as well."

"He gave it to you?"

"Not that one. I don't know what happened to it. I imagine he destroyed it himself to prevent its falling into the wrong hands. At any rate, Anita Escobedo was quite persistent, and apparently she was dissatisfied with Dr. Simmons's response to her complaint. She took the matter to your predecessor, Harold Benton. Fortunately for us, Mr. Benton contacted Simmons before doing anything about it. It turned out to be less fortunate for Benton than it did for Simmons.

"Simmons talked your boss into giving him a little time. Then he talked to me about the situation. He proposed a hypothetical. 'What if someone ingested a massive dose of digitalis?' he asked. 'What would happen?' Naturally, he knew that person would suffer heart failure and die. That was the last I heard about it until I read about Benton's unfortunate heart attack in the newspaper.

"It seemed pretty coincidental to me that Simmons just happened to be there at the time, so I invited him to my new office. At first he refused to admit anything to me, but I reminded him of our agreements. Then he told me."

"Told you what?"

Berroa nodded knowingly. "Of course you need an admission, don't you, in order to use it against him in court. All right. Simmons told me he put a massive dose of digitalis in Benton's coffee the morning he apparently died of a heart attack. When Benton collapsed, Simmons waited long enough to be sure he was dead, then summoned assistance and administered CPR. When the paramedics arrived, they had to force him to give up his heroic effort to save Benton's life.

"He knew that if he was present and could sign off on the death certificate, there wouldn't be an autopsy, and no one would ever know what he did. And that's exactly what happened, isn't it? Too bad they didn't run a tox screen on Benton's blood before they cremated the body, it would prove what I just said is true."

Kathryn stared at Granz, then turned to Berroa. "You have your deal, Mr. Berroa."

"Not so fast. I want it in writing."

Kathryn pulled out a legal pad and started writing, signed it, and handed it to Berroa.

"See you in court, Counselor. Too bad you can't use this against me."

49

Donna Escalante handed her boss a cup of coffee and removed the lid from her own. "Can't start my Wednesday morning without it," Escalante said, slurping from the steaming cup.

Kathryn Mackay laughed. "Me, neither. Or Thursday through Tuesday, either. Thanks. Late night?"

"Yeah, and I've got some bad news. San Jose Airport Police found Simmons's Mercedes in short-term parking. Fields and I searched it last night."

"What did you come up with?"

"Not a damn thing."

"Should we stake it out in case he returns?"

"I don't think he's coming back anytime soon."

"Why not?"

"I logged onto IRSC with my laptop and—"

"What's IRSC?"

"An on-line information service available over the Internet. You can find almost any kind of information about a person you want: bankruptcies, court filings, professional licensing, voter registrations, all sorts of personal and business data. I checked Simmons's credit reports."

"Looking for what?"

"Real estate holdings, bank accounts, and credit cards."

"What did you find out?"

"He owned two hundred acres of undeveloped land near Ben Hur, in Newton County, Arkansas, a four-plex in Russellville, and a house in Dover. Sold all three of them within the last few months. His condo here was free and clear until August, when he took out a quarter-million-dollar mortgage. Proceeds on all those transactions went into his account at Wells Fargo. He had more than a million bucks cash in checking, savings, and time deposit accounts last week."

Kathryn whistled. "We should have been doctors."

"For sure. You'll probably get some complaints about my attitude: I leaned on a few people. I checked on his credit cards, too. The usual: Amex, Visa, MasterCard. I have a friend who's a Visa-MasterCard fraud investigator in San Francisco. Travels all over the world, but we see each other occasionally. I got lucky and caught him at home last night. He agreed to check the charges on Simmons's bank card accounts."

"When do you expect to hear from him?"

"Already did. I made a couple of promises in exchange for prompt service."

"What kind of promises?"

Escalante smiled. "Let's just say they're the kind I won't mind keeping. Anyway, Simmons caught a Continental flight out of San Jose to Houston yesterday at 9:15 A.M. Bought a first class ticket at the gate and paid for it with his credit card."

"How does he know? When I charge airfare on my Visa, the statement shows the airline name, but no flight information."

"That's true, but my friend called direct to Continental's ticketing counter at San Jose International. They still had the charge slip."

"Why Houston?"

"Probably the earliest connection he could make out of the country. He left Houston at three-forty-five, their time, on Mexicana Airlines."

"To where?"

"Mexico City."

Kathryn pursed her lips, then sipped at her coffee. "Eventually, we'll find him in Mexico."

"Is Simmons bilingual?" Escalante asked.

"He's fluent in Spanish. Why?"

"That explains things. My friend called in a favor from a colleague at Mexico City Visa-MasterCard. Simmons charged a ticket on Aero InterUrbano last night from Mexico City to Caracas, Venezuela. Aero InterUrbano's a shoestring operation that doesn't even fly jet aircraft."

"He bought a ticket to Venezuela?"

"Yep. He also booked seats on flights to San Jose, Costa Rica; Belize City; Quito, Ecuador; Santiago, Chile; Rio De Janeiro, Brazil; Lima, Peru; Bogotá, Colombia; Montevideo, Uruguay; Buenos Aires, Argentina; and Barcelona, Spain."

"What's the hell's he doing?"

"Covering his tracks. Most of the tickets were on third-world airlines that don't even keep passenger manifests, much less turn them over to American cops. There's no way to know which country he actually flew in to or, for that matter, whether he left Mexico at all. Makes sense that they're all Spanish-speaking countries. If he's fluent in Spanish, he can move around without drawing attention to himself."

"We can flag his credit cards," Mackay suggested.

"No way, those cards are history. They're either shredded up in a garbage can someplace, or he left them lying around so someone would steal them, which shouldn't be much of a challenge in Mexico City. Simmons is too smart to use them again, and if someone else does, they won't tell us diddly-squat about where Simmons is."

"What's he going to do for money?"

"I'm sure he hit the ATMs for the max. He took a Visa cash advance en route to the airport at a bank in San Jose that opens early. Took more cash advances in Houston. My guess is he hopped a taxi and had it drive him from bank to bank. Same for Mexico City. About fifteen thousand dollars, total."

"That won't last long."

"It will some places in Spain, Mexico, or Central or South America. Plus, it looks like he got scared and started liquidating assets. Remember, I said he had a million bucks in Wells Fargo last week?"

"Don't tell me."

"Right. It's not there anymore. My guess is he wire-transferred it offshore, maybe the Cayman Islands, where bank security regulations are like Switzer-land's: don't ask, don't tell. Eventually he'll wire it to Mexico, then to wherever he's at, or he'll travel back and forth to the Caymans or Mexico City to get it in increments. We'll never trace it back to him."

"Maybe a murder warrant would make it easier."

"What are you talking about?"

"Berroa gave up Simmons for Benton's murder last night. We need to convene the grand jury right away."

"What do you need me to do?"

"For starters, bring me everything seized as documents, papers, or records, on this," she said handing Escalante the Evidence and Property Report from the search of Simmons's home.

"Will do. How soon do you need them?"

"Five minutes ago."

"There wasn't much seized as documents," Escalante said, tossing a few brown paper evidence bags on Mackay's desk and reading the Evidence and Property Report. "What are you looking for?"

"A couple of eight-and-a-half-by-eleven pieces of paper, handwritten rather than typed, probably hole-punched, that look like maybe they were ripped out of a file folder. Secreted someplace, probably not in his desk with checkbooks, electric bills, and his routine papers."

"Let's see," Escalante mused as she flipped through the listing. "The stuff's inventoried by room. Here's something unusual. Seized from the bottom of a dresser drawer beneath some underwear. Two hand-written sheets. Bag three."

Kathryn tore open the evidence seal on the bag marked "3" and pulled out two pieces of paper. She opened a manila folder and lay each sheet, one at a time, beside the physician notes in Esther Fuentes's medical record.

Kathryn looked at Escalante. "Exactly what I was looking for."

50

―――

"Are you on your way out?" Mary Elizabeth Skinner asked.

"I was just leaving to pick up Emma," Kathryn answered. "Can it wait?"

"Afraid not. You need to catch the six o'clock news. McCaskill's on."

"What's he up to now?"

"Talking about the deal you made with Berroa."

"How did he hear about it so fast?"

"JNN," Skinner said, referring to the prisoner grapevine that those in law enforcement referred to as the Jailhouse News Network.

Kathryn aimed the remote at her television and scrolled until she found Channel 7 News.

"Mr. McCaskill," Steve Wallace said, "is it true that you have resigned your position with the District Attorney's office?"

McCaskill wore suit pants and a white shirt, but his tie was loosened and his shirt sleeves rolled up. He stood in front of an office that had "Campaign

Headquarters and Law offices of Neal McCaskill, Esq." painted on the door.

"Yes, I resigned to devote all my attention to an election campaign to become your next District Attorney. Kathryn Mackay's latest debacle proves I made the right decision."

"What do you mean?"

"Last night, Mackay made a deal with a rapist in exchange for his testimony."

"Isn't that kind of deal common in your business?" Wallace asked.

"Not the kind of deal Mackay made. She dismissed sexual assault charges against Dr. Eduardo Berroa, a rapist, in exchange for his testimony against a man who is no longer even in this country, thereby unleashing a dangerous predator onto the streets of Santa Rita, endangering all of our wives and daughters."

"The man who's out of the country, who is he and what is he alleged to have done?"

"Dr. Robert Simmons. Head of County Public Health. Mackay carried on an affair with him immediately after taking office. Suddenly he leaves Mackay and Santa Rita behind, and the woman scorned claims he murdered District Attorney Benton. By her actions, she has disgraced the office of District Attorney and endangered our community. I'm calling on her to do the honorable thing and resign immediately. If she refuses, I will begin circulating recall petitions."

Wallace looked into the camera. "That's it from here at the campaign headquarters of Neal McCaskill in Santa Rita. Back to you in the studio, Arliss."

Kathryn switched off the television and turned to Skinner.

"What?" Kathryn asked.

"Can I be candid?" Skinner asked.

"Of course, you're chief deputy. I expect you to be straight with me."

"McCaskill just dealt you some serious community safety issues and put you in bed with a murderer to boot. You've got to do something fast or you're not going to survive a recall, never mind an election."

Kathryn handed Skinner two pieces of paper.

"What are these?"

"Part of Rita Rios's medical records," Kathryn said, handing her Fuentes's and Valenzuela's records, as well.

Skinner looked up. "The same doctor."

"Right. Berroa. Last night, he said he was Valenzuela and Fuentes's doctor. When I asked about Rios, all he would admit to was that she hemorrhaged to death following an abortion. He said Simmons removed part of her medical records. These are what he removed. Take a look."

Skinner read them silently. "So, he performed an abortion. Nothing illegal about that."

"Keep going."

"She had hemophilia."

"Correct. Berroa knew Rios was a hemophiliac. He performed her abortion, but he didn't take precautions to ensure she wouldn't bleed excessively from the procedure. He was reckless. Because of his recklessness, she bled to death."

"He committed a lawful act, abortion, without due caution and circumspection. Sounds like involuntary manslaughter to me."

"Me too. We'll call Berroa before the grand jury tomorrow and get our indictment against Simmons for Hal's murder. I fulfill my end of the bargain by dismissing rape charges against Berroa. Then we have him arrested for the manslaughter of Rita Rios."

"Involuntary manslaughter only carries a two- to four-year sentence."

"It's the best we can do, Mary. It's not a perfect world."

51

The District Attorney's press conference was held in the Board of Supervisors chambers at four o'clock Thursday afternoon, two hours after a special grand jury session adjourned.

Kathryn Mackay stared into the bank of lights. "Good afternoon, ladies and gentlemen. Thank you for coming on such short notice."

Inspector Donna Escalante sat to Mackay's left, and Mary Elizabeth Skinner on her right.

"It's late, and you have deadlines to meet, so I'll make a brief statement, then take a few questions," Kathryn began.

"This afternoon, the grand jury indicted Dr. Robert Simmons, former head of county Public Health, for the murder of District Attorney Harold Benton. A warrant has been issued for his arrest."

A reporter asked, "Why did your office previously report that Benton died of a heart attack if you knew he was murdered?"

"The evidence proving he was murdered was obtained only yesterday."

"Neal McCaskill said you made a deal with Dr. Eduardo Berroa, whose testimony enabled you to get the indictment, but that Simmons has fled the country. Is that true?"

"A manhunt is under way. Robert Simmons will be tracked down and returned to the United States for trial," Mackay responded. "I intend to try him for the murder of District Attorney Benton, and seek the death penalty."

"Why have you decided to seek the death penalty?" another reporter shouted above the murmer of the crowd.

"Robert Simmons was on a crime spree. He—"

"What do you mean a crime spree?" The question came from someone in the rear of the chambers.

"Let me finish, please, and I'll explain," Mackay answered. "He murdered District Attorney Harold Benton. He attempted to murder me by inducing a heart attack and almost succeeded. By his criminal conduct he allowed a rapist to run free, and his conduct facilitated the death of several young girls. When the victim of a murder is a prosecutor and the murder was intentionally carried out to prevent the performance of the prosecutor's official duties, the penalty is death. Forensic tests confirm Berroa's testimony that Simmons poisoned Harold Benton. Murder by poisoning is a special circumstance case, punishable by death as well. If there was ever a poster boy for the death penalty, it is Robert Simmons."

"McCaskill also said Dr. Berroa himself is a dangerous man," another reporter said. "Is he right that you've put the women of Santa Rita at risk by setting a rapist free on our streets?"

Kathryn smiled inwardly. "Dr. Berroa has just been

arrested on charges of involuntary manslaughter. He is presently incarcerated in county jail on a no-bail hold."

"How do you explain McCaskill's statements?"

"Mr. McCaskill is conducting a scare campaign to get himself elected DA. Dr. Berroa will remain in custody at our jail until he is sentenced to state prison."

"Is it true you have decided not to file charges against Raymondo Miranda for the death of Esther Fuentes?"

"Our investigation concluded that Raymond Miranda was not responsible for Ms. Fuentes's death. No charges will be filed against him."

Kathryn stood to leave, but was interrupted by a reporter whose face she couldn't see, but whose voice she recognized.

"One last question, Ms. Mackay. Neal McCaskill has called for your resignation and threatened to start a recall drive if you refuse. Will you resign?"

"Absolutely not."

"So you intend to seek reelection next spring?"

"I certainly do, Mr. Wallace, and I'm counting on your vote."

The crowd was laughing when Kathryn left the board chambers.

52

SEVERAL WEEKS LATER

Ms. Mackay, there's a FedEx shipment for you. Shall I bring it in?"

"Who sent it, Nancy?"

"John Doe."

"From where?"

"I can't make it out. It's an international air way-bill. I can run it through FedEx's tracking system if you want."

"No need. Bring it in, please."

Kathryn recognized the printing and pulled out a letter with trembling hands.

Dear Kathryn:

I'm sure you have heard some terrible things about me by now. Please don't believe them.

Ed Berroa bitterly resented the way I implemented my vision for the clinic. He called me a racist, but that was entirely untrue, it's just that the plan could not have succeeded any other way. But under the circumstances, I had no choice but to go along with him.

Then his problem surfaced. No good could have come of making Escobedo's allegations public. You understand that the victims could not have benefited by destroying the clinic or me. Berroa's resignation solved the problem.

Hal couldn't leave it at that, though, and neither could you. By then, events had been set in motion which couldn't be stopped.

I came to you, Kathryn, to learn what you knew about Hal's investigation. When I found out you wouldn't let it alone, your fate was as inevitable as his. But, my judgment became impaired as soon as I fell in love with you. If you had just stopped, the events of that final Sunday evening would have been unnecessary.

I'm glad I failed.

Kathryn, when you finally forgive me, you will realize I am not a bad man, just a good man who did bad things because I was thrust into a bad situation.

Never forget that I love you.

I sit in this paradise knowing someday you will join me here to lie in the sun, swim in the warm surf, and make love on the beach. You don't realize it now, but that day will come. When it does, I will be waiting.

> *Until We Meet Again,*
> *Robert*

Kathryn slipped the letter back into the FedEx envelope and locked what was now evidence in her credenza.

"You bastard," she said aloud, "I don't care why you did what you did, where you are, or how long it takes, I'll find you. And that's a promise."

Epilogue

The California Board of Medical Examiners received a well-documented complaint and revoked Eduardo Berroa's medical license.

At a press conference on the eve of his manslaughter trial, Berroa denounced the institutional racism that resulted in his prosecution for a crime he didn't commit and vowed to return home to Monterrey, Nuevo León, Mexico, immediately following his acquittal, to establish a privately financed health clinic for the poor.

Berroa's trial began November third. He filed a Farretta motion with the court to act as his own defense attorney. The prosecution objected on the grounds that it was not timely made. The judge granted Berroa's motion, acknowledging a defendant's constitutional right to represent himself, but warned him of the perils of doing so.

Eduardo Berroa was convicted of involuntary manslaughter on November seventeenth. He waived a probation report and demanded the judge impose his sentence the same day. Judge Jemima Tucker sen-

tenced him to four years in state prison, the maxi-
mum punishment allowed by law.

He was transported to Soledad State Prison the
following day to begin serving his sentence, and was
detailed to work as an orderly in the prison infir-
mary.

Kathryn Mackay didn't speak with the media following Berroa's conviction and sentencing, nor did
she watch Neal McCaskill's television interview on
Channel 7 News, at which he again called for her
resignation, but didn't mention his previous threat to
circulate recall petitions.

Dave Granz phoned Kathryn at home to extend his
congratulations and invited her and Emma to spend
Thanksgiving with him and his parents in San Diego.
Kathryn told him she needed to think about it, but
called back fifteen minutes later and declined.

Since Emma's school recessed for the entire
Thanksgiving week, Kathryn took four days' vacation. Wednesday morning they had coffee, hot chocolate, and scones at Starbucks, then spent the rest of
the day running errands in an El Niño–driven rain-
storm.

They ducked into Bookshop Santa Rita on Plaza
Mall to escape a sudden downpour, and Kathryn
bought large wall maps, travel guides, and a pictorial
account of the making of the blockbuster movie
Titanic for Emma.

Their last stop was at Deluxe Foods in Laguna Del
Mar. Kathryn bought a turkey, stuffing mix, cranber-
ry sauce and other fixings, a bottle of Martinelli's
sparkling apple juice, two champagne glasses, two
dozen pushpins, and ten spools of thread in different

colors. Then they went home and ate tuna sandwiches for dinner.

After dinner, while Emma watched TV, Kathryn hung the maps of the United States, Central and South America, and Spain on the wall beside her Stairmaster. She stuck pushpins into the cities of San Jose, California; Mexico City; San Jose, Costa Rica; Belize City; Quito; Caracas; Santiago; Rio De Janeiro; Lima; Bogotá; Montevideo; Buenos Aires; and Barcelona.

She stretched red thread between the California and Mexico City pushpins, then yellow between Mexico City and Caracas, blue between Mexico City and Belize City, and a different color between Mexico City and each of the other cities.

She opened one of the travel guides, *Paradise Found: The Ten Best Beach Resorts in Spain, Central and South America.* Laboriously she connected each city to each resort, using that city's thread color. When she finished, she stood back and studied the maze. It looked like a psychedelic spider web.

"What's that, Mom?" Emma asked.

Kathryn put her arm around her daughter. "A puzzle, honey."

"What're you gonna do with it?"

"I'm going to solve it."

"It looks like a mess to me."

Kathryn laughed. "It looks like a mess to me right now, too, but I'll figure it out eventually. I have to."

"I'm good at puzzles, Mom. I'll help if you want."

"Thanks, sweetie. Now let's go to bed so we can get up early and cook Thanksgiving dinner tomorrow."

Thursday afternoon, while the turkey roasted,

Emma did her homework, and Kathryn read the travel guides and studied her wall maps. She quit for dinner, but knew she would not give up until Simmons's whereabouts were no longer a mystery.

After dinner, she drafted her candidate statement and stapled it to the election papers. For reasons she didn't understand, she dialed Dave Granz's home phone number and listened to his recorded voice on the answering machine. The message said he was in San Diego for the holidays, but didn't provide his parents' number.

She wrote a $750 check to pay the filing fee and attached it to her candidate statement and election papers, which she filed with the County Election Department the following Monday.

Visit the
Simon & Schuster Web site:
www.SimonSays.com

and sign up for our
mystery e-mail updates!

Keep up on the latest
new releases, author appearances,
news, chats, special offers, and more!
We'll deliver the information
right to your inbox — if it's new,
you'll know about it.

2350

More to relish from
CHRISTINE McGUIRE

Until We Meet Again

Until the Bough Breaks

Until Death Do Us Part

Until Proven Guilty

Available from Pocket Books